THRACE AND THE CENTAUR:

The Hundred-Handed

Keith Bender

Book I

Thrace and the Centaur: The Hundred Handed is a work of fiction. The names, places, incidents, and dialogue are drawn from the author's imagination and are used fictitiously. Any resemblance to any person living or dead, or events is purely coincidental.

ISBN-13: 978-0615956466
ISBN-10: 06159566467

Edited by Deborah Reilly

Cover and Brand logo by Alison Brynn Ross
www.alisonbrynnross.com

Painting by Megan McLoughlin

Authors' note:

First, I would like to offer my kindest thanks and sincerity to my editor, Deborah Reilly, for her sharp mind and endless patience.

To friends; Steve, Tim, Andy, Mark, Gannon, Jenny, Bob, Terry, Conner, Owen, Parker, Scott, and Anthony. Thank you for your endless support and encouragement. It made the creative times easy, and saved me during the difficult times.

I would also like to thank those literary minds who brought me here in the first place; Hesiod, Homer, Heraclitus, Xenophanes, Pythagoras, Zeno, Plato, Aristotle, Diogenes, Xenophon, Aristophanes, Sophocles, Aeschylus, Euripides and Apollonius Rhodius.

For my Mother and Father; no matter my path, wise or reckless, your enduring support allowed me to follow my heart. Thank you so very much.

Prologue

All-Seeing and Bright Helios sailed across the sky blue heavens as he had done for centuries casting light and witnessing events unfold daily upon the mortal realm. The repetition would wear upon lesser beings, but he was the son of the great Titans Hyperion and Theia. He brought forth light for the mortals, and his sisters, Selene, careened the sky at night and lovely saffron-robed Eos, the Dawn, awakened the Heavens. He crossed the ancient homelands of his long ago worshippers and recalled a different time, one of courage and heroism. A time, he felt, long lost. As he made his final stretch across the sky blue heavens high above the island of Crete in the wine dark Aegean Sea, he spied three long shadows upon a hidden plain. He knew what events unfolded beneath him, and he made haste to the west and home, as Dark-winged Night prepared for her journey.

A rumble and a roar echoed across the hidden plain that stretched from a coal-dark cavern along the side of Mt. Dicte, the birthplace of Mighty Zeus, Olympian King. The ground shook and the scent of fear branded the small hidden plain. A terrified wail bellowed from within the deep despairing darkness of the coal-black cave. The sound of great fear, the sound of death embraced the air and the land. Then silence.

Three lone figures did not move nor flinch at the violent sound of death, but waited. A thin figure with hollowed eyes, thin lips and dressed in black as if trying not to be seen stood silently with a small smile etched upon his thin lips. A step to his left, a taller, leaner figure appeared to float in a long dark robe as if a shadow though it appeared his eyes were everywhere. Each stood behind a larger man, though 'man' would be an understatement for he was magnificent and glorious in stature. He wore an oil black Armani suite with a crisp crow black shirt and a glossy blood red tie and a matching handkerchief. His long black mane circled his carved and statuesque features and rested gently upon his wide broad shoulders. A look of disappointment burned in his small charcoal black eyes.

"Father," the hollowed-eyed man said in a barbarous whisper, "God of War, allow us to complete this task for you. You have waited far too long for its completion."

"Spare me your meager attempt at heroism my son Phobus, for Panic is simply all you are. And do not attempt to speak either Deimus, for uniting Fear with Panic would not succeed. For my task to be successful, I require the ancient human wisdom of Aristotle; the courage of a man who is full of rage, and I need this man eager to rush into danger. All of which you two lack."

Great Ares, Stormer of Strong Walls, and Olympian God of War proceeded forward across the plain toward the cave. A breeze neither brushed the blades of grass before his feet nor the leaves upon the trees at the plain's edge. Fear and Panic had ebbed nature's flow. A rumble once again echoed from within the coal-black cave. A lifeless form flew through the air, and with a sudden thump, the lifeless figure fell at the feet of the God of War. It was a young teen, one who had yet to taste life.

The mangled young boy, blood-stained, broken and covered in claw marks lay at the feet of Merciless Ares. With his shiny black Kenneth Coles, the God of War rolled the boy's head forward and back. The lifeless brown eyes of the youth stared off into the world of Hades and the land of Tartarus, where his soul would ride across the River Styx with the boatman Charon, but no coins would be left for his passage.

"I have waited many, many years to find the right son," stated Ares in disdain. "But all of you have been weak and feeble. Even with the path drawn out before you, you continually fail and perish so quickly. Your mentor, Peirithous will pay for his continued failure."

"Shall we kill him father, the centaur, kill him?" Phobus asked with a tone of excitement.

Ares the Quarrelsome responded quietly. "No. It is time for a new mentor, and my next son is soon to be of age"

"Shall you school your son," spoke Deimus in a whisper.

Ares turned with his charcoal black eyes burning with flames toward his Immortal son. "How inept you are Deimus, for your ignorance parallels your lovely mother Golden Aphrodite. Terror or false kindness would not bear wisdom. And to believe I would waste my precious time teaching a mortal." Ares the Deceiver returned his attention to his dead mortal son, "It is about time Peirithous' son became of use instead of buried in books cowering in his cave. I shall exploit each to my advantage, something I could not do with his father, Peirithous."

The God of War stepped away from the mangled body of his son. He pulled the blood red handkerchief from his breast pocket and leaned over to brush the dirt from his Kenneth Coles. He shined them to black glass and returned the handkerchief to his pocket. "Though few events may still be out of my control, I have time to prepare." A quick spark of a flame imploded, and the God of War was gone.

Fear and Panic stood before their dead disfigured stepbrother with amused smiles upon their barren eyes and hallowed faces. Phobus picked up the dead boy by his broken arm and dangled the corpse like a puppet before his brother.

"For a stepbrother, he is sad and lifeless." Deimus whispered.

"How many has it been, how many? What number are you?" Panic asked in a mocking tone. "You remind me of the broken body of Hektor, Breaker of Horses, after Achilles slaughtered him and dragged him to the Greek camp and around his dead friend Patroclus. Ah, the good old days. There are no more heroes left in this feeble and lazy world, no more. In the end we will be needed."

"We will be needed." Deimus whispered in agreement.

Phobus tossed the dead mortal son of Ares back toward the blackness of the cave upon Mt. Dicte. He grinned revealing sharp, bile yellow teeth beneath his thin lips. Deimus watched his brother, his face solemn and cold. In a dark puff of grey smoke, the sons of Ares were gone.

CHAPTER 1

A voracious clang and clatter stretched through the corridors as if the great warriors upon the plains of Troy had once again taken up arms: Diomedes the spear-thrower, Hektor, breaker-of-horses and swift-footed Achilles. These ancient heroes have long since passed as have their epic battles replaced by more verbal conflicts, though no less destructive, and unlike the battles of old, continued off the battlefield.

But, this is not the Plains of Troy where Paris was swept to protection from Menelaus of the War Cry by the Goddess of Love, Aphrodite. It is an arena of education. Though not the Agoge, where the great 300 Spartan warriors trained for battle and claimed glory at Thermopylae, nor is it Plato's Academy or the Lyceum where Aristotle would speak of moral virtue and the extremes between excess and deficiency. This was an average high school where excess and deficiency were a way of life.

A young man of average stature and build, wavy auburn hair and pale blue eyes made his way onto the education battlefield with a quick pause to peer back toward the grey Volvo wagon making haste from the school parking lot. It was not intrigue or excitement that gleamed from his pale blue eyes as it did the rest of the student warriors, but anguish and fear. Today, he wanted to be here no more than Hades wished to rule the Underworld. But unlike Hades, who drew lots with his brothers, Great Zeus of the Lightning Bolt and

Earth Shaking Poseidon, for areas of govern, Thrace was dropped off by his mother, the driver of the grey Volvo wagon. *Guaranteed*, by Eddie Vedder, his mother's favorite musician, still lingered in his ears.

Thrace glided between the student-warriors as he did each day like a rainbow trout through a Rocky Mountain stream, never seen. He arrived at his locker and spun the combination lock as he did every day for the past two years, but today was different. He felt fearful and afraid, though did not know why. Over breakfast, this fear spawned a fight with his mother, something which happened rarely between them. Over the years they had moved a couple of times; his mother accepted different teaching positions at various colleges. She was not interested in status or money, but she wanted a good college in a location she enjoyed living. There was a college that concerned itself more with athletics than academic, and though she was a college track and field athlete, she put education first. He recalled how she would complain at dinner about lack of funding for her department. The Dean asked her how much money lectures on ancient architecture brought in. Thrace was young and did not care either way; but he did not really care for the people. *The people are really loud*, he told her at dinner. They moved at the end of term. Next, they lived in a big city, but the noise and congestion bothered them both. She took Thrace to see a variety of museums and cultural experiences, but he did not care for the arts or theatre but preferred the museums for the solitude. His mother did too, especially since she taught Ancient Greek and Roman history. After a long search, she accepted at position at a small liberal arts college in the mountains of Colorado. After only a week they had both loved it. She loved the college; they both loved the mountains, and most of the people were really friendly. They have been here many years and felt completely at home with not so much as a single fight or argument. So, why did I get so upset and angry at her for asking me to try out for track and field next year, he wondered?

"Thrace. Thrace? Anyone in there?" spoke Parker.

Parker, a smaller boy with straight dirty blond hair and dark brown eyes, hid beneath large mirrored sunglasses atop a nose too small for his head. He paced anxiously around Thrace attempting to get his attention. The day Thrace and his mother moved in, Parker, who lived across the street, came running over to introduce himself. Their friendship has grown exponentially since then. There was a natural comfort between these two like a Spartan warrior and his shield.

"Hey, sorry Park. What's up?" Thrace asked.

"I overheard Mr. Grissom in the office this morning, and I think he is going to talk to you about trying out for track team next year." Parker's grin was riddled with excitement.

"You're kidding me?"

"No. I think one of the professors at the College saw you and your mom out tossing the javelin and gave the coach a call."

Thrace returned to his locker and began exchanging books, and felt a twinge of anger boil somewhere deep within.

"Hey, what's going on?" Parker asked with genuine concern.

Thrace closed his locker and looked at his only friend. He heard the concern in his voice and even through those mirrored sunglasses. It was a question Parker tossed out because he knew Thrace wanted to talk to someone about it.

"Mom and I got into an argument this morning. She said I should try out for track next year."

"You and your mom never fight," he stated with surprised, "and how do you get into a fight over a question?"

"That's it, I don't know. I said no, she asked why since I seemed to enjoy practice at the college. Then something about me needing the practice, 'cause it could be good for me, as if it would help me. And then, I don't know. I got afraid and angry and told her to stop butting into my life. We didn't speak all with way to school, even when she dropped me off."

"Note, I won't ask you why then." Parker smiled, lowered his mirrored sunglasses and said, "Why?"

Thrace held back a laugh and then could not. A simple thing, but it was Parker. Certain people can make you laugh when others would not understand.

"I don't know. I got all summer to think about it."

"And, we'll be Juniors next year. Life gets exciting the last two years." Parker said, adjusting his oversized backpack that made him look smaller and added, "Just apologize to your mom when you get home, she's cool."

"Yeah, she's cool. You know the worse part, I felt my heart pound in my chest like it was gonna explode. It made me even angrier. I just wish I understood." His mind replayed the scene over and over.

They both sat at a small kitchen table, bowls of grain cereal with fresh fruit and a glass of orange juice before each of them. His mother spoke about an upcoming lecture on comparative myth in the ancient world and asked if he would be interested. He said yes and that even Parker may enjoy it, especially since each night they played *Gods vs Titans* on-line, and Parker drilled Thrace with questions on ancient myths. After a quick moment, she made a simple comment.

"You seem to enjoy throwing the javelin, whether after my classes or camping, and you are better than some of the students at the college. Have you thought of trying out for the high school team next year? I think it would be really good for you. You never know what's coming or what's in store for you."

That was it. He felt his blood boil, his heart pound and rage swell through his neck like a war machine designed to storm great walls, and this rage machine stormed his mind. He barked at her like Cerberus the three-headed dog upon the gates of Tartarus. She said nothing. She quietly stood, gathered her dishes, placed them in the sink and walked out to her car and awaited him. He sat there dumbfounded and as he climbed into the car, he was too consumed with fear and anger; he did not know what to say.

A sound erupted throughout the corridor like the shriek of a beautiful Siren and scattered the students in all directions as they found safety within rooms along the corridors. Thrace and Parker where no different, they moved in haste for cover and the continuing steps of daily wisdom. The corridor sang a song of silence and emptiness, except for a lingering cloud of grey smoke.

CHAPTER 2

Again, this was not the Academy, nor was Plato discussing Politics and the role of the philosopher king with an enthusiastic and inquisitive youth craving knowledge. It was a modern high school. The Academy had evolved into a social forum of acceptance. The lazy-eyed youths sat at their desks like transparent shades looming in the realm of Tartarus, ruled by the son of Cronus, Black-eyed Hades. The students stared blindly at their teacher, who adamantly attempted to cut through the layers of video games, daydreams and youthful visions of beautiful Paris' or Helens. Coincidently, a Helen sat quietly in the center of the room, as if she were on a throne. Parker sat beside her; his eyes drifted toward her as her eyes shined, as vivid as bright Helios, who was lingering slowly across the spring sky.

Beside Parker, Thrace slumped in his desk by the windows in the back of the room. His eyes peered onto a pasture and the steep majestic mountains in the distance with a small blanket of snow upon their peaks. The mountains of Colorado had become a home he had envisioned for many years. The lush green-brown forests offered the sensation of warmth and welcome as if they were alive and excited he was among them. The great mountains had given him a sense of shelter as if the great Titan Atlas stood beside you holding up the Heavens. It also offered his mother and him the comfort of solitude, a solitude they often pursued into the forest which warmed them like a fleece blanket. Thoughts of his mother drifted through his mind like an unmanned trireme ship of ancient Greece upon the vast Aegean Sea, without a captain, lost and without guidance.

He recalled a Greek party at their house his mother hosted where all were drinking the traditional wine and water blend with honey and grain. He was sent to bed early in his toga (for he was only eight) but sat by the door listening to their work chatter. He enjoyed it because many of the conversations were debates on Greek and Roman history and myth and whose translations were more accurate. He remembered a woman older than his mother asking who his father was. With a haughty laugh, she replied, "Why Ares of course!" It drew great laughter at the party. Thrace recalled even laughing himself and from a shelf he brandished a plastic short sword and brought forth imaginary battles upon the furniture in his room. This, of course, brought his mother in to send him back to bed. The thought of a Greek God father soon trailed from his imagination, and he did not think about it until a couple years later, when he did ask. She informed him his father was another doctorate student she dated while she was in Greece. When she got back, she could not find his address or number. She could have searched harder for it but chose not to. He lived in Greece and did not wish to burden him, so did not concern herself with it, just with her son. After that, he did not concern himself with the information either.

Thrace caught movement across the green pasture beside the school. A man appeared from behind a tree fifty yards from the window. No, not a man…a horse. It had a deep chestnut brown coat with a trimmed mane as if it had had a haircut. The horse moved from behind the tree and approached the building. It paused twenty feet from the window and stared directly at him. The horse nahhed.

"Thrace?"

"Hey Thrace." Parker whispered.

Thrace turned his head to Parker then realized Mr. Grissom was attempting to get his attention.

"Good, you have seen a horse, and it appears to like you. But can you help with this question. Can you give me reason or cause of the Revolutionary War?" Mr. Grissom asked with his arms crossed upon his chest, his coarse brown beard trimmed to a square perfection upon his face giving a stern appearance, except for his soft brown eyes sprinkled with specks of light green revealing a flavor of understanding and wisdom.

Thrace slowly collected his thoughts having a difficult time taking his eyes away from the horse, for the horse did not remove its eyes from Thrace. It appeared to know him.

"Control?" Thrace responded absentmindedly. "People don't like to be controlled, especially from far away. So, they fought to break the control."

"Good. The British Empire taxed all its colonies, though the New World was taxed less than other colonies, most of the people were English and felt...controlled...manipulated..."

The shriek of the Siren echoed again throughout the school to cut off Mr. Grissom's final thought. On the one hand, Aristotle would not have tolerated this disturbance during his classes with young Alexander the Great. It did, on the other hand, activate a classroom of formerly sleepy-eyed youths to awaken as if Swift-footed Achilles called out with zeal to his Myrmidon warriors to prepare for their next battle on the plains of Troy.

"Remember, final exams on Monday, and hint, know the cause and effect of the Revolutionary war. And have your essay ready to turn in before the test." Mr. Grissom shouted above the noise.

The students departed the room with an urgency that Mr. Grissom wished they had for the wisdom he bestowed upon them. Fair-haired Helen got up from her desk with less urgency dropping her pencil to the floor. Parker, without haste, retrieved it for her from his seat and handed it back to her. She whispered "Thank you" that felt like a kiss upon his check as her soft green eyes sparkled like dew when she smiled. Parker sat motionless attempting to speak, and uttered something that two thousand years ago would have been a compliment.

"You are an ox-eyed beauty Helen."

"What?" she replied with a puzzled stare and stormed off.

Parker sank into his desk as that storm that just departed depleted the wind from his sails, and he sat dead in the water.

"Why when your mom says it about someone it means she's hot?" Parker muttered to Thrace, though primarily to himself.

"It meant their eyes weren't close together, which was attractive." Thrace said as he continued to peer out the window oblivious to the scene and unable to take his eyes from the horse, which appeared to mirror him. The horse nahhed once again.

"Thrace? May I speak with you a minute?" Mr. Grissom asked.

"I'll wait for you outside." Parker stated with a large grin and a wink.

Thrace approached his teacher's desk, with difficulty pulling his eyes from the horse that watched him.

"What may I do for you Mr. Grissom?" Thrace asked standing before his history teacher. He was a fit man, but not a broad man. His beard gave him a sense of strength, yet his eyes were as calm as a mountain pond persuading you to swim.

"I have it from a few good sources that you are quite the athlete, especially in track and field." He stated kindly and with a bright smile added, "Probably like your mother."

Thrace knew this was coming, but the words reminded him of his argument with his mother, and again, it brought forth the rage he felt over breakfast. "I don't know Mr. Grissom. I'm not really one for competing."

"Well, we lose a few students with this graduating class, and it cannot hurt to come by in the fall for a practice to see what you think."

"Thanks Mr. Grissom, I'll think about it over the summer."

"I'll hold you to that." He replied with a knowing smile and went back to his work at hand.

Thrace left Mr. Grissom at this desk to collect his daily toil. Outside the door Parker stood like a spring willow awaiting Zephyrus, the gentle west wind on a hot summer day.

"He asked you, didn't he?" He asked impatiently.

"He did."

"You said, 'I'll think about it'," Parker said mimicking Thrace the best he could.

Thrace ignored his last comment. "Did you see the horse outside the window?"

"Yeah, so? We live in the mountains."

"I don't know. It just seemed to be staring at me."

"Maybe it thought you were cute." Parker said as he slipped his mirrored sunglasses upon his small nose. "Let's get out of here."

"Where you going?" A sharp voice quipped from behind the two. The boys turned to see Chad who was surrounded by a small entourage of boys and girls. He had moussed hair in a messy fashion with a hawk-like nose and owl-like eyes. He stood with his long arms on his hips as his entourage spanned around him like a flock of crows awaiting a bloody battle and a plate of remains.

"Hey Chad, we're just heading home," Parker answered.

"I wasn't speaking to you," Chad responded, his eyes directed at Thrace. His entourage cooed over his words.

"We're just heading home," Thrace responded with a flavor of sarcasm.

"I heard Coach G talk about asking you to try out next year. He's right; we lost some good Seniors, but next year's Seniors and many of the Junior's will post better numbers than this year. What we don't need is someone who hasn't been here since his Freshman year; who's never played a sport, and who will break up the unity of the team."

"I wasn't planning on it," Thrace responded honestly. "I just told him I'd think about it, so he wouldn't harass me later." He watched as Chad accepted his response and found it amusing that Chad had never spoken to him until this day.

"Oh," Chad replied, puzzled by the response and upset by the lack of confrontation. He paused unable to recall a retort as the whispers increased around him as if a boxer at the Olympic Games decided not to fight, both fighters lost glory.

"By the way," he added, "what kind of name is *Thrace* anyway?"

Thrace, for a moment, believed he saw a glimpse of grey smoke drift between him and Chad. "Ah, I don't know. My mom teaches ancient history; it has something to do with Greece." Thrace replied. He knew why his mother named him but did not want to become entangled in a personal and historical conversation with Chad. Chad was the star track and football athlete, and most kids in school knew him, but Thrace felt his personality and ego was greater than his ability.

"I saw that his middle name is *Ares*," said Marge, a petite red-head with ivory white skin and a sharp aristocratic nose peeking around Chad, her fingers gently touching his shoulder as if not to break him. Thrace knew she worked mornings in the office, and now he knew she spent her time reading up on students.

"What!?" Chad yelled. "Are you kidding me, like the zodiac sign?"

Thrace felt his heart pound within his chest and his blood boil. He had been picked on before, but he always walked away. He grew two inches last summer and most of the bullying shifted to Parker, whose wiry and dry humor always diffused the situation. This was different? These were petty comments from an individual he knew to be petty; he should walk away, but he could not stop the anger and rage that ebbed in his veins and along his spine.

"It's not Aries like the zodiac, it's Ares like the Greek God of War." Parker stated matter-of-factly.

"That's even better!" Chad bellowed with laughter as if it had been a joke. "God of War?!" He echoed. Though there was little amusing about the name, it spread like a virus to Chad's entourage as a flock of birds all chirping to the same tune.

Thrace's heart pounded behind his rib cage as if Pollux, the great Olympian boxer, was training within his chest. His mind could not focus on simply leaving. To make matters worse, it was as if the Great North Wind, Boreas, brought forth a whirlwind of a tempest within his mind swirling with thoughts of blood and violence. Without thinking he took one step toward Chad, whose laughter eroded and was replaced with a dark smile.

The laughter in the corridor also diminished as Chad's flock of birds took a step back expecting a fight. Parker stepped toward Thrace and pulled at his arm telling him they should just get out of there. Thrace turned toward Parker and stared at himself in those large mirrored sunglasses. Thrace watched as his pale blue eyes turned to dark ambers of coal ebbed with orange flames. Within his mind he heard a great wail and fear struck him like a lightning bolt from Mighty Zeus. Pain stretched along his spine and throughout his limbs like the tentacles of a giant squid taking his breathe away. Seconds later, he was consumed with pain, a great and violent pain of flesh and blood. Thrace let out a wail he could not contain. In the distance he heard laughter, but it did not come from the corridor. Then everything went black.

Within the darkness Thrace heard his name. He fought to climb out of the yawning void calloused with pain and blood. He felt a tingling vibration throughout his body like an electrical current. In a glimmer of light he saw Parker, fortunately no longer wearing his mirrored glasses, hoping to erase the image of the coal-dark embers within his own reflection. Another face came into view. It was Mr. Grissom and his square beard and calm eyes. With each blink of his own eyes, he saw a fury of arms with long claws attacking him. He sat up in haste and fought to keep his eyes open wide.

"Thrace, you okay?" Parker asked.

"Yeah, I just…had a splitting head ache and then kinda fainted." Thrace said keeping his words simple. Chad was no longer there, but he witnessed the grey smoke once again lingering nearby with what he would swear was a face and then vanish.

"Thrace, head down to the nurse's office before you leave." Mr. Grissom said as he helped Thrace to his feet.

Getting to his feet, the images slowly faded from his mind, but not from his memory. He looked around for the grey smoke, but it was gone as well. Parker handed him his books as he steadied himself between his friend and his teacher. He wanted to get out of this school immediately.

"Thrace, did you hear me?" Mr. Grissom asked. "You should see the nurse."

"Sure Mr. Grissom. It's probably nothing. I missed breakfast and skipped lunch. I just need to eat." Thrace replied.

"Either way, just see the nurse, and I will have a talk with Chad."

"No problem Mr. Grissom," Parker said attempting to lead Thrace away. "I'll make sure he sees the nurse and gets something to eat."

They walked down the corridor, turned and moved quickly past the nurse's office, the main office and out the front door into the bright light of Helios. Thrace paused to feel the warmth of Helios upon his face as if it would erase the dark yawning void filled with pain and blood. After a moment, he continued down the front steps of his school. Parker followed without a word, putting his mirrored sunglasses back upon his face. He watched as Thrace continued to move his hands and fingers as if they were numb from sleeping on them. After three blocks, Parker could not contain himself and stopped.

"Okay, what in the world happened in there? I ate with you at lunch and you had two plates."

Thrace walked a few more steps before stopping. He did not know how to answer his best friend, nor could he stop the electric tingling throughout his body. He turned and set his backpack upon the ground and stretched his arms wide as if to feel them once again. He turned his head as if to crack his neck, trying to shake the violent images that lingered before his eyes.

"Honestly, I don't know. The obvious decision was to walk away, but all of a sudden I was angry. I mean, really angry, like I was over breakfast with mom. But this time, I wanted to destroy him. It's like it wasn't me. Then I looked at you, and you had those mirrored sunglasses on. I didn't see my own eyes, but something else."

"Like what?"

"They were like burning pieces of coal," he said almost embarrassed. "Then I felt this pain, like my skin being shredded off by hundreds of claws." Thrace pulled a pencil from his back pocket and moved it over his chest and arms as if sketching the marks he felt. "I had claw marks all over me."

Parker took off his glasses, looked at his own reflection and put them in his backpack.

"What about your hands?" Parker asked. "You keep shaking them."

Thrace looked at his own hands as if for the first time. "Again, I don't know. I have this tingling sensation all throughout my body that won't stop."

"Maybe you should see a doctor?"

"I don't want to see a doctor. I just need some sleep."

Thrace looked at the pencil he was still holding, and could visual imagine the scar marks over his body. As if by impulse, he took the pencil and threw it like a dart. Like a lightning bolt from Mighty Zeus, it raced through the air and pierced a tree ten yards away.

The boys froze and turned to one another in amazement. Parker dropped his pack and ran to the tree. Thrace followed. The pencil was four inches deep inside the tree. Parker attempted to pull it out, but to no avail. Thrace also tried, as the pencil snapped where it entered the tree.

"How in the Rocky's gorge did you do that?"

"I don't know." Thrace responded looking at the broken pencil in his hand.

CHAPTER 3

It was a cool late May as the chariot of the God of Sun, Apollo, pulled bright Helios who sees everything high across the sky allowing the clouds a day of rest. The trees still bare awaited the return of Persephone from Hades to her mother Demeter, Goddess of the Harvest, and the coming of spring. Though snow still arrived this time of year, the mountain town residents prepped their lawn with chemicals and additives as if it were their own children. Large shiny metal trucks and SUV's adorned the driveways, each larger than battle armaments of wars in years past and used simply to retrieve food and children.

Thrace and Parker walked along the sidewalk in front of matching sculpted homes adorned with an array of naked trees. Parker continued to sharpen pencils and Thrace tried to explain that he had no idea how to teach someone to throw a pencil like an arrow.

"I'm telling you, I don't know."

"Maybe if you hold a pencil first, and then hand it to me. Give me some of that tingling sensation." Parker said taking the pencil from Thrace, then he took aim at a tree. He fired the pencil, and it drifted casually toward the tree, turning end over end and lightly hit the tree falling quietly to the ground. He looked at Thrace and shrugged his shoulders.

Thrace laughed and picked up the pencil. Past the tree stood another about twenty yards away. Thrace quickly fired the pencil like a javelin and in a single breathe, it pierced the bark in the center of the tree.

"Ow."

"Ow? I didn't hit you." Thrace said.

"I didn't say anything. I'm still standing here in amazement. That was awesome and the furthest so far. I wonder if there is any way we can make money off this?"

"You didn't hear anyone say 'ow'?"

"Just you." Parker replied as he approached the tree and pulled the pencil from the bark. "Not as deep at that distance."

"Ow."

"There it was again!" Thrace stammered.

"There what was again?"

"I'm telling you I heard someone say 'ow' again."

"What? Like the tree?" Parker turned toward the tree. "I'm sorry little tree."

"Thank you."

"There! Did you hear that?" Thrace asked.

"Hear what?"

"The tree or something, said 'thank you'."

"All right. You were brilliantly cool firing off those pencils, but now you are starting to weird me out." Parker said to his friend with a smile. "I'm out. I will see you on-line around nine, and we will battle some Greek Gods versus some Ancient Titans. I like fighting with the Chimera. It gives Ares such a hard time."

Thrace stood staring at the tree. "Yeah. You got it."

"Later and get some rest."

Parker turned and jogged across the street toward his perfectly symmetrical house and manicured lawn. Thrace remained staring at the tree. He slowly reached out to touch the bark.

"Thrace!"

Thrace stopped his hand short of the bruised bark and turned toward Parker who was standing on his front porch.

"How about the fair in two weeks, maybe put together a competition or win few prizes?"

"Sure Park," Thrace said amused. "I'll see you on-line later."

Thrace turned back to the tree for a second and then laughed at himself. He made his way to the sidewalk toward his house. It was a small white two bedroom cottage with blue shutters and a blue awning and resembled any other house along the block except for the two Ionic columns supporting the awning. His mother had them installed just after they moved in. She said it made her feel 'at home', which he did not truly understand, but she always loved the ancient world. He turned back toward the tree he thought said, "Ow". He saw the blemish where the pencil had pierced. Up the street movement caught his eye. A bush and large tree shook, and the same horse appeared. Thrace rubbed his eyes and looked again. It was not a horse, but a man, in a dark brown suit and short hair. He was watching

Thrace. Thrace waved, but the man did not return his gesture. With a look of concern, Thrace lowered his hand and entered his house.

Thrace stepped inside his house as he had a hundred times before. In the front living room a small couch sat before a nineteen inch television and an old DVD player upon a little wooden stand that you would find at any thrift store. The walls were adorned with prints of red figured vase paintings with scenes of ancient combat and celebrations and shelves garnished with replica vases and statues of Ancient Gods, Goddess' and warriors from the time of the first Athenian leader Theseus to the Hellenistic time of Alexander the Great. Resting alone, atop the bookshelf was her prized replica black vase with the burnt orange design of the God of War in battle which she had made herself while in Greece from remnants of a shattered vase she had uncovered. A small worn wooden desk with a laptop was dwarfed by bookcases flooded with books on Ancient Greece from writers from old Hesiod to young Fagles and topics ranging from Ancient women and sexuality to Greek Architecture in the Archaic period. He browsed the shelves admiring the collection his mother had acquired. He pulled *The Odyssey* from the shelf and flipped through the pages. As far back as he could remember, each night his mother read the tale of Odysseus' journey home, always reminding him that no matter how difficult the journey, he could find his way home. He found a particular passage he recalled as a child.

> *Telemachus, walking the beach now, far from others,*
> *Washed his hands in the foaming surf and prayed to Pallas:*
> *"Dear god, hear me! Yesterday you came to my house,*
> *You told me to ship out on the misty sea and learn*

If father, gone so long, is ever coming home...

He wondered why those lines out of so many had crossed his mind. Was it a long lost concern for his father? Admittedly, he had hoped to meet him someday, but there were mixed feelings along those lines as well. The hope of who your father could be, and who he actually was may not run along parallel lines. He felt better off than some kids who actually knew their father though never saw him or spent time with him. He did well in school thanks to his mother often making him redo his homework whether it was right or wrong as he would complain and she would say, "Repetition is the key to learning". They would hike and camp even more than they did before they moved here. At the campsite, she taught him how to throw the javelin out of homemade limbs upon forest floor. Growing up, she always found time to play ball with him and the other neighborhood kids, and she, being a great athlete, usually won. She taught as she won as well. It might have been nice to know my father, Thrace thought, but I have done quite well without him; he realized.

Thrace placed *The Odyssey* back on the shelf as he dragged his fingers along the bindings of the remaining books. He had read few and skimmed many, but had barely dipped his toes in the water of ancient wisdom before him. The tingling sensation in his body was amplified as his fingers traced along an older book with a worn binding. The title read, *"The History of Thrace"*. The history of me, he thought amusingly. He thumbed through the book realizing he had never seen this one or never noticed it before. He fingered the pages and a glimmer caught his eye. In the middle of the book, a circle of bronze was tucked tightly into the binding along with a brown leather cord. He pulled the leather cord from the book and held a necklace before him. It resembled a bronze coin from ancient Greece with the leather cord weaved through a small hole atop the bronze coin. He held the coin in his hand to get a closer look. It felt heavy and old as if he was holding time itself. The image upon the coin was that of a ram, though in amazing detail having been made so long ago. He turned the coin over; it was bare and smooth except for two droplets of shiny gold upon it. Thrace caressed the gold spots upon the coin that smeared like blood upon his thumb. Slowly, they moved independently upon his thumb. Then, they were gone as if consumed by his own flesh, and his heart began to race.

Images once again exploded upon his mind like the ancient volcano at Santorini with debris and fire burning and destroying life within him. He saw a flailing body of a boy, three lone figures upon an open plain, the sound of a wailing creature echoed throughout his mind and small coal black eyes engulfed in flames closed in upon him. Everything once again went black.

Again, Thrace heard his name in the distance through the deep, dark yawning void. The image of the coal black eyes lingered in his mind as his own eyes fought to open and find light. Before him he saw Parker, once again at his side.

"What are you doing here?" Thrace asked.

"What am I doing here? I called because I got the new *Titans* expansion set and there was no answer, so I came over. What are you doing on the floor again?"

Thrace sat up and attempted to shake the images from his mind, but they were burned within him, as if a memory of a memory. He felt sore from head to toe as if he had fought the great Cretan Minotaur himself deep within the labyrinth of Crete. He stretched his arms and remembered the necklace in his hand. He held it in the air, and it calmly twirled before his eyes, the ram on one side and the bare smooth side on the other no longer carried the spots of gold. He looked at his thumb and the gold was not there either. Was the gold alive, he thought? He recalled how it appeared to absorb into his skin.

"Did you see those images again?" Parker asked.

"Yeah, but these were different. This gold stuff, kind of absorbed into my skin. Then, I saw these eyes, these dark eyes."

"Like the ones in my sunglasses?"

"No, these weren't mine."

"Can you stand? 'Cause I feel like I'm working at a nursing home the way I keep picking you up off the floor."

Thrace slowly got to his feet; a smirk etched upon his face. He stretched his muscles, which for some reason he did not understand, felt sore. He put the necklace in his pocket and placed *The History of Thrace* back on the shelf as he caught his breathe.

"Are you going to tell your mother?" Parker asked.

"I don't know. I don't think she's here."

"Mom?" Thrace yelled slowly making his way through the living room into the kitchen. It was Friday and his mother finished classes at noon, usually went for a run and was home by now buried in a book or doing research upon her laptop. He grabbed a bottle of water from the refrigerator. The cool water eased the tingling within his body. He made his way to the back patio and Parker followed. He found his mother.

She was on her knees in the backyard, head bowed. Before her stood a beautiful and elegant woman that glowed with the brightness of Helios. Her golden hair was pulled back with soft strands dangling before her majestically carved features with skin of soft cream. The woman held a flower in her hand and the petals matched his mother's auburn hair.

His mother turned her head slowly toward her son. She smiled softly, a smile of love only revealed between a mother and her son. A tear escaped her pale grey eyes and caressed her cheek. The beautiful woman before his mother softly blew the flower from her hand, and it drifted along the breeze like a melody and settled upon his mother's head. His mother bowed her head once again.

"Thrace, why is your mother kneeling before a bird?" Parker asked.

"A bird? What?" Thrace responded confused. "Excuse me, but mom, what are you doing, and who is that woman?"

"What woman?" Parker asked with a look of concern toward his friend.

"That woman!" Thrace barked pointing directly at her. Just as quick as he spoke, he watched as the woman stretched her arms out wide, glanced toward the heavens and transformed into a dove. The dove took flight into the sky and vanished into the cloudless blue above. Thrace turned to his mother whom he watched fold like a soft blanket upon the ground.

"MOM!" Thrace ran to his mother's side. He continually called her name as he held her head in his hands, but she would not respond. From upon his mother's head where the auburn flower gracefully fell upon her, another sprouted. The center of the flower was a soft pale grey, the same as his mother's eyes, surrounded by petals of bright auburn, the same luscious color as her hair.

A siren screamed from the ambulance that awoke the quiet cool May afternoon as it pulled into Thrace's driveway and abruptly stopped. A young stout woman in a white uniform made her way from the ambulance to the front door followed quickly by tall lanky man in matching whites. They pushed through the house and burst onto the back patio and arrived at the spot Thrace's mother, Cybele, lay upon the ground.

"Why is there a flower growing out of my mother's head?" Thrace asked unable to let go of his mother's hand as the EMT's started their examination.

"I think he's in shock," spoke the lanky EMT to his counterpart.

"Some woman blew a flower toward my mother, and now a flower is growing out of her head," he mumbled quietly, his lips quivering.

"Sorry," Parker jumped in. "He hasn't eaten today and is a bit loopy. We came out back and found his mother on the ground."

Thrace looked directly at Parker and wanted to yell at him, because that was not what had happened, and once again his blood began to boil. The question was…what had happened? Twice he had felt great pain and blacked out as violent images ravaged his thoughts. Could he just be seeing things? If so, twice? One thing for sure, no matter angry he felt right now, Parker was right, the priority was his mother, and they needed to find out what is wrong with her.

"Young man," the stout young woman said to Thrace. "We believe she had a stroke." She turned toward Parker, "Can you help get him to the ambulance and we'll get them both to the hospital."

"Sure." Parker said. He helped Thrace once again get to his feet as he finally released his mother's hand though his eyes were still transfixed upon her.

A small crowd had gathered in the front of the Kraft house to witness Cybele being loaded into the back of the ambulance. Parker's mother and father, a bookish brown haired couple who could pass as brother and sister, ran to the side of the ambulance seeing their son escorting Thrace from the house.

"Son, what happened?" Mrs. Wells asked.

"They think Thrace's mom had a stroke."

Thrace stood behind the ambulance as the two purveyors cloaked in white loaded his mother into the back. His eyes were consumed by the increasing number of flowers that began to sprout from his mother's flesh. What was real, he thought? Why can no one else see anything? Or am I simply going crazy?

He saw movement at the end of the driveway by the tree he pierced with a pencil less than an hour ago. From within the tree stepped forward a young girl with green brown hair, who appeared in an outfit of leaves and branches. She had a patch of leaves over her stomach as if covering a wound. She looked at him sadly as if she felt his pain. Then a look of fear consumed her features as she looked past Thrace. In haste, she disappeared back within the tree.

Thrace watched as she vanished and wondered; who she was, where had she gone and what had frightened her. There was too much happening too fast, he thought. A sensation of something breathing down his neck chilled his spine. He turned to see a shadow of a man standing behind him who appeared to be floating. The figure had a black smile upon his face. Then the dark figure itself froze in fear realizing Thrace was looking directly at him. In a whirl of grey smoke, he disappeared.

"Thrace." The stout young EMT said. "Get into the ambulance, and we'll take both of you to the hospital."

Thrace looked around the entire front yard. A dozen of people stood before him, most of whom he knew. He watched as Parker explained to his parents what was going on. He saw Mr. and Mrs. Clayton from next door quietly whisper back and forth; their age old wrinkles moving more than their lips. The Johnson kids from down the street sat upon their bikes and stared in wonder, but he saw no young girl dressed in leaves and branches, no dark shadow of a man and no beautiful blonde woman who had done this to his mother.

He realized Parker was now beside him telling him to get into the ambulance. Thrace climbed in and took a seat beside his mother as Parker jumped in and sat beside him as the lanky EMT closed the door behind them. He was so confused and the warmth of his boiling blood kept his mind spinning with images and thoughts of concern. He was glad Parker was there, for he was the only person he could talk to besides his mother, and right now, his mother was unconscious with flowers slowly stemming from her body.

CHAPTER 4

Thrace sat in the waiting room with Parker and his parents, face buried in his hands, his mind racing like the Athenian long distance runner, Phidippides, who ran to Sparta from Marathon to request help against the Persians, to no avail. Help is what he needed now, he thought. Nothing about what he witnessed made any sense. If it were true, how does one cure flowers from growing from one's body, he wondered? Maybe he could ask the little girl living in the tree in the front yard. She would know, then again, maybe she only knew trees and not flowers. Maybe she was still upset with him for piercing her with a pencil. He could get her a gift or a Band-Aid and let her sleep inside on the couch. It must be cozier than the tree. His mind spun crazy thoughts, and he wondered if maybe he was losing it.

"Parker, can I talk to you?" Thrace asked leaving his seat and making his way along the hallway.

Parker nodded and followed his friend away from his parents.

"So, you didn't see a woman standing before my mother?"

"I saw a white bird. I don't know…a pigeon or a dove."

"This may sound crazy, but I saw that woman turn into a dove." Thrace said with an amused smile at the sound of his own words. Parker did not respond. He stood waiting, knowing his friend well enough that he was piecing something together.

"Now, this is going to sound even weirder?" Thrace added.

"Weirder than you blacking out twice in one day and getting weird images of black eyes and then seeing a bird-woman...I'm all ears my friend." Parker said attempting to lighten the moment.

"Yeah, this is weirder. By the ambulance, I saw a young girl come out of the tree dressed in tree clothes. The same tree I pierced with a pencil."

"Was she hot?"

"Stop." Thrace remarked. He knew Parker would continue to soften this, but he needed his friend to listen. Parker's face calmed without amusement, and Thrace knew there would be no more comedy.

"This tree-girl looked scared and then went back into the tree, and I turned to see..., bear with me, a shadow-like figure smiling at me. He gave me the chills. I mean scared chills, then, he vanished in some grey smoke."

"Okay," Parker interceded with his focused tone. "Say you're not Lohan crazy and everything you saw is real. Who or what are they?"

"Well, this may make me Lohan crazy, but what if the woman I saw, the bird you saw, was...the Goddess of Love, Aphrodite?"

"Well, was she hot? I mean, she would be, being Goddess of Love and all. I'm just saying, that's one way to narrow it down."

"Yeah," Thrace responded with a smile, "she was hot. But the images I saw when I blacked out...violent; and just before that, these gold spots I touched from this necklace that, I don't know, absorbed into my thumb; then, the woman turned into a bird as my mom turns into a flowerbed. It kinda fits a lot of those ancient Greek myths."

"So, what do we do?" Parker asked.

"What, you believe me?"

"You're my best friend, and I think I know you pretty well. One thing I do know, you're not that creative."

"That's true. Thanks." Thrace said glad he had a friend this close who was at his side.

"So, what do we do?" Parker asked.

"I don't know," Thrace said in disappointment. "I know some Greek myths and history, but mom was the Professor. The only thing I can think of is checking the books at home and seeing what's on-line."

"What about a sacrifice?" Parker asked. "In that *Titan*'s game we play at night, to get help from Gods, you have to kill some goat and burn it and then type in help to the Gods?"

"You are brilliant!" Thrace replied, his excitement renewed. "Yeah, meat and grain I believe. I'll have to check the books."

"Thrace. Parker." Mr. Wells called out to the boys. They saw the doctor approach and hurried to join Parker's parents in the waiting room.

The doctor was short in stature and balding, but his large owl-like eyes gave the sensation of wisdom and confidence. Thrace was glad of the confidence, but he needed the wisdom more, ancient wisdom. Who else besides Parker would believe him?

The doctor stood silently before them expelling a feeling of uncertainty, quite contradictory from his appearance.

"Hello, I am Doctor Sheridan. It appears she had a stroke. Right now she is in a coma, but stable. We are still unsure of what brought on the stroke." His tone filled with concern. "Thrace, the EMT mentioned that you said something about a flower. Did she ingest anything that you know of?"

No, Aphrodite blew a flower from her hand toward my mother who then fell asleep, then she turned into a dove and flew off as the flowers with auburn petals began sprouting from my mother's head. Can't you tell by the dozens of flowers growing from her entire body? Yeah, that would go over well, he thought.

"She was in the backyard when I got home. I don't think so," he said. This doctor wasn't going to help his mother. Maybe he could talk to the girl in the tree. If any of this was true, it could not hurt.

"We are going to run a CT exam and a MRI and monitor her through the night. I suggest you go home and get some rest, and in the morning we can hopefully let you know more."

"Not unless you're Asclepius," muttered Thrace.

"Who?" asked Parker?

"Thrace," Doctor Sheridan said. "I do not believe an Ancient Greek physician could help your mother better than this hospital."

Thrace was surprised by Doctor Sheridan's quick comment, but not as surprised by the events that unfolded today, or that he wished Asclepius was still alive.

"Thrace, why don't you come over, have some dinner, and you can sleep at our house tonight if you like. We'll bring you back early in the morning," suggested Mrs. Wells.

"Thanks Mrs. Wells. I am hungry. There are some things I need to get at home though." Thrace replied as he nudged Parker.

"Thrace, we will see you in the morning and if any information arises before then, I will call myself." Doctor Sheridan offered.

"Thanks."

Doctor Sheridan offered a brief smile, turned and was gone.

"Before we go, I want to see my mother."

"Sure, we'll wait right here," said Mr. Wells.

Thrace went down the hallway and entered a small single room of white with reflections of soft pastels of auburn and pale grey upon the walls. The color stemmed from the beautiful and full auburn petals that shined a soft light throughout the room. She lay there peacefully with an array of small flowers sprouting from her athletic shoulders and glimmering from the lights beaming down from above. The sheet covered most of her body and pinned down the small garden that had begun to grow since her arrival and fought to reach out and reveal its beauty.

"With all the stories of Ancient Greece you told me growing up, I never thought you would become one of them, or I am going crazy. I don't know if these doctors can help you, but I'll find something. No matter what, I'll find something. I promise."

The first flower that spawned from his mother fell from her head and onto the pillow beside her. Thrace picked it and realized how beautiful the flower was and how the petals so closely resembled his mother's hair. As he looked at the pale grey center of the flower, it was as if his mother was watching him.

"I promise."

CHAPTER 5

Mr. Wells parked the spotless white minivan in their driveway alongside their manicured lawn as if each blade of grass had its throne upon the yard. Thrace stepped from the van and peered out upon the mountains to see All-Seeing Helios finish his journey in the west as Dark-Winged Night spread her black wings over the sky. The ancient starlit images took their places upon Night. Thrace saw Mighty Herakles and the Virgin Huntress to the south and the Twins, Castor and Pollux to the North. Thrace watched Pollux sparkle upon Night's wing and wished he would spend more time there than pounding within his chest. He turned his attention to his own house across the street. It looked cold, dark and empty. He thought of his mother and was reminded of so many years with late night tales of Prometheus, Bellerophon, Theseus, Echo and Narcissus and especially Crafty Odysseus all of whom kept him dreaming of great adventures throughout most of his youth. As he got older, he realized these tales where just that, tales, and though his mother no longer read them, he realized that Ancient Greece lingered in his subconscious. In school, the discussion of the Civil War reminded him of Athens versus Sparta, or as he did research on The Great War his mind leapt to Leonidas of Sparta fighting at Thermopylae and Themistocles of Athens in a naval battle just off shore, both united against the mighty Persian Empire. Even simpler things, like Parker in History class, consumed by Helen, he could not help but think of Helen of Troy as Paris first saw her, though Paris may have had more confidence than Parker, he thought. In time, the myths faded from this youth to more factual historical references. But now, it was myth that was reborn before him.

"Thrace, are you hungry?" Mrs. Wells asked sincerely. "I can make some soup or something."

"Sure. I'm just going to get some stuff from my house."

"Do you want me to go with you?" Parker asked.

"Yeah."

The young boys made their way across the street. Thrace stopped on the sidewalk and looked back as Parker's parents climbed upon their porch, both sides symmetrical in plants and chairs. They waved and the boys did the same. As they vanished beyond their front door, Thrace moved to the tree he witnessed the young girl vanish into. Parker watched as Thrace ran his hands around the tree and tried pushing his hands where she hand entered. Thrace did the same to the other trees as Parker continued to watch silently. After all the trees were checked, Thrace stood looking defeated.

"I guess the girl's not around?" Parker asked.

"Maybe I just imagined her."

"Maybe not," Parker said reassuringly. "Let's go grab some books and find out about that sacrifice. Then at my house, we'll check on-line."

"Yeah, like Wikipedia will have a page on animal sacrifice." Thrace said sarcastically. He looked at his friend with a feeling of guilt. He was simply trying to help. "Park, sorry. You know, the last time I spoke to my mother, over breakfast, we had a fight." Thrace said. "We never fight."

Parker approached his friend. "I'll admit I have never seen you two argue, much less fight, but that look she gave you this morning…she definitely wasn't mad at you."

Thrace smiled at his friend's words and together they went inside. Parker was correct, that was not a look of anger. He could not keep his thoughts on track, but he needed to stay focused to help his mother, even if he did not understand any of it. He was glad his friend was with him; no matter what he could or could not see.

"So where do we start?" Parker asked.

"You look for sacrifices," Thrace said. "I think you may find something in *Prometheus Bound*. I can't remember which playwright it's in. Check the *Iliad* too, the beginning."

Parker roamed the shelves and pulled out a couple of books. Digging through various books on Greek Tragedy, he realized, Thrace's mother had quite a collection. He finally found *Prometheus Bound* by Aeschylus.

Thrace found three different books on Greek myth and joined Parker on the couch. He started with the one he remembered, Echo and Narcissus, but skimming the story, he already knew there would be no answer here. Narcissus was lovely, beautiful and pursued by both women and men. He stared into a clear pool of water and for the first time, saw himself. In love with his own beauty, he remained until he died. His body was transformed by the Gods into the beautiful Narcissus flower. This was no cure, nor did he recall any myth that ended well when a mortal came up against the Gods. He needed help.

"All I found here is Prometheus giving mortals fire and getting punished for it."

"Let me check these books; this row is all on ancient myth."

"Should we check on-line?" Parker asked, knowing how it sparked Thrace earlier.

"We should. Wikipedia probably has a page on sacrifice to the Greek Gods."

"Sadly, it probably does," stated Parker setting down the *Iliad* and moved over to the laptop to search the internet.

The boys sat silently upon the couch, their eyes poured over pages of text and colorful web pages. There were no words exchanged between them, simply a comfortable silence only true friends understood.

"Here we go." Thrace said, his finger scanning the page. "Prometheus tricked Zeus into having mortals sacrifice the fatty part of the animal instead of the meat."

"So, we have to offer fat?" Parker asked. "That's kinda disgusting."

"Yeah, and who keeps fat in their fridge?"

"There's something here too." Parker added, attempting to find the passage once again on the laptop. "In the book I just put down, the *Iliad*. It appears to be Agamemnon shouting to Smintheus?

"That's Apollo." Thrace answered.

"Sure," Parker said.

> *If ever I have roofed a shrine to please your heart,*
> *Ever burned the long rich bones of bulls and goats*
> *On your holy altar, now bring my prayer to pass.*

44

"Again, more bones and fatty meat of livestock." Thrace said.

"Watch ya got in the fridge?" Parker asked.

Thrace got up with books in hand and stuffed them in his backpack and went to the kitchen. Parker added his books to the pack collection as well. In the refrigerator they found fresh meats and vegetables, milk and juice, but no animal fat.

"Wow! That is a pretty healthy looking fridge," Parker pointed out.

"Yeah, mom was always about eating well. We have some sweets, but few. That old Greek proverb, 'Nothing in Excess'." Thrace said. "I do crave ice cream from time to time, but we always have just yogurt."

"Well, we could try that nice ribeye right there or simply cook it up real quick for ourselves."

"That's right, I forgot your parents don't eat red meat." Thrace said. "Why not? What can tossing a steak on a fire hurt? Plus we have that cool brick hearth in the back."

"Yeah, that can be our holy altar. I'll get the fire started." Parker said as he grabbed some matches from the counter, and today's paper still sitting on the kitchen table and hurried outside.

Thrace pulled the steak from the refrigerator and followed Parker. He watched as Parker crumbled newspaper pages and began piling them up. From beside the hearth, he took small kindling and stacked it like a pyramid above the paper. He recalled how his mother had taught him how to do that, and she taught Parker when they took him camping. His parents did not like camping or the outdoors or anything that could not be counted or configured. They enjoyed the comforts of home and modern conveniences. His room was littered with computers, video games, the newest iPhone and electronic gadgetry that was mysterious to Thrace, who rarely used the flip phone he carried. Their parents were quite the opposite, he thought, but both had done a pretty good job of raising each of them.

Parker churned the fire to a bright orange flame. He added more wood and the flames consumed the wood with a ravaging hunger. Thrace approached the fire and could feel its warmth, its comfort on this cool May evening. The flames appeared to dance before him as if enchanted and there for his pleasure. So enamored by the flames, he wished he could join them in their gaiety. From the coals, he saw two black eyes he had seen in his mind, and they appeared to be watching him.

"A little gift from Prometheus. Thanks Promy." Parker said looking around as if the Titan was there, but he could not see him. He noticed Thrace was not paying attention. His eyes were transfixed upon the flames and a glazed look enveloped his face.

"Thrace!"

"Yeah, sorry." Thrace replied nervously, his eyes moving to his friend to the flames and back again.

"You weren't going to black out again were you?"

"No. Let's just get this done."

'Get this done', he thought. Get what done? They were about to toss a good steak on a fire, allowing it to burn and ask for help from Ancient Greek Gods. He must be going mad, but he didn't know what else to do. He pulled the auburn flower from his pocket and stared at its grey center. It was the same color as his mother's eyes. He wished it could speak; tell him what to do. But it did not, and he was on his own and had to try something, anything. She was all he had.

"Well, what do we do?" Parker asked.

"We toss the steak on the fire; it burns and smokes. The smoke reaches the heavens, and we ask some god for help."

"Which one?"

"I'm gonna ask Aphrodite. She's the one that did it."

Thrace pulled the steak from its plastic wrapper and placed it atop three small logs of wood within the flames. They watched as it slowly cooked and then burn. A dark grey smoke emanated from beneath the meat and Zephyrus, the gentle West Wind, carried it toward the Heavens. Thrace took a knee (for it felt like the right thing to do) and Parker joined him.

"Aphrodite, Goddess of Love, I offer this meat to you. I am asking if there is any way you can help or just tell me how to help my mother from this…curse, that has been placed upon her?"

His eyes followed the smoke toward the heroes that littered Night's dark wings. His eyes spied the heavens above for a bird or dove. There was not a cloud nor was there any wildlife near or far. He felt anger burn in the back of his throat and the great boxer Pollux return to practice with his heart as it beat with a fury.

"Olympian Zeus, Son of Cronus, if you are out there, what about you? Can you help at all?"

Thrace waited with every attempt at being calm, but his blood began to boil like the fires of Tartarus, as he stared at the heavens above, but the ancient heroes just sparkled back and revealed nothing to him. His eyes returned to the fire as if seeking resolution or warmth. Once again he saw those coal black eyes staring back at him. They appeared almost to smile.

"CAN ANYONE DO ANYTHING!?!" He yelled as his heart beat in turbulent fury.

"Maybe I can help." Thrace and Parker both turned toward the sounds that came from behind them.

"Hey, it's that horse from school. It does like you." Parker said.

But Thrace saw something much different. "That's no horse," he replied.

Before him stood a great mythical creature, a Centaur; a being with the head, arms and upper torso of a man and the body and legs of a horse. He had broad shoulders and thick arms of a warrior and close-cropped hair and beard to match his chestnut coat. His dark brown eyes were laced with gold and penetrated each of the boys as if absorbing all knowledge within them. His presence was elegant and wise, yet fearful and strong. He carried a beautifully carved wooden bow slung over his broad shoulders along with a quiver of arrows and a short sword at his waist. He appeared surprised that Thrace could now see him for who he truly was.

Thrace slowly approached the centaur. If all were true, it was yet another myth brought to life before his eyes, though he could not believe what his eyes revealed.

"Parker, what do you see?"

"I see a horse standing in your back yard. You?"

"A Centaur." Thrace replied.

"No way. Awesome."

"I am Sophos, grandson of Cheiron the Wise, who was teacher and mentor to Herakles, son of Zeus, and Achilles, son of Peleus. I am here to assist you in helping lift the curse of Golden Aphrodite from your mother." Spoke Sophos the Centaur in a deep and calm voice.

"Dude, the horse just nahhed a bunch of times. Was it talking?" Parker asked.

"Yeah. His name is Sophos," replied Thrace.

CHAPTER 6

Thrace ate a warm and thick tomato soup at the dinner table of the Well's family. It was a larger house than Thrace's and decorated in cube shapes and the simplicity of black and white. The Wells were organized in everything they did; they were accountants and desired structure, balance and organization. The dinner table was quiet except for the random slurping sound from Parker. The boys hastily drank their soup as if they had not eaten since the reign of Ouranos, the starry heavens, grandfather of Zeus. When they finished their meals, they quickly took their bowls into the kitchen and placed them into the sink.

"Thanks Mr. and Mrs. Wells. It was great." Thrace said.

"Would you like more or something else?" Mrs. Wells asked.

"No thank you. I'm just going to get some sleep."

"All right. If the hospital calls, we will wake you immediately."

"I appreciate it. Good night."

"Good night Thrace." Mr. Wells said. "Your mother will be all right."

"Thanks Mr. Wells."

"Good night Mom, Dad." Parker said as he made his was around the table to pass cheek kisses to his parents.

The boys disappeared from the dining room toward Parker's room. Mr. and Mrs. Wells looked at one another with stark surprise by their son's actions. Upon their return from Thrace's house, there was an eagerness followed by a sense of urgency. Not the expected condition with a mother in the hospital in a coma.

"Let's just let them get some sleep. The severity of it has probably yet to sink in." Mrs. Wells stated.

"You're probably right." Mr. Wells added, as they both began clearing the table.

Parker's room was one of disarray as if the Spartan King Leonidas and his Three Hundred fought the great battle of Thermopylae there just this morning. Posters of snowboarders and video games hung from the walls. An ocean of clothes littered the floor as the boys swam through the debris to the desk supporting a computer, which appeared to have been cleaned daily. It was a temple in a room of chaos.

"So," Parker asked. "What's the plan?"

"You know you don't have to go."

"I'm not letting you take off alone on some adventure with some random Centaur."

"Because you know so many." Thrace chided. "What about your parents?"

"Well, I'll leave some kind of note. Not the truth of course, but something." Parker spoke as he attempted to convince himself.

"We need to stop by my house to get our camping gear." Thrace said.

"We have all kinds of organic health bars in the pantry. I'll snatch a bunch of snacks." Parker said and added, "Do we need hay?"

"Nah, and not so funny."

"Well, just don't say 'nah' around the horse."

"Better not let him hear you say that?"

"Agree. What do you know of Centaurs?"

Thrace pondered for moment trying to recollect what his mother has told him over the years. "Well, Cheiron the Wise trained Herakles and Achilles, to name a few, and was the wisest of all Centaurs. Generally, they were a warring bunch who fought one another."

"Well, kinda like humans," Parker said with a smirk. "Let's see what Wiki says." Parker pulled up a seat at his desk and typed away with quick and nimble fingers upon his keyboard. "Let's see....men on mounted horses; well we know they are real. Violent by nature, good to know. Oh, thought to have been destroyed. Again, not true. Well, nothing really helpful for real-life situations."

"I think for most of what's coming, we are going to be winging it." Thrace replied.

With a nervous sigh, Parker responded. "When are we meeting the horse, ah, Centaur?"

"It's Sophos and just before midnight."

"Are we going to be riding him?"

"I'm not sure."

"It would be weird riding behind a human body. Would he turn back to chat with you? Then he wouldn't see where he was going? But, you could give him a massage while your weight hurts his back." Parker getting up from his desk as he nervously packed.

"He said we have to go somewhere in the mountains to get the cure." Thrace said with a smile. He knew Parker was nervous because of his endless attempts at humor. He was as well, but somehow, it felt right. "He also said it wouldn't be easy."

"Okay, your mother gets turned into a flower bed by the Goddess of Love, and a Centaur shows up for you to go on some quest. Name me one quest your mother every read or told you that was easy?"

"Now that makes me nervous." Thrace said apprehensively. "I'm not sure how big this is going to get."

"It's a good thing for you I've been sharpening pencils all night." Parker says with a smile.

It was a moonless night and the heroes, and victims of old riddled the sky offering little light except for two shaky beams of white. The boys pedaled north toward the mountains along a dark road following Cassiopeia who was placed upside down in heavens by Poseidon, God of the Sea, for her treachery to Perseus, son of Zeus and slayer of Medusa. Thrace gazed upon the array of stars on the dark blanket of heaven and thought of the vanity of the Gods that had brought so much pain to so many.

Their packs weighed them down, but Thrace even more with the burden of his mother upon his shoulders. He questioned his own courage. He was not trained for battle in the Agoge of Sparta like all Sparta's youth or raised since birth by the great Centaur Cheiron the Wise for a life of adventure. He was a sophomore in high school and not even sixteen yet. Though he was athletic, he was not competitive, was not some high school jock or a popular kid. He was just someone who liked camping and played video games with his geeky best friend. Now, he had met a Centaur, Cheiron's grandson, and was being led into the wilderness to save his mother. At least his geeky best friend was with him.

"What did you leave in the note for your parents?"

"We left and they were asleep. They won't get it until they awake, so I told them we woke early and went to the mountains for a quick hike and some fresh air. We'd be all right and home soon. They know how much you like the mountains."

"Well, it's not really a lie."

"Hey, is that it, or him?" asked Parker.

From the tree line beside the road a black silhouette of a Centaur appeared from the darkness of the forest from their two flashlights. Without the moon and only the stars upon Night's wings, his dark outline revealed a monstrous presence, but a comforting aura. He appeared as a guardian, a mentor. If there was trouble, Thrace felt, or hoped, he could protect them. But what trouble, he thought? The heroes upon the night sky killed most of the ancient monsters.

The boys stopped their bikes by the road where Sophos stood. The Centaur instructed them to move their traveling devices into the woods for they would not need them. Thrace and Parker obeyed and hid them within a large bush. They moved to join Sophos then Thrace paused as his eyes danced in amazement. He saw movement even as Night herself was all around him. Beautiful girls covered in leaves and limbs were running, singing and dancing though the forest.

"Who are they?" He asked Sophos.

"They are Hamadryad, or tree nymphs. They live in and nurture the forest, though it appears there is less forest then there used to be." Sophos stated.

"What did he say?" Parker asked.

"There are tree nymphs dancing around the forest."

"Oh, I need to see this." Parker stated adamantly.

One of the Hamadryad danced slowly toward the three of them. Her dancing was natural and innocent and gave life to the forest around her as if both rain and sunshine. She passed by Thrace and Parker. Parker did not even notice. He anxiously watched Thrace who slowly turned watching the young tree nymph dance around them. Thrace recognized her as the young girl from the tree out in front of his house. He smiled at her as she smiled back.

"I'm sorry. About the pencil," Thrace said quietly.

She smiled and danced between them and waved her hands before Parker's eyes as a soft song ebbed from her lips. He blinked continuously as his hands went to cover his eyes. "Oh, my eyes burn."

He attempted to open his eyes blinking quickly as his hands wiped away the tears. He cleared the water and his eyes erupted in wonder.

Parker witnessed dozens of tree nymphs who danced and sang in and around the trees. The music was serene and caressed his eyes, his ears, and his heart. He turned toward Thrace in excitement and for the first time he saw Sophos the Centaur.

"Holy fourteener."

"It is a pleasure to meet you Parker, son of William," said Sophos.

"AAh, nice to meet you Sophos…ah…" he looked at Thrace, puzzled.

"That would be grandson of Cheiron the wise, teacher of Herakles and Achilles." Thrace informed Parker.

"Cool. So, who's your father? Who did he teach? Who else have you taught?" Parker asked with childlike excitement.

"Many questions from the witty one. My father is another tale and as of today, Thracian Ares Kraft, Son of the Ares, God of War and Slaughterer of Men, you are my first," respectfully stated Sophos as he bowed before the son of Ares.

The boys stood silent. Sophos the Centaur had just stated that Thrace's father was Ares, the God of War and, by the way, he was a Slaughterer of Men.

Thrace stood fighting for words. When he asked his mother growing up about his father, she informed him he was someone in college she knew on a dig while in Thrace, Greece. She explained that is why she named him so. She added that the name Ares came from the Temple of Ares where they spent many hours at the dig site. He never questioned his mother's answer because she had never lied to him, and he felt in his heart her words to be true. But now as this mythical world had crashed before him, like waves upon the sandy shores, he knew not what to believe. Were the tales his mother told him as a child exciting bedtime stories or for understanding his lineage and the world associated with it? Even after his mother's flowering illness, seeing tree nymphs, and a living Centaur, he still had difficulty grasping all of it. Sophos had now shot an ancient bronze arrow into his heart. His father was the God of War. He pulled the auburn flower from his pocket that had fallen from his mother. Its grey eye stared back at him.

"It's just a dream," said Thrace in anguish as he fell back against a tree.

"I am sorry; it is not," said Sophos. "I apologize that you had to learn this information in such a fashion, but there is much to do and little time."

"Okay, so…I guess I need to talk to my father?" Thrace asked.

"Not yet. First we must consult the Oracle of Delphi."

"Uhm, sorry. I don't mean to interrupt," said Parker. "But did you say Oracle of Delphi? Isn't that in Greece?"

"That is correct," said Sophos.

"Why can't we just get Ares here and ask him to reverse the curse that Aphrodite placed on my mother?" asked Thrace.

"Young Thrace there is greater things at work here. First, Ares the Quarrelsome cannot help you, and he will not help you. If your mother has taught you anything of our ancient world, you must know a little of your father."

Thrace nodded, thinking back to stories he had heard or read about the God of War, the Slaughterer of Men. He was the most hated of the deathless immortals, a God whose only passion was that of war and the death of men. That was what he knew of an Immortal labeled his father.

"We must reach the Oracle to set us on the path for saving your mother." Sophos said.

"I mean, we're in Colorado there Sophos," said Parker. "It's gonna be hard to get to Greece, especially with a horse. No offense, but, you know, when people see you they see horse."

"Mortals see what they expect or want to see: that is all. There are other forms of travel besides a horse, as you said, or your wheeled devices. Now if you will follow me, we have much ground to cover." Sophos turned quickly into the forest and made his way toward the mountains.

Thrace and Parker stood for a moment lost in thought pondering the new world which existed all around them. The tree nymphs around them changed their song. It was one no longer of serenity but of victory. They danced and sang filling the boys with courage.

"You don't have to go." Thrace reminded Parker.

"I will admit...I am little more nervous than I was when we left. I can't let Thrace of the Pencil go out on a quest alone; can I?"

"Thanks." Thrace said quietly. "Of the pencil?"

"Let us go!" bellowed Sophos from deep within the woods.

"What are the odds he has a sense of humor?" Parker asked.

"One hundred to one." Thrace said with a smile as both Thrace and Parker ran into the forest after Sophos the Centaur.

CHAPTER 7

The stars upon the heavens silently drifted over head, and the Hamadryad and their song sailed purposely through the leaves. The wind howled like Cerberus, the monstrous three-headed dog and protector of the entrance of the realm of Hades, as the trio came upon the jagged edges of the mountain protected by great pines along the mountain ridge. With each step upon leave and branch, their sounds echoed throughout the forest as if the ancient mountain nymph, Echo, still craved attention, and searched for a two way conversation. The sounds sent chills down the boy's spine. Sophos did not notice her voice and moved as graceful and silent as a soft breeze.

The Centaur crossed into a small opening through the trees near the mountain's edge. Lifting his front, left hoof, Sophos pounded the ground four times and waited. Thrace and Parker once again passed familiar and puzzled looks. A rustle of branches followed a humming sound that traveled along the wind and passed between the boys. They watched a great tree with its leaves moving independently from the wind dancing to a song only it heard. It was sheathed in brazen bark except for a large circular knot about two feet by three feet where one could see the pale colored wood of the tree itself. A beautiful young girl with dark blue-black hair and arctic blue eyes stepped from the opening as if passing through a doorway. She was covered with white wool woven from mountain sheep. A warm light emanated from her illuminating milky white skin giving our weary travelers warmth and comfort. Thrace could not withdraw his gaze from her. Seeing him stare, she paused near the bush revealing her shy and cautious nature.

"It is all right Anthia, Mountain Oread, daughter of Gaia. These are the heroes I spoke of. If you could guide us to the Oracle of Delphi, much would be appreciated." Sophos spoke with great admiration.

"He called us heroes." Parker whispered to Thrace with pride.

Anthia stood motionless as the warm light from her skin caressed the mountain side. She nodded and turned back toward the great Sequoia doorway and passed once again through the large opening in the bark. Thrace and Parker stared in amazement and exchanged amused glances. Parker tightened his pack and quickly made for the knot in the tree. Just before rushing in, he paused nervously as he reached his hand forward, which passed through the pale wood of the inner tree as passing through mist.

"This is so cool." Parker said looking over his shoulder at Thrace.

Seconds later, his eyes erupted and fear consumed his face. Thrace rushed to his friend's side, but it was too late. Parker was yanked quickly into the tree itself.

"I should warn you," Sophos stated. "The trees do not like being used in such fashion. So do not play around as your witty friend did, or they will suck you in and throw you out the other side."

"Ah, thanks." Thrace responded as he briskly walked toward the tree and into the knot/doorway.

He could only see a void of darkness. He took small steps forward with his hands outstretched. Only a few steps in he felt a pulling sensation in

60

the pit of his stomach. He tried to stop, but the more he resisted; the more it pulled. Then, in a moment, he was thrown forward. He tumbled through the black abyss. In a flash of light he hit the solid earth below him upon his back, the books jabbing into his shoulder. He rolled to his side to see Parker lying on the ground beside him attempting to catch his breath. He sat up and watched Sophos gracefully step though a small knot upon a thin and narrow tree with pale white bark.

Thrace got to his feet and helped Parker to his, as his friend took deep breathes to regain his balance. He peered into the azure blue above him to witness All-Seeing Helios streaming his way from the east on his morning run. Around him, a smaller mountain than the one he stood before moments ago rose to the north and rolling fields of green expanded south. An ancient symmetry surrounded him. He expected to see a shepherd tending a flock of sheep in this pristine land, untouched by modern construction. Toward the south and tucked away in a nest of white barked trees stood the remains of an ancient Archaic Greek temple, one he recognized from his mother's models and books, one that existed during the time of the Homeric heroes; Odysseus and Achilles. The base was intact and many of the Doric columns stood strong, though the roof had long since fallen.

"We are in Greece?" asked Thrace in bewilderment.

"We are young Thrace," said Sophos. "Let us set up camp down by the Temple of Artemis, The Goddess of the Hunt."

Sophos the Centaur and Anthia the Oread made their way through the green pastures toward the temple. Thrace followed and paused realizing Parker was not walking beside him.

"You all right?" he asked looking back.

"We're in Greece. We're in freaking Greece?! I mean that tree was weird enough. It grabbed me by the arm and tossed me out that tiny knot there, but this....we're in Greece."

"Let's go." Thrace said as he jogged after his immortal companions. With a yell of excitement, Parker ran alongside his friend.

The Temple of Artemis had grand columns that had stood strong and tall for thousands of years. Four of the six Doric columns remained at the front and two in the back of the rectangular shape, but only a few pieces of the Doric columns along the sides still survived. Its solid foundation was still intact as Sophos stood at its center watching as the boys paced around in wonder. It reminded him of himself with his father; he thought, when his father was around and not off on one of his quests. Then as quickly as his smile arose, it vanished.

"Let us prepare some food. We have many miles to travel. Young Parker, will you start a fire with wood Anthia will bring from the forest while Thrace and I will hunt for meat."

Parker ceased his admiration of the ancient columns as Sophos' commanding tone reminded him why he was there. He nodded to Sophos and jogged over to where Anthia had placed firewood in a circle of rocks. He paused to look back at Sophos and thought he would have questioned his own parents as such a request. Then again, his parents were not Centaurs.

"Sophos, why is no one here? This is an ancient temple. Shouldn't there be tourists or students studying it?" Thrace asked.

"Like much of many countries, all is not built upon every hill or blade of grass. Many of these ancient places we have hidden from modern eyes. Only those who have had the mist removed may see much of our; what you call, 'Ancient' world. We preserve our history as well young Thrace." Sophos said. He walked to the corner of the temple where an array of weapons lie.

"Thrace, will you pick up those spears next to the Temple's edge and follow me."

Thrace looked around and found three eight foot hand-carved wooden spears lying in the grass. Each spear had a sharpened iron pike on the end. He picked them up and tested their weight. Much heavier than a javelin he thought.

"Just think of it as a big pencil," said Parker.

"Oh, that helps," replied Thrace who turned and ran to catch up with the Centaur.

Anthia sat quietly on the temple floor leaning back against a column watching Thrace and Sophos head into the forest. Parker noticed her eyes follow Thrace and smiled.

"You like him?" Parker asked.

Anthia's eyes met Parker and her expression changed from one of embarrassment to anger as she scowled at Parker.

"Sorry, just asking." He said. "How about some magic?"

From his back pack he pulled out some paper and a pack of waterproof matches. As Parker had done only hours ago, he crumbled paper from his pack, built a stick pyramid above it and added stronger pieces of wood atop his pyramid. He smiled as he enjoyed these aspects of camping which he knew little about until Thrace had moved across the street. It was a form of adventure that he only witnessed in movies or video games. Thrace and his mother first took him to the woods, hiking and camping. But now, being an active participant with mythical beings and traveling through trees, this adventure was more exciting and vigorous than any video game, or book he had read.

Parker, adding a touch of clumsy flair, struck the match to flame and lit the corner of the crumbled pages he pulled from his pack, and watched them go up in flames. He gently blew on the small fire to ignite the kindling. The flames caught and a smile of pride arose on Parker's face. He looked at Anthia, who was ignoring his magic and was smiling off in the distance. A long bellow rose behind him. He turned and saw a face upon the wind as a strong gust came racing toward, through and past him. He fell backward upon the ground and to his left he saw an extinguished fire. He sat up and heard Anthia rolling with laughter in the grass.

"Friend of yours?" Parker asked.

The forest thickened the deeper Sophos and Thrace traveled. Sophos did not speak, but continued to walk through the forest, his eyes scanning every limb, every blade of grass. Thrace followed his eyes and attempted to do the same. He noticed creatures in the forest, but their movements were too quick for his eyes even with the mortal mist removed. Sophos paused and sniffed the air. Thrace replicated him, but sensed nothing but the fresh, earthy scents upon the air. Sophos pointed south. Thrace's eyes followed his mentor's finger to see a young deer eating grass in a small opening in the forest. Sophos nodded toward the spear in Thrace's hand.

"I've never killed anything before," whispered Thrace.

"This is not for sport, honor or amusement, but for survival, yours and your mother's. Your first lesson." Sophos replied.

Thrace stuck two of the spears into the earth and steadied himself to throw the third. In Virginia, when he was only six, his mother showed him how to throw the javelin. He proved himself a quick and able study. Once at the College, when he was awaiting his mother for a weekend camping trip with Parker, the track and field team was wrapping up from practice and left a javelin behind. Wondering if he could still throw, he picked it up and fired it like a lightning bolt from Great Zeus. Parker danced with joy and since then mentioned the track team. Parker left it alone after he said no; until, he overheard Mr. Grissom.

The deer was less than forty yards away and even with this heavier spear, he knew he could hit it; he just didn't know if he could kill it. He was hungry. The soup he had last night was not enough, but he was too excited to eat. He was nervous and excited about this quest and being in Greece. They had only just arrived. Now, he stood with spear in hand being asked to kill a deer for food. Stinging eyes were upon him, and he knew Sophos was waiting impatiently. So, with spear in hand, he pulled it back by his ear and launched it toward the deer.

Ten yards beyond the deer, a tree was skewered, but the deer fell nonetheless. Thrace ran toward the deer to see what had happened. He intentionally missed. He wasn't ready to kill anything. Not yet, and not ever actually. He knelt beside the deer to see the feathers of an arrow from the chest of the deer. A perfect shot. Thrace heard the hooves of his mentor behind him. Sophos stood like a giant behind him holding the two spears in one hand and his bow in the other.

"I knew you would not kill it. I saw it in your eyes and so will your enemies. But, you needed to see it die to understand."

"Understand what?" Thrace asked.

"Heraclitus said, 'Only understanding the central pattern of things can a man become wise and fully effective.'"

"What is that supposed to mean?"

"In this instance, death for this animal had to occur for our survival, but death does not always have to come at your hands."

Thrace stood confused and angry. He was hungry and wanted…needed to eat, but this was modern times, right? We do not hunt for food anymore.

"Stop thinking." Sophos demanded. "You must accept this wisdom and what has happened and move on. Now, throw the deer on my back, and we need to return, and prepare for our journey and for what lies ahead."

They walked through the forest in silence with only their footsteps to remind them they were moving. As they cleared the forest they saw a large fire by the Temple. He could hear the laughter of Anthia. It danced along the mountains and gave him peace in his mental whirlwind of confusion.

"I want you to be alert to the four elements young Thrace," quietly spoke Sophos.

"Aren't there like two hundred something elements?" he asked.

"You need to shake your mind of your modern thinking. You may break things down smaller and smaller and find an infinite number of smaller particles as one may also expand to see we may be mere ants ourselves. In our pursuit to find what lies beneath, we tend to look too far and miss what is right before us."

Sophos the Centaur galloped forward leaving Thrace to make the last of the walk alone. He didn't understand. He could analyze it to the moon and back and arrive at one hundred conclusions. What he did know from years of his mother's reading and teachings was that the answers were usually revealed to each in time. He did have patience, but did his mother have time? He pulled the flower from his pocket and though the auburn petals began to fade, the pale grey eye of the flower stared back with strength that brought courage to his heart.

At the camp Thrace saw Parker run nervously around the fire, as Anthia's laughter offered a comforting sound upon a quiet and still background. Sophos moved to the edge of the temple and with the blade he carried in the sheath at this waist; he cleaned, gutted and skinned the deer as if he had done it a hundred times before.

"Hey bro, can you help me out here?" asked Parker.

"What are you doing?" Thrace questioned.

"There's this thing on the wind. He blew out my fire…three times and now keeps sneaking up on me and scaring me to death, and all the little tree girl does is sit there and laugh." He said and added. "Oh, did you know the tree girl here can start a fire by snapping her fingers?"

"It's Anthia."

Thrace looked over at Anthia who attempted to hide her laughter with her fingers, but could not hold back her amusement. The bellowing howl echoed through the green plains along the mountain, and Parker jumped back to front with one of the sharpened pencils in hand. The howl became louder, and Parker spun and threw the pencil at the face in the wind. Thrace saw a warm smiling face racing in the wind. Parker's pencil traveled end over end through the smiling mouth of the wind.

"Be gone Zephyrus, the West Wind. Leave us!" Yelled Sophos with a commanding tone. The howl fainted off into the distance.

"Oh Zephyrus, the West Wind was hanging out to give me a hard time. It kinda reminded me of Chad." Parker said. "So, you got the deer?"

"No. I missed it."

"Thrace, you don't miss."

"I just couldn't kill it," said Thrace. "At least I am not like my father."

Thrace looked at Sophos who was staring at him in discontent. Thrace attempted to hold the Centaur's gaze but could not. From the corner of his eyes, he noticed Sophos had thrown something at him. He did not duck somehow knowing it would not hurt him. He reached out and caught a thigh of the deer wrapped in fat.

"You will sacrifice that to Artemis, The Virgin Huntress, Daughter of Zeus and Hera, and thank her for good hunting on her sacred grounds. Then we will eat, prepare food for the journey and move further down the mountain. We have much traveling to do tomorrow."

"I'm not sure how?" Thrace said holding the deer thigh in his hand remembering how his last effort failed.

"Just as you did at your house. I have barley to add and thank the Goddess. Then we will feast in her honor."

"I like feasting." Parker added.

Thrace placed the fatty thigh upon the fire. The fat quickly embraced the flames and black smoke drifted into the azure blue above. Then he offered the barley Anthia handed him to place upon the fire. The dark smoke reached a dark grey color and reminded Thrace of the face his saw by the ambulance. He watched but saw no eyes in the grey smoke. Zephyrus returned, silent this time, and swirled around the misty grey smoke. Thrace watched as the West Wind carried his offerings into the blue heavens above; then, his eyes returned to the fire. He remembered the coal-black eyes watching him before. He was transfixed by the flames as they danced like the hamadryad along the burning logs. He saw no black eyes with the coal, no darkness peering back at him.

"I offer these fatty meats to the Virgin Huntress, Artemis, daughter of Zeus, and thank her for the use of her temple and her sacred hunting grounds. May you give us a safe journey." Thrace finished and looked at Sophos for approval, but he offered none.

After the fatty thighs had burned, and the smoke reached the heavens, Sophos placed the remaining meat upon the fire, racking it upon spears placed on both side of the flames. He roasted the meat as if he had done hundreds of times before, and the boys quietly watched. The smell of rich roasted game teased the boys with hunger. Sophos carved meat for each and tossed it their way.

"You boys need to eat and get your strength about you. We will move south until Helios sets in the west."

"Sophos?" asked Parker. "Where in Greece are we?"

"We arrived just beneath Mt. Parnassus, and we must travel south to get to Delphi. Two days journey if we are quick."

"Not trying to be rude about the traveling situation, because it was cool, weird, but cool. But, why didn't we just get out of a tree in Delphi." Parker asked with a bit of caution.

"Because the journey is as much of the quest as is the destination." Sophos simply replied.

"Sophos, another question?" Thrace asked as he pulled the coin necklace from his pocket. "I found this in a book. Do you know what it is?"

The Centaur approached and took the coin from his hand and held it before the bright orange flames. It spun slowly as the Centaur examined it with concern.

"It is an ancient coin from the land of Thrace, though more refined than many during that time. More than likely used by the priests at the Temple of Ares," Sophos concluded returning the coin to Thrace.

"There were also some gold spots upon the back of it. I touched them, and well, they kinda moved, and I think they went into my thumb," Thrace said looking cautiously at Sophos rubbing his finger along his thumb as if it itched.

"Gold spots?" The great Centaur stated and slowly paced among the columns. "That would be ichor, the blood of the gods. More than likely, it was blood from Ares himself. The blood sensed you, being his son, and returned home. That is why you could see me for who I truly was at your house."

Thrace sat upon Mother Gaia by the fire observing the coin in his hand. He noticed Parker out of the corner of his eyes encouraging him. He rolled his right finger over in a circle, his personal sign for 'keep going'. Thrace understood what he meant.

"Well, after the…ichor got in me, I saw images. Images of a dying boy, three figures on a plain, coal-black eyes, and I heard the wailing of a monstrous creature," Thrace said, his eyes returning to the dancing flames upon the logs for comfort.

"And that wasn't the first time," Parker added. "He passed out in school saying he saw the same things."

Thrace looked up at his friend. He was not upset at him for adding to his already nerve-wrenching tale; it needed to be said. He was nervous; he was scared. He felt too young for this, but what else was he to do; his mother needed him.

"The ichor brought a quick connection between you and your father; you saw what he saw. The earlier image I cannot say." Sophos said looking up toward the heavens as if seeking council or advice; though his grandfather would not reach the heavens until the arrival of dark-winged Night.

"In a very short time, you have been given much information young Thrace. Not just about this world but about yourself. In any other time, you would be considered a man and take responsibility for your past, present and future. I know in your time, there are rules, age limits, and they are installed for your safety. But now, you are responsible for your safety and for that of your mother. You two should eat, and I will scout the area quickly before we travel south until Night takes her place in the heavens."

Sophos, the Centaur, slung his bow over his shoulder along with his quiver of arrows; he unsheathed his blade and sliced meat from the deer upon the fire and headed away from camp. Anthia smiled and nodded to both of them and walked toward the closest tree and stepped into the tree as if into a home. Thrace and Parker sat alone by the fire.

"How are you feeling?" Parker asked.

"I don't really know." Thrace answered. "You know, my mom made a joke at a party when I was a kid, that my dad was Ares. I overheard her and spent the next week with a plastic sword running around the house doing battle. I was like seven or eight. It seemed cool then."

"Well, being the son of a god could be cool. Weren't Hercules and Achilles sons of gods?"

"You may want to say Herakles, it's the Greek. Hercules is the Roman. They may get upset; it being their history and all. Anyway, Herakles killed his wife and kids, and Achilles, a great warrior, was a whiny child who died early."

"You don't have to be like them. Isn't the purpose of the study of history not to repeat it?"

"You sound like Mr. Grissom." Thrace said with a smile remembering the simple things of school. "Did you pack the *Iliad*?"

"Yeah," Parker stated and dug through his pack to find it. "Here it is."

Thrace opened the book and thumbed through the pages in search of history. He found the proper chapter, ran his finger down the pages turning them with ease until he found the section for which he was searching. He read.

> *But Zeus who marshals storm clouds lowered a dark glance*
> *And let loose at Ares: "No more, you lying, two faced…*
> *No more sidling up to me, whining here before me.*
> *You-I hate most of all the Olympian gods.*
> *Always dear to your heart,*
> *Strife, yes, and battles, the bloody grind of war.*

Thrace closed the book and looked at his friend who listened carefully at the words he read. He tossed the book back to Parker, who caught it and began flipping through it himself.

"There's my dad in a nutshell." Thrace said eyes back upon the flames.

"That's stupid." Parker remarked. "That's like saying I have to be an accountant, or if your dad's a crack head, you have to be a crack head. It's up to you…Thrace of the Pencil." Parker tossed his friend a pencil from his pack.

Thrace smiled as he caught it and turned it over in his hand. Thrace of the Pencil, he thought. Kinda funny. He looked around for a target, not wanting to use a tree again. Twenty yards away, he peered at a stone column. He turned on his knees and faced it. From the corner of his eyes, he saw Parker smile. His friend gave him encouragement. He let loose the pencil and like a lightning bolt from Zeus it crossed the twenty yards in a moment. It pierced the stone column with great force.

Both of the boys got up and ran over to the column. They saw only the eraser extending from the column as the other four inches were stuck within the column.

"Holy Mt. Elbert!" Parker yelled.

The boys laughed as they returned to the fire. Parker handed Thrace a handful of pencils he had sharpened and Thrace placed them in his pocket as Parker reminded him, 'you never know'. They sat by the fire as Parker asked him questions about Ancient Greece and how it compared to the video game they played nightly to get caught up as bright and shining Helios made his westward journey across the blue heaves above.

They saw the Centaur approach and finished eating quickly. He ordered them to put out the fire, back up, and they would travel for a few hours and camp. They packed as they had done on many camping adventures as Sophos sliced up the meat for the journey. Parker doused the fire as Thrace organized the weapons. Sophos quickly marched south as the heroes hurried to keep pace as Helios made his way west and soon Night stretched her dark wings across the sky as the heroes of old took their place to offer courage to the mortals below.

CHAPTER 8

The first day had been an arduous one for the heroes. Their camping and hiking had traditionally been on their terms, starting with a hike of a few miles at a casual pace followed by a playful campsite with packed food or a stint of fishing. It was no longer. In the morning Sophos was already awake preparing meat for breakfast. "You will need your energy", he reminded them. Parker had also been prepared and passed out cereal bars which Anthia enjoyed. The morning meal was quick lived as the fire was extinguished, and Sophos was on the move south. They did not stop for lunch nor breaks of any kind. Anthia just walked quietly behind the boys with a soft smile as if a quiet walk through the Gardens of Elysium. The boys, on the other hand, dropped their packs at dusk by a fire and slept until sunrise.

The next morning Dawn stretched her golden arms wide as Night made her way home to Tartarus along the river Styx, though it was a slow rise for Thrace and Parker, and again Sophos had a fire warming hot water with herbs and dried meat. It smelled divine, and the boys ate as if they had not eaten in days. They now understood Sophos', 'you will need your energy' statement. Even as they started off, they felt sore, but the hiking helped, even at Sophos' hurried pace.

"So, what happens at Delphi?" Parker asked walking alongside Thrace. "Is it kinda like the video game; kill a goat or lamb for answers to questions?"

"Sort of, but I think you can offer some priest money, then they sacrifice a goat or ox or cake to the gods, some priestess mumbles something and the priest you paid translates it for you."

"Well, couldn't the priest tell you what you want or don't want to hear according to how much you paid?" Parker asked.

"Good observation quick-witted Parker, son of William," Sophos injected. "In a time long past, there was a bribe to an influential priest, Cobon by Cleomenes, the Spartan King. It was revealed, and Cobon and the Priestess Perialla were banished from Delphi, but the oracle has benefited the Hellenes, or Greeks far more than it has hurt them. She has revealed secrets; instructed Lycurgus to reform Sparta to the military power it became which helped against the Persians; it began the colonization of much of the Aegean and saved the slaughter of the Athenians against Xerxes."

"So, how does that help us?" Thrace asked.

"The Oracle of Delphi is much different than it was then. During these so-called modern times, it has become a site of study and tourists come to visit a time long ago. It is presently maintained by the children of the Immortals, primarily the ancient Immortals, like Anthia."

"And you think a mystic will help us with Thrace's mother?" Parker asked.

"Does not your world seek advice from psychics, news people or television actors? The Greeks sought only one focal point, the navel of Zeus."

"You got a point there." Parker replied.

"How has it changed?" Thrace asked.

"She no longer receives many visitors, for only a handful have the mist removed. I believe the last mortal may have been your mother."

"What?!" yelled Thrace. "When was this? Why didn't you tell me?"

"That is for you to ask your mother." Sophos replied.

Thrace felt Pollux return to his chest to continue his training as his heart pounded and his blood begin to boil with rage. There was much Sophos knew and was not telling him. He recalled earlier the idea about answers being revealed to those in time when they were ready? As new information trickled toward him, he began to feel differently. The more he knew; the more prepared he would be. Like a test. He caught up to Sophos wanting to ask him more, but the Centaur marched hastily on, as if Thrace was not there. Thrace was beginning to lose his patience.

"So, what do we offer?" Parker asked trying to break the chilled silence in the air. "I've got a twenty, but I doubt they will take that."

Parker was nudged on his shoulder and turned to see Anthia standing next to him with her hands clasped before her. She lifted her top hand to reveal a large collection of ancient gold coins.

"A woman hording gold. Why am I not surprised?" Parker stated.

Anthia, not happy with that statement, nudged him unveiling a strength Parker was not prepared for as he tumbled to the ground, pack and all.

"Hey!" Parker yelled attempting to gather himself.

"Guys," Thrace said.

"Dude, she knocked me over!"

"I think we have bigger problems right now."

"Look what we got here." Spoke a sly lisping voice.

Before Thrace stood two large burly men in worn modern rags of dirty khaki pants and torn sweatshirts with sun weathered faces and toothless smiles. The taller one waved a large curled Persian sword before him as if swatting flies. The shorter of the two, though much stouter, had a thick short sword that resembled a modern day military knife.

As Parker's eyes made contact with the two large ragged men bearing weapons, he felt as if the other son of Ares, Phobus or Fear, seized his heart. He stood as still as a blade of grass. Parker looked at Anthia, but he did not see the Oread that had led him through the trees, but a White Mountain sheep. Sophos was still Sophos the Centaur standing beside Thrace.

"All right boys. What brings you two Yanks way out here in the middle of nowhere with a horse and a sheep, heh?" The taller one asked in a brogue English accent.

"They must be on holiday," the stout one said with a lisp through his limited teeth, "and look, they brought us gifts."

The stout one pulled a rope out from his waist as the taller one copied his friend's moves. The stout one tossed the rope around the waist of Sophos as the other tossed the rope around Anthia, the White Mountain sheep.

"Now," the stout one with the lisp said. "How about those satchels?"

"Are you going to do anything?" Thrace asked to Sophos.

"Hey look," spoke the taller one, "he talks to his little horsey. What do you want him to do? Does he prance or bow like those on the tele?"

"Or maybe he jumps fences. Let's hope so, then at least he can bring us some money." The Lisp said. "Now, hand over the packs."

Thrace and Parker paused, each looking at one another. Parker nodded, took his pack off and tossed it in front of the thieves. Thrace did the same seeing fear in his friend's eyes. The thieves picked up their packs, and each slung one over their shoulder.

"Nice doing business with you boys." The taller one said. The thieves turned and began walking away with Sophos and Anthia in tow.

"What are we going to do?" Parker asked.

"I don't know. I thought Sophos would have done something."

"Do you know how to get to Delphi without him?"

Thrace gave his friend a disgruntled look.

"Just asking?"

"We don't have time for this," Thrace stated, his heart pounded within his chest, his blood boiling. "Follow my lead."

"HEY!!" Thrace yelled.

The two thieves paused at the sound of Thrace's voice. "Oh, sounds like the little boys want to play." The Lisp said with a smile.

"We have cash on us. How about you give us back our pack and the animals and we give you the money?" Thrace asked.

Thrace watched Sophos who made neither a sound nor facial expression. He was simply an observer to the event as if an actual horse being bought and sold.

"How much you got?" The stout one asked and was quickly slapped on the shoulder by the taller one. "What?"

"About one hundred dollars, Amer…Euro." Parker barked out.

Thrace turned to Parker who shrugged a knowing thought that twenty dollars was worth very little, especially an American twenty in Europe. This exaggeration caused the two thieves to argue. Thrace became impatient even angry knowing Sophos just stood there doing nothing, and there were more important tasks at hand than these two stupid thieves. In the past his patience had been one of his strong points, but since that morning fight with his mother, his patience had started to waiver. Like the turbulent North Wind Boreas, time howled past and he did not need to be wasting it here with his mother in the hospital thousands of miles away. Now, only Rage wailed within him.

"You know what." Thrace spoke with a flavor of aggression in his tone. "How about you just dropped the packs and leave the animals and no one gets hurt."

The thieves' argument seized and both turned their attention to Thrace.

"Is that a threat boy?" The taller one asked.

"It is." Thrace said pulling the pencils from his pocket.

"You're kidding me right." The thief with the lisp gargled a laugh. "Pencils?"

Without a second's hesitation, Thrace hurled the pencil like an arrow from a taut bow and in a single breathe, it struck the stout thief with the lisp deep in his right shoulder. He let out a bellowing wail. Again, Thrace hurled the second pencil and in a single breathe it stuck the taller one deep in his left shoulder. He copied his friend and let out a second wail. Both thieves' fell to their knees in pain.

"Now." Thrace said calmly. "You will drop those packs and release our friends or the next couple of *pencils* will take out your eyes, and you will wander these hills blind like Oedipus." Thrace finished, not concerned whether or not they understood his analogy.

"Fine! Fine!" The taller thief yelped, dropping the packs and releasing the ropes.

"Sophos!" The one with the lisp yelled. "You said we wouldn't get hurt."

"What?" Thrace said.

"Not like your father indeed." Sophos said solemnly. "Now pick up your gear. We have wasted enough time here."

"What was that? Another test?" Thrace yelled. But the Centaur did not reply. He continued through the mountain hills toward Delphi in haste.

"Oh, I'm gonna get lead poisoning, I just know it." The tall thief said pulling the pencil from his shoulder.

"I told you we should have taken the money." The stout one retorted.

"Sorry about that." Parker said as he reached down to pick up his pack next to the thieves. "You may want to put some peroxide on that."

"What?" The taller one yelled, and Parker raced after Thrace and the Centaur.

CHAPTER 9

Thrace noticed that Sophos had picked up his pace through the rocky crags now moving west following All-Seeing Helios' path. He hurried to keep pace, though his mind drifted on the recent conflict. *What was the point of that last encounter? Did he want me to throw pencils at them? I had never thrown pencils at anyone before. Was he pushing me? Or was he telling me I am like my father?*

This confusion in his mind reminded him of the Fates; who weaved and manipulated this life unfolding before him. Clotho at her spindle who wove life and its adventures for each and Lachesis, with her rod measured each and every life. Thrace wanted to use the third Fate, Atropos' shears, who ended life, to cut through his thoughts and to seize this continued anger. He wanted to understand where the rage came from. More importantly, he wanted to be able to help his mother. He wanted to apologize to her.

The thoughts of his mother where cleared from his mind as he ran into the back end of Sophos who had stopped. He shook off his weariness and moved beside Sophos who stood on a rise overlooking the slopes of Delphi.

"Eyes always before you young Thrace."

"Yeah, that would be a good idea," Thrace replied.

Thrace's eyes spanned the small opening in a valley, a crevice looking west upon the craggy mountain slope which were Delphi. Staggered terraces climbed the mountain slope like a staircase; each offering new life and attractions to this once thriving city of answers. The Great Theatre curled along the recess of a crag which once held great theatrical competitions for ancient playwrights like Aristophanes and Sophocles. Further up upon the mountainside was the Great Stadium designed for competitions in wrestling and the footrace.

Thrace drank in the view of the scattered remains, rebuilt monuments and temples that adorned the steep mountain side. He knew that all the cities and peoples of Greece visited or sent emissaries to the Pythia for answers or assistance from the Gods. Throughout his years, his mother had told him tales of the wonders of ancient Greece, but rarely mentioned Delphi, which seemed odd witnessing such ancient beauty. His mother rarely told tales or read from ancient texts about what transpired here. He knew she had been here on her college travels, but with Sophos knowing she had visited Delphi, that changed the ancient prophetic land. She did nothing without a reason, and how would Sophos know? Like Sophos, did she keep things from him, like who his real father was? Was it for his protection?

"It's magnificent." Parker called out.

"Over time, only memories and tales remain, not objects." Sophos said gently, and added. "Only three columns of the twenty remain of the Temple of Athena of the Grey eyes. Today they believe since it was built round it was used for worshiping Hades and other underworld practices. How dark your world is Thracian Ares."

Thrace heard the sad tenderness in his teacher's voice and for the first time saw softness in his eyes. Of all the people who felt as if they do not belong in the time they live, maybe this great creature was one that did not belong in this time. Parker and Anthia arrive beside him for a closer look and witnessed Sophos' strength reappear like a thundercloud. He heard the deep breathing of his friend beside him and noticed he was exhausted, but he smiled at the ancient wonder before him.

"In the center you will see the Temple of Phoebus Apollo. A large hexastyle with fifteen columns along the sides and divided into three naves, the back nave, called the adytum is used by the Pythia, the prophetess. She sits in her bronze tripod which they believe represents the cosmic egg from which all of the universe spawned."

Thrace and Parker turned to see the two thieves standing behind them. They had torn rags tied over their shoulders where Thrace had pierced them with the pencils. Each smiled a toothy smile.

"You don't mind if we keep the pencils do you?" The one with the lisp asked. "You being the son of Ares and all. They could be worth something."

"Boys, meet Aemon and Battus, Battus being the stout one with the lisp. They, for some unknown reason, have never had the mist...unfortunately." Sophos said.

"Yeah," Aemon quickly said. "We could always see the Naiads, the Oceanids, and Hamadryads since we were kids, but Sophos was our first Centaur."

"Oh, the satyr too," added Battus.

"Yeah, we saw a satyr. He comes and plays the flute for the Hamadryads."

Thrace and Parker stood silently staring at one another lost in confusion as the thieves giggled like school girls looking at Thrace like English royalty. They bickered and whispered between one another.

"Fine!" Battus bellowed. "So, have you seen your father?"

"You two quiet!" Shot out Sophos and the thieves crumbled like the Nemean Lion did as Herakles permanently quieted the beast with his vicious club on his first of twelve labors.

"We stand at the navel of the earth. In a time long ago, it was foretold that devious-devising Cronus, who took control of the world from his father Ouranus with the great grey flint sickle, would be displaced by his own son. Upon the birth of his children, Cronus swallowed each one. His wife Rhea wishing to protect her youngest son Zeus, replaced him with a stone wrapped in a blanket and presented it to Cronus. In his arrogance, he simply swallowed the rock. Zeus was carried away to Crete at Mt. Dicte on the Aegean Hill where he was raised by Amaltheia. As Mighty Zeus grew he heard of the oppression of his mother Rhea and sought revenge for his brothers and sisters. He led a battle against the elder Gods lasting ten years. He released a few of the ancient Titans, the three brothers, the giant Hundred Handed, and he defeated Cronus the devious who vomited the stone replicating Zeus, and his brothers and sisters. Zeus himself placed it in Crete, but later moved it here, the navel of the earth." Sophos turned toward Thrace.

"Now, these two actors have made arrangements that we will not be interfered with for the remainder of the day," Sophos said with a bit if disgust. "You must find the navel of the earth and place your hand upon it. It will feel your question, your desire and reveal the path to the present Pythia."

"How do I find it?"

"You are the son of Ares the Immortal, you will know." Sophos said and took a step back to allow Thrace to proceed toward the ancient city of Delphi.

The heroes proceeded along the rocky terrain to the mainstay of Delphi and Thrace followed the Sacred Way leading to the Temple of Apollo. Ancient rock and chips of marble lay astray along the path as they passed the remnants of ancient treasuries. Even after a thousand years, many remains maintain the beautiful and delicate artistry of a period of detail and patience.

"This fully restored building on the left is the Treasury of the Athenians built after the victory at Marathon against the Persians," Aemon said.

"What are those pictures along the roof?" Parker asked.

"Good question young sir," Aemom said. "They represent the magnificent deeds of the great Athenian hero Theseus."

"You two, silence." Sophos said.

"By the way young sir," Aemon whispered. "We're not usually thieves, we're actors. We do theatre here and Battus and I play Might and Violence in Aeschylus' *Prometheus Bound.*"

Aemon smiled as Battus leaned over from behind Aemon and mouthed 'Violence' informing Parker which one his was. Parker nodded with a smile and laughed.

"What," Aemon said. "You don't believe us? You believed us when you thought we were…"

"I said Silence!" Sophos yelled. "Now Thrace, you should be able to feel a sensation within you, a warmth."

Thrace paused and turned back toward Sophos. "A warmth?" he asked.

Thrace proceeded forward. With every step he tried to feel each thing, but attempting to isolate 'a warmth' seemed impossible. He stopped before what remained of the Temple of Apollo just beyond the Alter of Chios. Only a handful of columns stretched out from the base of temple. He remembered the pictures and replicas his mother made with modern software over the years, and his mind could drum up a grand vision of a once magnificent building. The Temples bold thick columns stretching to a deep marble roof. Such a feat today would take a parking lot of machines and men, he thought.

"And they met together and dedicated
In the Temple of Apollo at Delphi
As the first fruits of their wisdom
The Far-famed inscriptions
Which are in all men's mouths,
'Know thyself' and 'Nothing too much.'

"Plato," Sophos finished.

Thrace knew the two coins of wisdom from his mother, but he had never heard that passage before. He watched his mentor as if recalling some long lost memory. There was something within this being that was far more than just a mentor helping him help his mother. There was concern as well, but not just for him.

Thrace walked around the temple reaching out and touching rocks in search of this 'warmth', but felt nothing. He finished his tour and stood at the original temple front, where many years ago people stood for hours searching for answers to question they could not answer or help in completing tasks they could not understand. I do not understand any of this, he thought. I'm just a fifteen year old. I still can't talk to girls. I just want my mother to be all right. Who cares if my father is some Greek God? I just want my mother back. I just want to say I'm sorry.

He felt a buzzing near his ears like a humming bird steadily drinking from a flower. His eyes panned the temple; he saw neither bee nor bird, but the fluttering continued. It grew stronger as he stepped to the front left of the temple steps. Buried next to the steps was an oval boulder reaching out from Mother Gaia just above his ankles. Upon it, a single straight line was etched into the rock. He stretched his hand toward the top of the rock.

"We believe that rock was placed to signify the first or most important temple." Aemon said as Battus quickly slapped him upon the shoulder.

Thrace paused and looked back at Sophos who stood stoic as always, but his chestnut eyes gave Thrace confidence. Thrace turned to Parker, who just shrugged and rolled his finger to get on with it. He dropped his back from his shoulders and returned his attention to the rock.

He placed his hand upon the rock, and a sensation of warm water surged from the rock through his body. It was soothing, like a warm bath on a cool night. In a moment he saw Mighty Zeus, son of Cronus himself placing the rock along the rocky plains of Delphi beside the Temple of Apollo. The rock was much larger than he imagined as Mighty Zeus pushed it deep into the surface of Mother Gaia. As the Olympian King finished, his eyes slowly panned the horizon and for a breath, the eyes of Mighty Zeus of the heavy thunder met Thrace. He was younger than the paintings and sculptures Thrace remembered. His beard was not as full and robust, though already a dove white, but that was the only softness upon his stern, yet tired face of a man. Not a man, an Immortal who had defeated his father, fought tireless battles with other Titans and Gods, and carried the burden of the mortals on his shoulders. He had the deep and dark eyes of a never-ending canyon, and Thrace thought he would fall in forever.

Thrace was thrown back from the rock and hit the ground hard upon his back. The image of Father Zeus was gone. The remains of ancient Delphi stood again before him. Parker was at his side as was Anthia. The Mountain Oread touched Thrace, and he felt the warmth of her surge through him as Parker helped him to his feet.

"You all right?" Parker asked.

"Yeah, I think so," Thrace replied still getting his bearings. "I saw…well I think I saw Zeus placing the stone here. Then he looked at me, and he didn't look happy."

"REALLY!!" Bellowed Aemon. "What did he look…"

"SILENCE!" The mighty Centaur wailed. "I forbid either of you to speak."

Aemon and Battus cowered like small children unprepared for the Spartan Agoge, the military middle school all Spartan boys attended, and hid behind partial columns as if they rendered them invisible.

The ground began to rumble beneath their feet, though no column or pedestal fell. The heroes stepped back from the temple, except Sophos who stood his ground. The first steps leading up to the Temple of Phoebus Apollo lowered themselves deep within the Mother Gaia, leading down to a lower level beneath the Great Temple.

"I guess that was the rock," said Parker. "Zeus throws you on your ass for one ticket to the priestess."

"You are often humorous young Parker," said Sophos, "but there will be a time when you will no longer be able to hide behind it."

Anthia stood before the steps leading down into the lower level of the Temple to the present Pythia, priestess of Delphi. She handed Thrace a large stick, the end wrapped in cloth. Holding her hand near the cloth, she snapped her fingers and like a match, the cloth lit. She then handed Thrace a pouch of gold coins she revealed to Parker earlier. She lit torches for Parker and Sophos and walked away from the entrance.

"You're not going?" Thrace asked. He wanted that same warmth her touch offered after being thrown to the ground. She softly shook her head.

"This is your request for information, so you will go, as will young Parker, and I and the Oread must wait outside." Sophos informed him.

Thrace, with torch in one hand, proceeded into the darkness. As the flicker of his light disappeared, Parker paused before the steps. He looked at Sophos.

"Nothing to say?" Sophos asked.

"I'm good." Parker replied and made his way down the steps after Thrace.

Thrace stepped in the darkness and held his torch high. Before him were three large columns that appeared Archaic in design, which he remembered from his mother's description of their Doric cylindrical tops. A flicker of light closed in behind him and within a minute Parker was beside him. The hooves of Sophos the Centaur echoed from behind.

"So, what do we do?" Parker asked.

"We need to offer someone money." Thrace replied. "Let's keep going."

The trio continued past the columns; the torches light off the columns left large shadows throughout the room. They came to the third column, and Thrace held his torch up high to examine the room. Torches along the wall sparked and blazed as if alive on the east and west walls of the heroes as they reached a passage revealing the furthest chamber. Two more wall torches awoke on their own in bright flames upon the back wall and between the torches stood a bronze half-moon bowl atop three iron legs and resting within the bowl sat a slumping young girl as if asleep.

"Thracian Ares." A voice spoke. "Taking the name of a God can place one in much harm."

"Who's there?" Thrace asked.

From behind the column a man appeared as if he stepped out of column as Anthia stepped from the tree. His eyes were a transparent green-white that shimmered in the darkness as the torches glimmered light off his clean shaven head. The man had no hair at all, not even eyebrows.

"I am Lampos, present Priest of Delphi." He said in a deep chilling voice. "What do you offer for the consul of the Amymone, Pythia of Delphi?"

"I offer gold." Thrace said holding out the pouch of golden coins given to him by Anthia.

Lampos the Priest accepted the pouch, reached his hand within, and his fingers felt the nuggets as if running them through a flowing brook.

"This shall be sufficient for one advisement." He said. "Be wise when asking your question, Thracian Ares."

Sophos and Parker stood in silence behind Thrace. He felt alone, even in their presence. Before him slumped a young girl covered in a woven white robe, and for some reason she was going to tell him how to help his mother. With all the odd things he had witnessed of late, this appeared to be the most unbelievable. His mother had come here for some reason, and now he had to do the same, for her. For that was all he wanted, nothing more…to help his mother.

"Ah, hello. I am here to find out how to help my mother from the curse placed upon her by the Goddess Aphrodite." Thrace asked.

There was a silence that felt like a lifetime and the slumbering Pythia did not move. As sudden as her silence, her head swiftly arose and her eyes flared white as the moon. She let out a long slow breath of air. Without a teardrop of air within her, a long whisper of a voice stretched from her lips.

Within the hundred,

lies the one.

Born of a god,

painted in red,

will return the love

and forgo the dead.

The Pythia slumped back forward as if life had been taken from her. Lampos stepped before Thrace with a small parchment of paper.

"Here is her consul, her voice etched upon this parchment for only your eyes to read. May it help you on your journey."

"What?" Thrace asked. "It's just a riddle, and it could mean anything."

"It is for you to deduce." Lampos said.

"Sophos, this isn't going to help…."

A wail from Priestess echoed throughout the chamber as the torches beside the Pythia blazed as if a hundred pyres circled the adytum. The priest Lampos leapt in fear and quickly bowed down before the Priestess. Her voice, no longer a silent whisper, erupted like a thunder cloud from Zeus throughout the room.

THE SEED OF DESTRUCTION
SHALL CALM THE WINE DARK SEA.
BUT BEWARE HIS POWER,
IT LIES NOT IN THE SPEAR
AND RIVALS THE LIGHTNING
OF THE SON OF CRONUS.

The room went dark.

A small beam of light stretched across the room and fell upon Amymone, the Pythia. The beam of light trembled upon the Priestess from Parker's small flashlight as his hands continued to shake. She had fallen from the bronze tripod and lay crumpled upon the stone floor like a piece of parchment. The Priest Lampos entered the light beside the Pythia; his hand caressed her face with the tender care of a lover.

"She is dead." Lampos spoke quietly.

"Dead?" Thrace asked. "I thought she was immortal. She can't die."

"Immortal means one cannot die of natural causes, say old age," said Sophos, "but it does not mean they cannot be killed."

"Killed?" asked Parker.

Lampos' transparent pale-green eyes did not leave the Pythia. "She was killed by the power of Phoebus Apollo, God of Light and Prophecy. His strength entered her, and it was too much for her."

"But the Gods slumber," stated Sophos.

"Yes, physically all but a few slumber, but the second prophecy has never been spoken outside the halls of Great Olympus when it was first prophesized by Lord Apollo so many, many years ago. Your father knew of the prophecy."

Sophos entered the light Parker placed upon the scene. His muscular arm snapped out and grasped the priest by his pale white neck and lifted him off the stone floor to stare upon him eye to eye.

"What are you speaking of priest!"

"Your father had been here many times before with many sons of Ares receiving the same prophecy. Each time he failed. That is why he suffers in the bowels of Tartarus for all eternity. Punishment from Ares the Cunning. He knew from his father of the second prophecy, but had never heard it. We only knew of it, but not it's content. Now, even in Great Apollo's slumber, he reaches out to reveal this son of Ares, your pupil, who will bring upon the change our world has sought for so many years. Are you ready for the task young Centaur?"

"How dare you speak of my father in such distaste?" Sophos barked. "I should take your life like that of this Pythia that lies upon this cold stone floor."

"If that is who you are Centaur, so be it," replied the Priest.

The hand of the Centaur tightly cinched upon the throat of the pale priest. Thrace witnessed his other hand held a short sword pressed upon the belly of the priest, fearless of death.

"I know who you are," Thrace said. "You are the grandson of Cheiron the Wise, teacher of Swift-footed Achilles, son of Peleus. You are Sophos the Clever, teacher of Spear-throwing Thrace, son of Ares, God of War and Slaughterer of Man."

Sophos the Centaur turned toward Thrace. This young boy of fifteen who originally looked scared, lonely and confused now stood strong. He had accepted this world and his place within it. If all else failed, this young boy, unlike so many in years past and present, knew who he was. This boy will not fail. I will not allow it, Sophos thought.

Sophos lowered the Priest, who showed no sign of fear and returned his attention to Amymone the Pythia. The grandson of Cheiron the Wise approached Thrace and stood before him.

"Sophos the Clever?" he asked.

Thrace looked at his mentor and smiled. Sophos matched it.

CHAPTER 10

The fire teemed with life as its flames danced in the center of the Temple of Pallas Athena upon the plains of Delphi. The three remaining Doric columns stood with the same strength in which they were built holding up the last pieces of an ancient frieze long worn by Time. Sophos the Clever paced before the columns with the trials before him and the thoughts of his father sifting like sand though his mind.

Thrace sat next to Anthia on the ground before the columns resting against a small rock wall. The warmth of her skin fed his courage. Courage he needed after realizing the grandeur of this quest. Courage he did not know if he could summon and a quest that involved more than just his mother. A mother, he had no idea how to save.

The last time he was in the mountains was with his mother. As always, they pitched camp six miles in and then kept hiking to the summit of Castle Peak. She always climbed to the top of the mountain as if to see something or be seen. Then back at the camp site, they ate, and she told the tale Bellerophon and his courage and his hubris. He always loved the way she told the tales, as if she had witnessed them herself. As night fell, she asked if he recalled the heroes in the sky. He recalled a few, and she pointed out the rest. She never forgot, no matter the season of year. Maybe she lived in the wrong time, he thought.

Parker stood by the fire watching the pacing Centaur, and Thrace, the son of Ares and the Mountain Oread sit against and old wall, and in the distance he could see Aemon and Battus sitting quietly hoping to be put to task. Everyone seemed to have a purpose but him. To help his friend, he needed to offer more.

"Question," Parker asked. "What did the Priest mean when he said that 'all but a few slumber?'"

Sophos stopped pacing, faced the dancing flames upon the fire and spoke. "For a reason not known, most of the Immortal Gods lie in deep slumber in their respective homes atop Mt. Olympus, all but Ares, the God of War and Aphrodite, the Goddess of Love. Many speculate that the wars of mortals awoke the son of Zeus since they now span the globe. It is thought that he awoke his lover, Aphrodite."

"So, how many 'Sons of Ares' have there been?" asked Thrace.

"I do not know. My father, Peirithous, would depart for a time, never revealing to me his whereabouts or his purpose. For my safety, he told me. Ares the Insidious would send him on a quest. My father would state, 'It is for the Gods, and my penance'. You must remember, Ares the Quarrelsome has been around for thousands of years."

"What happened to your father?" Thrace asked.

"I did not know until just now." Sophos replied. "He was sent on a quest and had not returned. Aphrodite approached me and informed me his quest was not complete, and now, I had one of my own." His eyes met Thrace. The two beings looked upon one another, each different in their own right, though both carrying the burden of their fathers.

"Aphrodite?" Thrace asked, "She was the one who cursed my mother. This could be some giant trap by both of them."

"I do not believe so, young Thrace." Sophos said. "Ares would not send his sons on quests for centuries without a final endgame. Aphrodite has always been associated to the purpose, but I believe she has a different agenda." Sophos paused witnessing the anger swell within Thrace when they spoke of Aphrodite. "She told me only that a son of Ares would need my help."

Thrace felt anger toward Aphrodite for cursing his mother, placing this burden upon him and threatening the life of his friend. It is said, we all have choices. I could go home, he thought, and wait until the doctors find something or my mother dies. Or I go after the cure. There are choices, but why does there only appear one path before me, he thought?

"So, what do we do next?" Thrace asked.

We must understand the prophecy given to us by the Pythia." Sophos said.

"I can't believe she's dead." Parker replied. "I mean she was weird and all, but she died right there."

"She died doing what she was meant to do. She was a powerful Priestess, Amymone. Powerful enough to pull an ancient prophecy from a slumbering God. Quite impressive." Sophos said.

Aemon and Battus quickly entered the center of the Temple of Athena out of breath and excited. Aemon is carrying a small deer and Battus had a snake in each hand.

"We got food!" Battus lisped a bark with a toothy smile.

"Yeah, we didn't want to interrupt, but figured you needed food." Aemon added.

"Snake?" Parker asked. "I wouldn't eat snake if I hadn't eaten in a hundred years."

"That's it!" Thrace yelled.

"What, you'd eat snake?" Parker asked.

"What, well, I don't know…maybe. Never mind that. But 'within the hundred lies the one'. Sophos spoke of Zeus taking down the Titans with the hundred-handed. What if that means the Hundred-Handed?" Thrace stated. "You know, in the hundred hands lies the one cure." He said looking for reassurance from his friends. "Plus it reminds me of the dream I had. Those serpentine hands…" Thrace added nervously.

"What's a Hundred-Handed? It sounds like a one man band." Parker replied.

"The Hundred-Handed or Hecatonchires: Kottus, Briareus and Gyes, are the children of Ouranus and Gaia. Each great Titan has one hundred intolerably strong arms, fifty each bursting forth from their massive shoulders. These shoulders are stacked upon an overwhelming body with incredible strength and supporting fifty heads. Ouranus banished them to Tartarus, but they were released by Mighty Zeus in his battle with his father, devious Cronus, son of Ouranus. Upon Zeus' victory, he placed the terrible three Hekatonkheires to guard the deep gates of Tartarus where the rebellious Titans were banished." Sophos informed young Parker.

"Oh, those Hundred-Handed," Parker replied.

"It is a keen observation young Thrace," Sophos said. "But prophecies tend to lean one away from expectations."

"Well, I don't really want or look forward to going up against one of the Hundred-Handed."

"He is right." A soft caressing voice tickled their ears as Anthia spoke her first words.

"And here I thought she was Anthia, daughter of mime." Parker said.

Ignoring Parker, Sophos stepped down from the columns to stand before the Oread as Thrace turned his complete attention to her and her glowing warmth. Realizing his joke was ignored, Parker made his way toward Anthia as quietly as possible.

"Ares the Deceiver asked Kottus, the Hundred-Handed, to guard a sacred vial at the cave of Dicte on Crete." Anthia said.

"Why didn't you tell us this before?" Thrace asked in haste.

"I was forbidden to speak of any knowledge I knew unless it was discovered by the travelers at hand or face banishment in Tartarus." Anthia spoke her eyes penetrated deep into Thraces' and revealed a truth she did not wish to keep.

"Ares the Cunning placed the cure where Zeus of the Thunderbolt was raised in secret from his father Cronus, the Devious. I am not surprised." Sophos acknowledged.

"Yeah, but how do you fight a Hundred-Handed?" Thrace asked. "Zeus freed the three to fight the reigning Titans and his father. I'm just a kid who can throw a spear well. No wonder the other sons died."

"This must be why my father failed. An impossible task. It must be why he suffers in Tartarus." Sophos said understanding his father's silence a little more.

A soft, delicate breeze gently caressed the ears and hair of Parker like a voice on the wind bringing a smile to his face, warmth to his heart and a thought to his mind.

"What about Perseus?" Parker asked.

"Perseus? The son of Zeus, defender of Andromeda, daughter of Cassiopeia and slayer of the daughter of Poseidon…"

"The Kraken." Parker said cutting Sophos off. "I saw the movie, *Clash of the Titans*, both of them, though liked the old one better."

"Good idea Park, but Perseus already cut off Medusa's head. And I think Athena has it on her shield." Thrace said.

"Well, if she's sleeping, she won't need it." Parker stated.

Sophos glared at Parker, his deep penetrating chestnut eyes bore a hole through Parker and seized his witty smile. The stern glaze faded as a rare smile arose upon the face of the great Centaur.

"Keep your quick-witted nature going young Parker, you may be onto something." Sophos said as he paced around the fire gathering his thoughts.

"There may be two opportunities for us. First, Medusa's head is not on the Goddess Athena's shield. Her shield is bronze and the Titan's image was blazed upon it by the Lame God of the Forge, Hephaestus. She has two sisters; Stheno and Euryale. These sisters are immortal, only Medusa was mortal. Poseidon, Son of Cronus, and Lord of the Sea, seduced Medusa at a Temple of Athena. The Goddess of Wisdom, felt betrayed by the actions of

Poseidon lying with Medusa at her temple. She transformed Medusa into the original nature of her immortal sisters, the Gorgon; a hideous, snake-haired creature with huge teeth and a protruding tongue. When Perseus killed Medusa, two children of Poseidon were born from her blood, fully grown; the Winged-horse Pegasus, first caught and rode by Bellerophon, and the warrior Chrysaor, 'the Golden Sword', bearer of the lightning bolts of Zeus. Perseus used the head of Medusa to turn the Kraken, as you call her, to stone. Perseus did this to many of the people who rose up against him. I know her head was retrieved by her two immortal sisters."

"Perseus, never rode Pegasus?" Parker asked.

"No, young Parker, his killing of Medusa gave birth to the winged stallion." Sophos answered.

"So, we must attempt to borrow the head of Medusa from two Immortal Gorgon sisters?" Thrace asked.

"Or we must take it from them." Sophos said.

"Well, I like it better than going up against the son of Ouranus and Gaia that has a hundred hands and fifty heads with a spear." Thrace finished, then realized going up against two Medusas did not bode well either.

"You know, with fifty heads, how does he know where he's going?" Parker asked.

Sophos shook his head in angst at Parker and turned toward Aemon and Battus. "You two, prepare a meal and a sacrifice to the Goddess Athena of the Grey Eye. Anthia, you will come with us. We are going to the Stadium. Our heroes need to train."

"Sweet," said Parker. "We just need some *Rocky* theme music."

Thrace gave a sardonic look at Parker then pursued Sophos and Anthia.

"What?"

Dominating the landscape and nestled by pines along the hillside is the stadium of Delphi. From the starting line, the competitors could see the temples in the distance and on their return the craggy mountain side. During the Pythian Games at Delphi, Greek athletes from around the region came to compete for honor, glory and a crown of olive leaves. No financial award was ever received, just the recognition of being victorious.

The heroes stood at the side of the stadium closest to the city of Delphi, the concrete seats added by the Romans were positioned to their left. Anthia carried a large log as if it were a sliver and two olive crowns toward the steps. She placed the log on the second tier of the steps then proceeded to the far side of the stadium.

"Quick-witted Parker," Sophos said. "Here is my bow and a few arrows. I wish you to practice hitting that log on the stadium steps."

"Yeah, sure." Parker said accepting the weapon with excitement.

Parker stood about twenty yards from the log. He stuck all but one of the arrows into the earth by his feet. The remaining arrow was placed in the cord of the bow. Aiming with delicate precision, one eye squinted, tongue out, he attempted to pull back the bow string. He could not. Parker looked back at Thrace who gave him the 'let's go' roll of his finger, and Parker tried again. He slipped the nock of the arrow into the string with the arrow aligned with the center of the bow once again. He took three deep breathes and pulled once again with all his might. As he pulled, the arrow pointed to every direction of the stadium, but the string upon the bow did not yield.

"Come on Sophos, this is too tight. I can't do this." Parker said.

"That is why we are here. Continue young Parker," Sophos replied. "Now, Spear-Throwing son of Ares, Anthia will carry a crown of olives and I wish you to throw the spear through the crown."

"What if I hit her?" Thrace asked picking up one the many spears at his side.

"I do not think that will be a problem."

Anthia morphed into a golden eagle with wide wings and sharp talons. She clutched the two crowns of olive leaves in her talons and took to the air. She glided above the stadium as if she was born to fly. Swooping down from the bright blue, Anthia, leveled above the stadium and began to circle. Then she dropped the first of the olive-leaved crowns. Thrace took his spear and with a keen eye, fired it toward the falling crown. The spear flew like a lightning bolt from Mighty Zeus and clipped the top of the crown. It continued on out of the stadium into the rocky crags.

"Again." Sophos the Clever said.

Anthia came back around and dropped the second crown. Thrace, already with spear in hand, took an extra second and released his spear with zeal. Again like a lightning bolt from Mighty Zeus it shot through the air in a single breath and cleared through the crown without touching a leaf.

"YEAH." Parker shouted with excitement.

"Yes, you are gifted with the spear, young son of Ares, but as I said, we are here for not what we can do, but what we cannot." Sophos said as he quickly pulled the short sword from his waist. "Defend yourself!"

Sophos came quickly at Thrace with his sword held high, its blade glimmering in the late afternoon light of Helios. Thrace stumbled backward to avoid the blade as Sophos brought it down just before the chest of the son of Ares. He fell back upon his hands and saw Sophos the Centaur rear up on his hind legs as if to stomp him to death. Quickly, Thrace rolled to his left and attempted to stand, but as he turned, Sophos was before him with the short sword at his throat.

"What's going on?" exclaimed Parker.

"If we are going south to the land of Argo in pursuit of the head of Medusa, where her sisters now take residence, they will more than likely not let it go easily. Throwing spears at distant objects can only help a warrior so far. Within the confines of the Gorgon lair, you may be confronted and challenged and have to defend yourself. Thrace, you will need to learn not only to throw the spear, but to fight with it; first with spear, then with the short sword. Parker, you will fight with that bow until you can pull it back and release an arrow."

Anthia landed at the steps near where she first placed the log for Parker and transformed back into her human form. She sat with her eyes fixed on Thrace and watched as Sophos came at him hard and aggressive revealing his ancestry of the Centaurs, known for their violent temperament. Theseus was forced to drive the Centaurs from their home in Mt. Pelion due to a blood bath at a wedding. Indifference between the Centaurs and mortals has continued, except for a few wise Centaurs who worked with the heroes of old.

Thrace jumped and leapt from each swing of the blade Sophos brought forth. On a few occurrences his spear blocked the blade of Sophos, which caught the surprise of Thrace, only to be pushed back to defend himself again. Parker, at this point, had the bow beneath his feet and was pulling the string with both hands. But, again, to no avail. He turned to see Anthia standing beside him.

"You can do better?" he asked handing her the bow.

Anthia took the bow as if she had handled one on many occasions. Quickly pulling an arrow from the earth, she strung it and fired the arrow dead center into the log. She smiled and returned the bow back to Parker.

"Show off."

"We are done." Sophos stated.

Parker looked over at his friend who was on his back in the stadium of Delphi attempting to catch his breath. Anthia and Parker walked over and Anthia offered her hand, which Thrace took thankfully. Her warmth and strength were obvious as she pulled him up with little trouble.

"Thanks,' he said.

Anthia smiled and walked toward camp following Sophos.

"I think she likes you," said Parker.

"She doesn't say much." Thrace replied.

"Well, that could be a good thing."

"How was the bow?"

"I need some work. The close combat?"

"I need some work."

They both laughed. Thrace and Parker realized even knowing the dangers ahead, they both, no matter if their father was an ancient Greek god or an accountant, a difficult road lied ahead; even knowing the path they were on. The scent of cooked deer with spices lingered through the Temple. They had forgotten dinner was being prepared by the actors Aemon and Battus. Their hunger eased their fears and awakened their spirit as they ran back to camp.

CHAPTER 11

The void of space pulled at Thrace within the darkness as he leapt forward, not wishing to be tossed upon the earth again. He did not enjoy tree to tree travel and missed his bike that was resting in a bush back home in Colorado. A bike would do him no good now nor did attempting to maintain his footing as he fell more gently this time upon Mother Gaia. Parker lay before him wiping dirt from the smile upon his face. He appeared to enjoy being thrown from tree to tree. Thrace heard the sound of crashing waves upon a shore. He rose and helped his best friend to his feet. The bright light of Helios shone down upon them, and Thrace saw the wine dark Aegean Sea stretched out before his eyes.

"If my mom knew I was in Greece and standing at the shore of the Aegean Sea, she would be stoked." Thrace said.

"She knows." Parker replied.

"I'm glad you're here my friend."

"I'll see how I feel after we face a couple of Gorgons."

"Well, who do we have here?" spoke a voice from the sea.

Thrace and Parker eyes turned toward the voice upon the sea to witness a beautiful woman rising from the crashing white waves. Her dark tan and swimmer's body were slightly covered in a green woven seaweed outfit, and upon her strong shoulders rested her bright golden hair, the color of the All-Seeing Helios. Sea green eyes sparkled upon an elegant face, as if something carved by the master Greek sculptor Praxiteles.

"Hello," responded Thrace quietly.

A coy look of surprise graced the woman's face as Thrace addressed her. "Handsome young boys without the mortal mist...quite the surprise. I am Halia, daughter of Nereus and Doris. I am a Sea Naiad." Halia said as she continued to rise from the sea and approach them with the gentle gait of someone who was use to both land and sea. "And who might you be?"

"This is Parker, son of William and I am..." Thrace paused unsure of the response he would get from this unfamiliar Immortal.

"He is Thrace, Son of Ares, God of War." Sophos the Centaur finished for him coming out from the darkness into the light of Helios. Halia paused at this response. "What brings you here Halia of the Sea?"

"As always you Sophos," she said with a soft smile and a sparkle in her sea-green eyes. "But it looks like it has begun again, though much quicker this time." Her face saddened as she took a long look at Thrace and Parker.

"You knew after all these years?" asked Sophos.

"Your father asked me never to speak of it. He never wanted this burden placed upon you." Halia of the sea replied.

"This is not like before Halia of the Sea." Sophos finished.

"Ares the Cunning is not sending you off like he did your father following the same prophecy of Delphi to this child's demise?"

"No, he is not."

"Yeah," Parker added. "And we got two prophecies this time."

"What?!" Halia said with a glow of excitement.

"Seize your tongue Parker!" Sophos barked.

"He is the Seed of Destruction?" Halia asked with a look of surprise as she apprised the son of Ares.

"How do you know of this?" Sophos asked.

"Your father spoke of a prophecy a long time ago after the passing of your mother, Theope the Lovely. He always knew Ares was sending him on a mission to fail, and Ares the Quarrelsome made sure of it. I have watched and cared for you for many years handsome Sophos. I do not wish you the same fate as your father."

"I will ensure you lovely Halia of the Sea…this is quite different than before." Sophos said his tone laced with confidence. It brought a smile to the Sea Naiad.

Anthia, the Mountain Oread stepped from the darkness into the light of Helios and stood beside Thrace and Parker, her warmth sent courage to the heroes.

"You travel with the Oread and a few mortals." Halia stated spying Aemon and Battus watching her from the shadows like two children not allowed in the room. "Your father only took the son of Ares on each quest. Do you need the assistance of a Naiad as well?" Halia asked as she approached Sophos to stand directly before him, her sea green eyes peering deeply into his stern and collected gaze. "I could be of assistance."

"I thank you for your offer, but we are here for weapons then are headed south to the new home of the Gorgon sisters in Argos."

"The Gorgons." Halia said admiringly. "Peirithous thought of that, but was unwilling to risk the life of the son of Ares against the sisters; though their lives were forfeit nonetheless."

"It was my idea." Parker said in dismay.

"It was." Thrace said with confidence. "And it appears enough sons' of Ares have died, as well as others, at the hand of my father."

"Bold words young son of Ares." Halia said approaching Thrace. "But be warned. Your father, Ares the Deceiver, has taken Stheno the Gorgon as his lover. Another reason Sophos' father, Peirithous did not take that route. You may not have been put on this quest by the God of War, and if you do succeed, you will bring great wraith upon yourself, son or no son of Ares."

"Thank you Halia for that information," Sophos said. "That may become useful. And please, do not speak of what you have heard on this day."

"I shall not. Be safe my love and if you need my help…" The Naiad said returning to the Centaur. She placed a hand upon his broad shoulder and peered deeply into the chestnut eyes of Sophos the Clever. From a green strap tightly wound around her waist, she unveiled an ivory horn carved in the shape of a spiraling dolphin and offered it to Sophos. "Call for me, and I will come to your aid. Do not have as much pride as your father."

Sophos said nothing as he took the horn from Halia and as their hands touched there was a moment the two looked upon one another as they had dozens of times before and again as if it was for the last time. Halia let go and made her way back into the wine dark sea. Sophos did not move as he watched her every step as she disappeared beneath the white cresting waves.

Thrace watched as his mentor could not take his eyes from the wine dark Aegean. Thrace thought of the concern for his mother as his hand grasped the auburn flower in his pocket. His mentor carried a much heavier burden than he realized. First, for the honor of his father, the feelings he hides for a woman whom obviously cares for him and the concern he has shown for he and Parker. With each step, this quest became more important and involved more people, mortal and immortal. They needed to succeed not only for his mother but for all those around him.

"I think she likes you Sophos." Parker said.

"Enough with your tongue today." Sophos spat pulling himself back to the task at hand. "Down the shore, there is a cave. Inside, we have weapons to acquire and traveling to do."

From behind the heroes, Aemon and Battus shot out from behind the tree and fell upon the sandy shore of the island like circus clowns. They barked and pushed at one another placing blame as they sluggishly got to their feet. Parker laughed at the lightened moment after being spurned by Sophos. Thrace, ignoring the ruckus, stood admiring the Aegean Sea. His mother had promised a sailing trip upon the Aegean visiting many of the islands after he graduated. He still wished to take that trip. But the Aegean sparked a different thought in his mind. *The Seed of Destruction shall calm the wine dark sea.* How do you calm a Sea? Or do I calm the God of the Sea, Poseidon? Another task I am unsure how to tackle, he thought.

Anthia's warmth brightened the cave as the heroes made their way through the dark corridors. Their pace was slow and cautious as if counting steps. The fluttering of bat wings echoed upon the cave walls followed by the eeriness of silence. Sophos, leading the way, paused before a large boulder against a cave wall. Beside the boulder rested a trunk of a tree. Sophos grabbed the tree trunk, wedged it beneath the boulder and with his broad shoulders and great strength lifted up on the tree trunk rolling the boulder away from him revealing another corridor. He returned the trunk against the wall and proceeded down the corridor and the others followed.

Thrace and Parker followed the warm light of Anthia as they entered the hidden room. Her glowing warmth glimmered like a light upon a pool as she moved around the room igniting torches along the cave walls. As the fire brightened the large room, it reflected off the bronze, iron, silver and gold of weapons and treasures stacked upon stands and racks along with wooden shelves adorned with scrolls, parchments and books that appear to have been written yesterday. It was a giant cave room reflecting the history of Greece.

"You gotta be kidding me!!" exclaimed Parker. "This stuff is got to be worth millions."

"This 'stuff' as you call it is the treasures and weapons of great heroes, cities and temples. They have been stored and maintained here to protect them from the greedy eyes of this world." Sophos replied.

"Well, Indiana Jones would put it in a museum," Parker muttered to himself. He ran around the cave picking up gold coins, gold laden vases and chalices and admired the brilliant craftsmanship of each.

"You grew up here?" Thrace asked Sophos.

"This was my home, while Father was sent on his quests." Sophos answered.

"Many amazing things, but quite…isolated." Thrace replied, not wishing to offend his mentor.

"Those books and scrolls kept me company along with Hamadryad of the forest and the Naiad within the Aegean. It is a life better than many of the Immortals who hide and live in fear of the ever-expanding mortal realm." Sophos stated simply as if talking to a friend, then anxious to change the subject his mind returned to the task at hand. "Thrace, you had much courage in your heart as you spoke to Halia of the Sea. Just let us make sure it continues to be courage and not anger, rage or revenge. Remember…

Being driven to face danger by pain or rage, then, is not courage. However, this kind of courage, whose impulse is rage, seems to be most natural, and, when deliberate purpose and the right motive are added to it, to become real courage."

"So, I don't want rage, but I do?" Thrace asked.

Sophos the Clever offered a rare smile as the young son of Ares pondered the ancient wisdom of Aristotle. "Thrace, if every answer was given to every question, no one would learn a sliver of wisdom on their own and who, if no one asked the questions, would seek the answers?" stated Sophos the Centaur.

"Fine, I will admit revenge is on my mind, but I also know you have not told me everything. Like Aphrodite being the one who put you on this quest."

"All will be revealed in time young Thrace. Sometimes knowledge is better gained and understood in parts."

Sophos gave Thrace a knowing stare and proceeded along the cave walls looking over the hidden treasure trove. Thrace watched his mentor

114

move on and then moved his attention to the weapons before him. His mother could gaze upon these weapons and probably point out the Club of Herakles or the Sword of Theseus. He simply needed to find something he could work with. He picked up bright silver spear heads that rested in a wide-rimmed golden chalice. Probably thousands of years old, he thought and the edges appeared as if they were sharpened today. He wrapped them in a cloth and placed them in his backpack.

Sophos grasped a large thick spear resting on a weapon rack. He turned and tossed it to Thrace who caught it but was unprepared for its unexpected weight. He regained his footing and slowly moved it as if preparing to release the long spear. Its large iron spear head was perfectly balanced with the length and weight of the shaft. It was thicker than any javelin or the spears he had thrown since his arrival in Greece. It felt heavy but balanced easily in his hands.

"It is the ashen spear given to Peleus, father of Achilles by my grandfather Cheiron. The shaft is taken from an ash tree from the summit of Mt. Pelion and smoothed by the Goddess Athena and the blade was forged by the Smith God Hephaestus. It is the same spear used by Swift-footed Achilles at the battle of Troy when he fought the horse-breaker Hektor."

Thrace gracefully turned the spear over in his hand in awe as if handling a delicate glass brooch. He knew the tale of Achilles and Hektor at the battle of Troy well. His mother read him *The Odyssey* in his crib, but she did not start reading *The Iliad* until his was older, not wishing to glorify war. He recalled hiding the book beneath his pillow like that of Alexander the Great and opening it at night to read more of the great heroes and their battles. Though Achilles is remembered for defeating Hektor, Thrace always felt his battle with the River Salamander was his toughest battle. In his youth, he admired spear-throwing Diomedes, son of Tydeus, who fought the God of War himself on the plains of Troy, but Thrace hoped he did not follow in his footsteps. He was not even sixteen and had no intention nor desire to fight his father.

"Hey, how about this bow?" Parker asked. He held up an elegantly carved wooden bow, taut and strong, curled at the ends like serpents tales.

"That was the bow of Atalanta, a fierce warrior and daughter of Iasus and Clymene. She was awarded the pelt of the Calydonian Boar by Meleager, son of Ares for drawing first blood. A wise weapon quick-witted Parker. If you can pull it back that is?"

"Wasn't Meleager cursed by the Fates though?" Thrace asked.

"He was, but he was the best javelin thrower in Greece and a great warrior." Sophos added.

"It appears being a son of a God has a lot of drawbacks." Parker said as he attempted to draw back the bow with much difficulty.

"It may appear so, but it offers great honor and glory that will last the ages." Sophos said with pride.

"I don't care about glory or honor," Thrace said. "I just want to get my mother better."

"I understand young Thrace," Sophos said approaching the young hero. "But it is your predecessors, these 'heroes' who leave behind the strength and passion you and many have read and admired. It is these weapons, their courage and strategy you will need and borrow from to survive and save your mother."

"I understand."

A metallic clang echoed though the cave. Sophos and Thrace turned to see Parker in a bronze corset hanging off him like a bathrobe and supporting a large Spartan helmet with a plumage of red horse hair across the top that dangled before his eyes. Anthia stepped before him and began to laugh, a laughter that warmed the room. Thrace followed her lead and whether contagious or not, Sophos joined in with a large baritone laugh.

"At least I got him to laugh." Parker said.

"Young Parker," Sophos said. "The bow is a fine choice but let us find you some more suitable attire. Against the Gorgons, you will have to be as quick as your tongue."

CHAPTER 12

Through the yawning void they made their way. The stillness of the air around them exaggerated their already nervous sensations as they prepared to be thrown from yet another tree. Anthia had selected armor for both of the heroes and herself, as well as, helmets and short swords to accompany their primary weapons. Sophos strapped on his helm and brazen chest plate, a gift from Hephaestus to his grandfather, Cheiron. Upon the center of the breast plate is the Wise Centaur rising up upon his hind legs with spear and shield in hand preparing for battle. Encircling the great Centaur were the bravest warriors trained by the great teacher; including Herakles, Asclepius, Jason, leader of the Argonauts, and Swift-footed Achilles. The breast plate was a work of perfection only created by the Smith God of Fire, Hephaestus. Slung upon the back of Sophos was the shield of Perseus, used long ago against the Gorgon Medusa. Spear-throwing Thrace inquired if Sophos had the helmet of Hades, Lord of the Underworld, within the cave to render them invisible as it had Perseus. Sophos informed him the helmet was reacquired by Hades, Lord of the Dead and rests in Tartarus a top his throne. Thrace's pack did have the invulnerable wallet used by Perseus to carry the head of Medusa. Well, two of three wasn't bad, he thought; then again, fighting two out of three might be.

Thrace felt the warmth of Anthia which gave him courage seconds before he came through the knot of a tall ash tree. His feet hit the ground this time as he attempted to catch his balance, but the weight of the weapons and pack threw him forward upon the soft ground of Argos. He saw Parker also on the ground before him, dirt covered smile upon his face as he coughed laughter and dirt sprayed from his lips. He knew Parker was scared, as was he, but he enjoyed the journey as only Parker could. His fear was always masked by anything he could find humorous, but this upcoming battle would have no humor. Parker had been there when he heard the news of his father, then seeing mythical beings was one thing, but doing battle against a Titan was something else entirely, he thought. They would need more than luck on this battlefield.

Fear of what they were to encounter crept upon the heroes like a serpent. They had encountered many mythical beings including the Immortal Goddess Aphrodite; but as of yet, none had attempted to hurt or kill him, for that matter, either of them. They were approaching new water, and this was unlike any water young Thrace had ever crossed. This adventure resembled the hated river nymph Styx, whose dark waters travel deep into Tartarus, and the same dark waters where oaths are sworn over and when broken, bring the deceiver to a deep slumber or death. These ancient myths & legends, (now not so mythical) crept into Thrace's mind often now. He watched as Aemon and Battus adjusted one another's gear and liked the idea of having extra bodies alongside him.

The heroes made their way toward Helios as he finished his westward journey as black-winged Night began to blanket the land. The trip was silent as Sophos took the lead followed by Thrace who now walked beside Anthia in her chain mail armor, a short sword at her side and walking with a thick staff. He noticed her dark hair shimmer in the late sun and her arctic blue eyes sparkled with warmth like hot springs.

Parker walked behind them and noticed Thrace and Anthia taking casual glances at one another as if avoiding what each was thinking. Parker was nervous and unsure of what was about to happen. Right now his best friend was unknowingly flirting with an immortal Mountain Oread, walking behind a centaur and about to attempt to negotiate with two Immortal Gorgons for the head of their monstrous sister Medusa. Yeah, he was nervous. He wanted to help his friend, but he wanted to live a while longer too.

"So, Thrace...do we have a plan?" Parker asked.

Thrace appeared to awaken from a trance as he looked back at his friend. He could see the fear in his eyes, and it matched the fear in his heart he was trying to ignore. He walked beside Anthia to feel the warmth and courage, hoping it would help him on his quest. Seeing Parker, he realized he did not need to be dependent on something that was not always there. His friend had come willingly, not knowing the danger, (though neither knew), and now he was scared. Thrace looked at Anthia and saw the warm glow of her skin fade. She withdrew her warmth sensing that he needed it like a drug. He needed courage on his own terms. He smiled as he felt her glow dim as she sensed what he felt. He needed courage, there was no doubt, but he needed more than courage.

"Sophos...thoughts on a plan?" Thrace asked his teacher.

"We will camp at the base of that ridge tonight. There are a few ideas we need to discuss. We must decide if we are attempting to enter and take the head of Medusa or attempting to reason with the two immortal sisters."

"Can they petrify you like Medusa?" Parker asked.

"Medusa was originally mortal. She was cursed by Pallas Athena to be forever the snake-haired Gorgon. Her two sisters, being immortal, can appear beautiful and captivating, but can also transform to their other natural form, the Gorgon. If the sisters so chose, they can reveal their true form and petrify you. Be on guard, for it is difficult to fight someone you cannot face eye to eye. Also, if they transform into the hideous creature, their black eyes will fear the light."

Along the base of the mountainside, Aemon and Battus started a fire in a small altar they were instructed to build. Sophos the Clever offered some deer meat and wheat with spices to Apollo, Lord of the Silver Bow thanking him for the vision he offered at Delphi and for good fortune for their confrontation the next day. Thrace dug through the books of Greek myth he brought, but found little information on Stheno and Euryale. Parker tossed him some camping food he had brought from home, then toyed with his iPhone attempting to help Thrace with his research, but was unable to get any service. He cursed AT&T under his breath as he offered Sophos a whole grain bar. The Centaur simply shook his head, for the thought of eating it was disgusting. Parker ate quickly, shoved his phone in his pack, pulled out his bow and attempted once again to string and fire an arrow.

"Have a thought," Thrace said tossing his book back in his bag. "How about Sophos and I approach the temple and request an audience with Stheno and make a request for the head of her sister, which we will return. I believe Parker pocketed some gold which we can offer them as a gift."

"What, gold…I wouldn't, didn't…" Parker said fumbling with the bow and falling on his back after realizing he was caught with his fingers in the candy jar.

"I hope you did; we'll need it." Thrace responded.

"Well, yeah, of course I took some gold. I mean." Parker said sitting up, and trying to sound confident, "Everyone here always wants to trade, so I thought."

"You took gold from my cave?" Sophos questioned.

"Uhm, well…Thrace just said we needed it."

"We shall approach with the attempt to reason with the Immortal Gorgons," Sophos said glaring at Parker, then turning his attention back to Thrace. "If that fails?"

"I guess we work on a plan B." Thrace said. He himself had no idea on how to steal anything, much less fight an immortal.

"I'm hoping you may have some suggestions?" Thrace said to Sophos.

Dawn of the yellow-robe awoke and rose from her immortal bed sending dark-winged Night back to her slumber in Tartarus. Spear-throwing Thrace and Sophos the Clever stood before an ancient temple of Hera nestled beside a small ash-laden forest. It was not a worn and dilapidated temple like those at Delphi, for the roof was still intact as were the columns. Steps led up to four columns that braced the front as if a small porch, which was also the host to two very detailed stone statues of two men very unhappy about what they saw. A doorway led into a darker chamber within the temple. The morning sun rose with the help of the sun-chariot of Helios stretching long shadows from the heroes as they climbed the steps of the temple of Hera.

At the temple doorway, Thrace used a waterproof match from Parker to ignite two torches for both he and Sophos as they entered the darkness. Inside the temple the flames from their torches exposed stone statues of man and women alike revealing faces strewn with fear. There was no prejudice among these immortals. A voice echoed throughout the room. It was as beautiful as Apollo, Lord of Music, on his golden lyre.

"What brings a young boy and a centaur to our temple?" the voice asked.

They had agreed not to mention that he was the son of Ares to these immortal sisters, for they did not wish to bring forth Rage and Jealousy in an immortal Gorgon.

"I am Sophos, grandson of Cheiron the Wise, and we have come on a quest. This young boy's mother has been cursed by Crowned and Flowered Aphrodite, and we seek a cure, which the Delphic Oracle has informed us is being guarded by Kottus the Hundred-Handed. We kindly request the head of your sister, Medusa, to petrify the Great Titan and retrieve the cure for his mother. We offer gold and shall return your sister's head safely back."

From the darkness a beautiful woman elegantly approached the heroes dressed in a superbly woven white tunic announcing her physical perfection. She had shiny walnut-colored hair that appeared to absorb the light from the torches. Her ox-eyed face rivaled that of Aphrodite, Thrace thought, as her deep green eyes sparkled like jade.

"I am Stheno, daughter of Ceto by Phorcys. It has been many, many years since I have seen a centaur or a young man on a quest. A lovely young man indeed. I must ask, why would lovely Aphrodite curse your mother? Young…"

"Thrace," he said. "She accused my mother of blasphemy."

"Accused?" Stheno asked.

"I guess there was truth in it." Thrace replied.

"The Goddess of Love has grown bitter in time. More bitter than usual, I must admit. Especially since most of the gods slumber. I believe she is bored. But why should I help you? The great Titan Kottus helped Olympian Zeus defeat Cronus the Deceiver. He and his two brothers, Gyes and Briareus, guard the great underground prison in Tartarus. Why should he be doomed to save a mortal woman?"

"Beautiful ox-eyed Stheno, if there was another way I could retrieve the cure, believe me, I would. But I know of no way of battling a Titan as great as Mighty Kottus without the head of Medusa." Thrace said.

"Winged words young man," Stheno said as she approached. Her elegant arm reached out as her hand caressed his face.

"You could stay here with me, and I could reveal to you a world you could never imagine, a world beyond that of fighting and warring."

"I will admit it sounds intriguing lovely Stheno, but I can do nothing until I help my mother." Wisely spoke Thrace.

"So admirable." Stheno said coolly. "Did you teach him that Sophos, grandson of King Cheiron, or did he learn that from his father?"

"He learned that from his mother," spoke Sophos.

"It must be why he is so adamant to save her. Did Ares send you on this quest? It does smell so much of him?"

"You mean your lover, Ares the Quarellsome?" Sophos added.

"Ahh, so you know. It does explain why Aphrodite has so much time to curse silly mortal woman." Stheno said with a coy smile. "OH, Aphrodite sent you on this quest."

"Who sent me on this quest does not concern the task at hand nor this boy's mother." Sophos stated.

"But it does. The petty Goddess of Love curses this young boy's mother and sends you off to help him. Both of your parents suffer. Do you not see the common thread upon the webbing?" Stheno chided. "Understanding is the first thing that must come from a teacher…Centaur, your wise grandfather must have told you that much."

"We sought understanding at Delphi, which has led us here. Our quest shall reveal understanding for each of us as all journeys do." Sophos stated.

"Quick words that mean nothing. I do not believe the Pythia sent you here for Asclepius' cure." Stheno pointed out. "So, now you are here attempting to buy my assistance? What if my cost is more than payment in coin? Perhaps this young boy? He would be less burdensome than the Ever-Conniving Ares. He would make a playful…"

"ENOUGH!" Thrace yelled. His much loved patience waivered once again as Rage slowly slithered though him; Pollux put on his gloves, stepped into the stadium within his chest and beat upon his heart. "I am no one's bartering tool. Unless you know another way to retrieve the cure, I want the head of Medusa."

"How dare you order me around boy?! I am an Immortal, a Titan, daughter to Ceto!" Stheno's barbed tone echoed through the room.

"I am Thracian Ares, son of Ares the Cunning. I guess your lover is not as faithful as you imagined." Thrace spat back at her.

Hearing those words from the son of her lover, Ares the Betrayer, enraged the Titan Stheno with the fire of a volcano. Her eyes filled with Rage as her form shimmered in the darkness.

"NOW!" Thrace roared!

Sophos reared back upon his hind legs as if to trample Stheno and delay her from a hasty transformation. She stepped back quickly to move away from his muscular front legs as he pawed the distance between them. Thrace rolled to his left taking cover behind a statue of a terrified young man. Peering around the statue, Thrace could see Stheno move back through the distant statues with cat-like agility as her beautiful walnut brown hair began to turn coarse and green. The Gorgon sister did capture the shock of beauty to the beast so well, he thought. Thrace watched as Parker pushed three balls made of grass and twigs about three feet in diameter into the temple like giant bowling balls baring down upon the once mortal statues. He ran to a statue beside Thrace for cover and from the top of the demigod's lungs he yelled, FIRE. From two large cracks in the roof along the frieze, flaming arrows begin to rain within the temple like arrows from Apollo's silver bow upon the black ships of the Achaeans on the shores of Troy. The three wooden balls erupted into a blazing fire lighting the temple of white-armed Hera. The flaming arrows continued to rain down throughout the temple as is seeking any target.

"Thrace, the head of Medusa is at the far end of the temple upon a pedestal." Sophos called across the room. "Aemon and Battus, would you fools aim and try not to hit us!"

A golden eagle flew into the temple through the front door carrying large torches in her talons. Anthia returned to her training form and dropped torches in a pathway leading to the pedestal upon which sat the head of the hideous Gorgon Medusa. Sophos galloped along the path toward the pedestal. Euryale, the other Gorgon sister, stepped before him as beautiful as her sister, though dressed in armor for battle.

"You will not touch my sister's head Centaur." She wailed as she raised her sword above her head to strike down the centaur. Quickly Sophos brought up the shield of Perseus to block her blow and then drew his own sword.

"You remember the shield of Perseus Gorgon?" Sophos yelled going sword to sword with Euryale. The two immortals engaged in battle, Sophos slowly pushing the fight away from the head of Medusa.

Thrace and Parker, both still hiding behind the statue, watched Sophos violently engaged in battle with a beautiful armored Gorgon.

"There's another one out there right?" Parker asked.

"Yeah," replied Thrace.

"I'll be the diversion."

"What? Are you crazy?" Thrace said. "I saw her turn into the snake-haired monster. You can't look at her."

"I can with these." Parker said pulling out from his pack his mirrored sunglasses. "I'll go the other way, toward Sophos as if to help since they've moved away from the pedestal. She'll try to look at me, hopefully it won't work. You run by and grab the head, and we get out of here."

"Let me wear the glasses and go." Thrace demanded.

"Dude, you're the son of Ares. You may need to help one of us. You're the one with the spear who can hit anything." Parker said slipping on the sunglasses. "I'm off."

Parker peaked around the corner and dashed to the next statue before Thrace could stop him. Through his mirrored glasses the blazing balls of fire glimmered dimly in the darkness. Shimmering light shined off the weapons and armor of Euryale and Sophos as their blades met in heated combat like two Spartan warriors long depraved of battle. He saw no one else. He stood and quickly ran toward a center column near the battle of the Centaur and Gorgon and through the darkness his eyes followed the torches toward a pedestal that supported Medusa's head.

He could grab it himself, he thought. Everyone here had a part or a role, but him. He was small enough to sneak by column to statue and grab it while the others fought. I just need an opening.

Thrace slowly stood and peaked around the statue. Parker was swiftly making his way from statue to statue. His bow and quiver slung over his shoulder and his short sword bounced in rhythm of his pace off his thigh.

128

Thrace watched as Parker was now only ten yards from the head of Medusa, and he knew that his friend was going to make a run for it. Above the statue where Parker hid, Thrace could see snake heads wriggle about, peaking over as if scouting the scene.

"PARKER, LOOK OUT!" Thrace yelled.

Too late. She slithered like the giant Python out from behind the statue. As Parker attempted to make a run to the next statue, a long arm reached and grabbed him by his wrist. Parker fought to get away, but the Gorgon was too strong. Dozens of snakes squirmed upon her head above dark black eyes and sharp protruding teeth. Parker pulled out his short sword and aimlessly swung it toward her. As quick as the snakes upon her head, she grasped his sword wrist to stop his feeble attack, bent it back, and Parker relinquished his blade.

"Who do we have here," Stheno hissed, her forked tongue wiggling between her sharp protruding teeth.

"I am Parker, son of William." Parker said courageously.

"How brave," she said then her head tilted slightly, puzzled why this young boy was still fighting to get free.

"What are you wearing?" She asked with a coy smile revealing her barbed teeth. "How cute, mirrors for eyes. How about I remove these?"

Stheno released his other wrist and reached out to pull the mirrored sunglasses from Parker's face. Her long clawed fingers stretched out reflecting in the mirrors upon his face. Parker kicked at her snake-like figure trying to break free, but her scaly surface was too strong. His free hand grabbed her hand as it reached for his glasses trying to stop it, but her strength defied his. Then, her fingers stopped. Stheno the Gorgon, daughter of Ceto by Phorcys let out a temple crushing wail.

Parker looked down through his mirrored glasses to see the glimmer of the ashen spear head of Achilles protruding from the chest of Stheno the Gorgon. She dropped Parker, who fell back watching the hideous monster flail upon the ground in pain. Thrace, son of Ares, killer of Gorgons stood behind her, holding the spear of Achilles he pulled from the great Titan.

Sophos and Euryale stopped their battle at the sound of wailing Stheno. Euryale stared at her dying sister gasping for her last breathe upon the floor of the temple of Hera. She turned toward Sophos and swung her blade hard and violent at him. He quickly brought up the shield of Perseus to defend himself. As he blocked her deadly blow, she rushed toward the head of her sister Medusa and brought her sword down upon it, shattering it like that of crushed stone.

"Your mother will die as did my sister." Euryale wailed as she quickly ran out of the back of the temple.

Sophos galloped up to Parker and Thrace who stood watching the Gorgon slowly die. She transformed back and forth from the hideous monster to the beautiful woman until her last breath. The beautiful Stheno lay dead upon the floor of the temple of Hera.

"Her sister Euryale has destroyed the head of Medusa." Sophos informed them.

Thrace looked down at the body of Stheno, a beautiful woman with walnut colored hair and jade eyes. It was the first time he had killed anything. He did not know how to feel, though his heart still beat like an Olympian boxer in his last round. The horrifying beast he saw effortlessly capture Parker was no human. She was about to turn his best friend to stone. He could not allow that to happen. He killed this being not for sport or food, but survival as Sophos had taught him. Anthia, still as a golden eagle, flew in and rested upon a statue of a scared fat old man next to Thrace. They watched as blood ran aggressively from the beautiful body of Stheno upon the temple floor.

"Thanks," Parker said looking at his friend.

"No problem," Thrace replied.

"We must go and now." Sophos said with haste.

As the blood made its way across the temple floor, it appeared to be alive and like hot molten lava; it began to boil.

The heroes ran from the temple. Sophos galloped past Aemon and Battus at full speed and the young heroes attempted to follow as quickly as their human legs would take them. The actors, Might and Violence stood dumbfounded, and wondered what had occurred. From deep within the temple, a dark howl erupted through the land rocking the Earth like Poseidon, the great Earth-Shaker. Aemon and Battus turned in fear and chased their new friends as quick as their legs would take them.

CHAPTER 13

Thrace and Parker finally caught up to Sophos and Anthia as they walked on without a word until dark-winged Night spread her wings and covered the land. Parker fell upon the grass exhausted and tired before the sacrificial altar Sophos was constructing. Anthia stepped from the forest with wood in her arms and her steps stuttered as she saw Thrace approach. A gentle smile graced her lovely, youthful face revealing concern for Thrace's well-being and honor for his courage. Within her lovely features was an old spirit who found honor, not in the killing of Stheno, but the friendship he shared with his best friend Parker in a time of conflict and stress. She placed the loose kindling and logs upon the altar and stood quietly beside Thrace, this time absorbing the warmth from him. The latter stood staring at his mentor Sophos the Centaur.

His mind was spinning with a diversity of thoughts as rich as Poseidon's Great Ocean. First he realized he was not as tired as he would have imagined running such a distance; especially, after seeing Parker on the ground gasping for air. Being a part of this world was slowly changing him, mentally and physically. How much more it would change him he did not know, nor did he have time to contemplate. Now, he stood before his mentor, the lingering effects of fear at the horrible howl that erupted from within the temple chilled him. What drove the pounding of his heart was that each of their quests was orchestrated by the Alluring Goddess, Aphrodite. He felt Stheno may have been correct in them not understanding the final purpose. Once again, his patience failed; he was tired of waiting for answers.

Sophos finished the altar and turned toward Thrace whose stare he could feel the moment he arrived. Sophos' silence allowed Thrace to relax, gather his thoughts; Thrace did not want to say something he might regret. Sophos could see within the young Son of Ares' eyes his endless confusion about himself and this journey.

"You have questions young Thrace?" Sophos asked.

"I have a question." Parker jumped in. "What was that noise from the temple?" He asked, but noticing the staring competition between Thrace and Sophos. "It's not important," he finished.

"Yeah, a few." Thrace said trying to collect his thoughts as his blood boiled within. "O.K., why would Aphrodite send you to take me on a quest and then curse my mother? You were at the school before my mother was cursed, so…you knew it was going to happen."

"Would you have gone otherwise?"

"There would have been no need! Now my mother may die, just like dozens of other mothers and sons of Ares!" Thrace stammered.

"She does not have too." Sophos quietly stated looking over this altar. He offered a long pause to allow Thrace to calm himself and slowly approached the angry son of Ares. "Aphrodite came to me and said, 'A son of Ares will need your help'. There are greater tasks at hand young Thrace."

"Does not have to? Greater tasks?" Thrace repeated. "The only task at hand is the cure for my mother." He knew he was not going to get straight answers from Sophos, and no matter what the answers were he still needed to go on and still needed Sophos' help.

"Can Aphrodite save my mother?" He asked.

"She cannot."

"What about Ares, can he?"

"He cannot. As Stheno pointed out, the cure for death created by Asclepius will succeed in saving your mother. Centuries ago Hephaestus the Smith God crafted a metal vial to protect it from the ages. It was in the hands of Mighty Zeus for many years, but since he slumbers, Ares must be in possession of it. Only a single drop and she will live again."

"First, what if Ares doesn't have the cure? Second, didn't your grandfather teach Asclepius medicine?" Thrace asked impatiently.

"First, then we will find another way. And second, yes, but I cannot. Asclepius was trained by Cheiron and Apollo of the Light. He created this medicine himself. For it, he was killed by Mighty Zeus of the Thunderbolt for fear that mortal men might attempt Immortality and rival the Deathless Gods. The cure he had in his possession was the last."

"Ares has sent other of his sons on this quest, so why does Aphrodite curse my mother and send me? I don't get it!" Thrace said, eyes blazing with rage at Sophos.

"As I have explained, you are my first student. Aphrodite informed me you would need my assistance in saving your mother. The Gods can be petty and have punished…." Sophos dialogue was cut off as a fire erupted within the altar.

A fiery spray of red, yellow and orange sparks brightened the night sky as grand as a giant firework cone Parker saw last Fourth of July. From the raging yellow and red sparks and flames a face arose within the fire. Ares, God of War, Slaughterer of Men stepped from the blaze. His long wavy dark hair whipped in the fiery blaze and a blinding white smile stretched upon his face as his dark beady eyes took in the scene from his audience. He was not wearing the traditional white tunic in which the Gods are often depicted, but in a sleek black Armani suit, crisp black shirt and red tie. Ares noticed two large toothless men take long steps backward and laughed. He appeared to like the stage.

"So, how's it going?" Ares the Cunning said with a smile. "That's what you moderners say isn't it?"

The God of War slowly paced around the heroes admiring them up close for the first time. He took long slow steps as if absorbing the tension around the fire, breathing it in. He paused before Sophos, but not before brushing the ash from his suit.

"Sophos the Centaur, son of Peirithous, it is finally good to meet you. So many years I witnessed you peering out at your father and I chatting at the mouth of that cave along the Aegean. How is old dad anyway? That's right, he's suffering in Tartarus. I should know...I put him there." Ares laughed at his own amusement. He turned toward the boys and smiled.

"Has he told you of his father? Then again, he doesn't really know." He stated with a coy smile of a thespian on a one God show. Seeing the blank faces upon the boys, he continued. "For centuries of failure, unlike his Wise father Cheiron, who rests upon the starry heavens above, he starves, strapped

135

above a mirrored pond. The pond reveals his reckless youth where he abandoned his father's teachings that eventually led to the death of Sophos' mother, Theope. But, like my step-brother Herakles, he wanted retribution. Yet, after years of study and training, he was still unable to teach one mortal son of mine anything, hence their deaths. Now he watches his sad existence over and over and over again."

Sophos lowered his head, the pain obvious in his eyes.

"Maybe being your son curses us all toward death." Thrace said.

"Ah, my son...brave young Thracian Ares." Ares approached Thrace, his eyes leading the way. He watched as Thrace stood confused and smiled. "Though the name itself lacks originality, it does remind me where your mother and I met. It's finally a pleasure to meet you. I am your father, Mighty Ares, Ruler of...well, everything." The God of War offered his hand.

Ares remained holding out his hand, but Thrace stood his ground. For years he wondered who his father was someday hoped to meet a man he expected to be a college professor or fellow student of his mother's. Now, before him stood his father, an Immortal Greek God who had been alive for many a millennia and just stepped out of the fire before his eyes in an Armani suit. Upon meeting him, Thrace despised him.

"I need the cure for my mother," he simply stated not accepting his father's hand.

"Straight to the point." Ares replied, though a bit perturbed his son did not accept his hand. "Your mother...she was an athletic, beautiful and sensual woman. She would have lived well centuries ago in Greece and probably rivaled the mighty Atalanta. Anyway, I heard your questions and even your anger all the way atop Mt. Olympus. I have kept tabs on you, as with all my sons and daughters through the ages. Yes, what you said is correct. I have organized this little quest. Though, not all of my children are selected for this quest. Some are weak, others soft, or simply not up to task at hand. I select only the best. You were not to be selected. You're a good kid, but quiet, not really athletic or competitive and you hide in the mountains. Without realizing it, you heard the Hamadryad singing; I believe that it is why you spend so much time there. I thought you more a nymph yourself, which is odd knowing your parents...me, for one...a god, and your athletic mother. Back to the point, as you know, the end game has always been failure. Sophos' father knew how to acquire the vial, but wouldn't take the path, hence his eternal suffering. For some reason, Lovely Aphrodite put *you* on the quest. I was amused and at such a young age too. On top of that, The Goddess of Love whispered the path to the end game, not to my son, not to Sophos, but to this young mortal here, Parker is it?"

"No one whispered anything to me." Parker stated.

"The Centaur agrees, and off you go to Argo to battle Gorgons. Fantastic." Ares said, ignoring Parker as if he did not even speak. He paced around the fire watching the reactions of those before him. His son held his gaze. Stronger than I suspected, Ares thought and continued. "As you probably figured, Aphrodite has been upset with me for so long I cannot even remember. Primarily, because of my affair with Stheno and well, a few others. But, why should she be? I mean, she's married. Hephaestus is sleeping, but still. I think she believed we would rule this world like some romantic couple…women." Ares paused once again and appeared to be talking more to himself than the audience around him as if he missed the attention.

"Where was I…oh, the endgame. Aphrodite wanted to end this little game of mine, so she set *you* on the path. You see, in this modern world, the youth are not men until their eighteenth year. Years ago, they were men as early as twelve, but today, it is assumed they cannot be ready, which means mentally they are not ready…so many rules. Anyway, the path you are on, young Thracian Ares, you were not even supposed to be on. Your mother should have never been harmed. Aphrodite with all her beauty is wiser than many believe. I must admit, you have done better than any before you." Ares said as he approached his son and patted him on the shoulder.

"Done better?" Thrace asked. "The head of Medusa is destroyed and there is no way to get the cure from the Titan Kottus without it…unless you help."

"Are you asking your father for help?" asked Ares. "A minute ago you wouldn't even shake my hand."

Ares, the Destroyer, made his way toward Parker, who was standing calmly attempting to work as much courage as he could before the Immortal God.

"Parker, son of William," Ares said as he rubbed the head of Parker like a pet. "Mirror glassed…ingenious."

"You didn't answer my question father." Thrace said drawing attention from all encircling the altar by his use of the word 'father'.

"Father," Ares said lavishly. "I have not heard that from a mortal in many years. Too bad you are not the one I wish to hear it from."

Ares, Slaughterer of Men, turned and stood before the fire roaring upon the altar. The light flickered and shined upon his dark black hair as his eyes appeared to consume the flames.

"In the beginning the quest was to find a worthy son. I needed someone strong to rule beside me. With the other Gods slumbering, there is so much to do. But all my mortal sons have been unworthy. I blame it on your soft and cowardly modern world with its video games and reality television. But I did need you...son. I needed you to kill my lover Stheno. That was the real quest. Which you did, wonderfully I might add. You see, the quest had nothing to do with your mother. Either one of you would be what your world calls 'collateral damage'. You see, the lovely Aphrodite whispered the idea of Perseus on the winds to your friend Parker."

Parker looked at Thrace confused. He remembered the breeze and the thought of the movie leapt into his mind, but he did not recall any Goddess' voice. Had he accidentally brought on this dilemma?

Thrace watched his friend, whose eyes again were filled with fear, and this time they revealed the pain of someone taking blame. Thrace knew it was not Parker's fault. He also sensed what Ares was about to say, and he realized they had all been pawns of Ares, the Cunning.

Ares smiled as he watched guilt take its place upon the young mortal's face. "Stheno has been carrying my offspring for centuries, but because of being an Immortal and a Gorgon, she needed to be slain for my offspring to be born. So, thank you son, for your kindness and in bringing my endgame closer to fruition."

Ares, the Destroyer raised his hand to sky. All eyes followed his hand to lay witness to the coming destruction. A giant flying mare swooped down from the black Night sky and landed before them, but this was no lovely white-mane Pegasus. The giant Syrian beast was coated in black with reptile-like wings stretching the length of four men and black smoke and fire flared from her nostrils, and that was not the worse. Upon her back sat a great muscled warrior with two coiled horns of a ram protruding from his smooth bald head. He and the winged Syrian beast carried the same jade green eyes as their mother, Stheno, the only soft spot among these two giants Immortals.

"I would like you to meet my son, Cresphontes and my daughter, the winged Deinus. Together, we will continue to wage war upon the mortals, but now on a greater scale."

"Father," Cresphontes said in a grizzled dark tone. "May I kill the mortals?"

"No." Ares replied. "Let them continue on. I think Kottus is bored and could use some amusement."

Ares, the God of War, Slaughterer of Men, bowed before his son, the mortals, the centaur and Oread and departed the way he arrived through the blazing flames. The fire within the altar imploded and went cold. Dark Night once again consumed them all.

Deinus let out a painful grunt as flames showered from her nose and the altar was reawakened. The enormity of the immortal son and daughter of Ares erupted as their shadows encompassed the heroes.

"Hopefully, Thrace, mortal son of Ares, brother, we shall met again." Cresphontes growled as Deinus leapt into the air to take flight. The large reptilian wings carried the newborn immortals off into the black wings of Night.

They all stood in silence around the altar, the light from the flames revealed the sorrow and defeat felt by all. None had expected what befell them. Each one had been deceived for a purpose or 'endgame' far greater than saving Thrace's mother or Sophos regaining the honor of his father.

"I am sorry Thracian Ares Kraft. It appears I have been deceived." Sophos the Centaur, son of Peirithous said with grief.

"It's not your fault." Thrace replied. "There was no way to know. We have all been used like pawns in a chess game. I am sorry about your father Sophos."

Sophos nodded as their eyes met and each felt the sorrow that consumed them. His father knew the consequences of the killing the Gorgon Stheno and avoided it. Stheno had pointed out 'understanding' was what a teacher should know. An understanding he must reach for what lay in front of him.

Again, a soft breeze caressed the hair on the nap of Parker's neck like a whisper on the wind and kissed his ears. Again, he smiled.

"We've got to keep going," he said.

"What?" Thrace asked.

"Remember when Ares said that Aphrodite whispered the idea of Perseus to me. Well, then the idea just hit me like the wind on your face. Just a second ago, the same sensation hit me…this kinda warm breeze. All of the sudden I feel like we are only halfway there. Like, all this was supposed to happen."

"Maybe Crowned and Flowered Aphrodite is as wise as Ares, the Cunning, pointed out?" Sophos added.

"If she is, why allow those two creatures to be born?" Parker asked.

"As the Gorgon pointed out to me, we must understand all. Something I did not do, which my father knew well. If there is a purpose beyond the birth of these immortals, we must seek it."

"I have to go no matter what Aphrodite says." Thrace stated. "I still have to save my mother."

CHAPTER 14

Thrace stood at the end of a football field. He was dressed in red athletic shorts and a yellow tank top which read, "BHS" for Bemus High School. In his hand he held a javelin. A rowdy noise turned his attention to this right. He saw a crowd of red and yellow blanket the stands of his high school football field. They cheered for him. Behind him he received encouragement from his team, Chad most of all, as his coach Mr. Grissom approached.

"All right Thrace," Coach Grissom said with enthusiasm. "You're the last one. If you throw as well as you did in practice, you'll cover Fairview's furthest throw by twenty yards. So, just relax, have fun and let it rip."

Mr. Grissom gave Thrace a pat on the shoulder, a nod of encouragement and returned to his players. Thrace turned back to the crowd and saw his mother in the stands on her feet, clapping and screaming for his son to, 'kick ass'. Thrace smiled at the sight of his mother and her encouragement, despite the displeasure of her comment obvious in the other parent's faces.

He focused his attention toward the length of the field and the flags representing the other tosses. Chad was beaten out by John Reese, a Fairview player, by less than a foot. Thrace raised the javelin to his ear, began his short sprint and fired the javelin high and strong down the field. It soared like a golden eagle through the air. What a beautiful eagle, he thought, as he watched it elegantly soar upon a backdrop of bright blue. The eagle was then split in half by a mighty brazen double-sided axe. The two pieces of the eagle fell to the ground, just short of Fairview's mark. The crowd sighed. Thrace stood in disbelief staring at the suffering eagle.

Hovering in the air was Deinus, her reptilian wings stretched wide as she glided overhead supporting her mighty brother Hideous Cresphontes. Black-winged Deinus plunged toward the earth and landed beside Thrace.

"It appears you lost brother," Cresphontes said with a growl.

Thrace looked at Deinus as she brought her nose up, smoke lingering from her nostrils. The black-winged Syrian mare placed her snout under the hand of Thrace as if wanting to be pet. From behind him, the band stuck up and marched onto the field. He saw Parker leading the band with a lyre. Beside Parker, his mother, Cybele came dancing onto the field with a satyr. Sophos galloped past his mother and raced toward Thrace.

"WE MUST RUN." Sophos yelled, holding his bow taut with arrow.

Thrace turned toward his half-brother Cresphontes. His horns appeared to glimmer as if Hephaestus the Smith God sharpened them to finite point. He forced a muscular smile upon his beastly face, his jade eyes sparkled like green flames.

"It will be over soon." He said.

Thrace turned back toward the approaching crowd singing and dancing. From behind the crowd he saw dozens of serpentine arms stretch out from around the bleachers. The mighty Hundred-Handed Kottus was upon them.

"RUN!!" Thrace yelled.

No one listened. They sang and danced to the music of Parker and the band. Parker approached Thrace with a smile, the music from his lyre was magical.

"Come on Thrace, dance." Parker said playing away like Apollo, Lord of Music.

"We've got to go, Kottus is right behind us!" Thrace said in angst.

"Who?" Parker asked and continued to play.

Above the dancing and singing crowd, Thrace could see the Hundred Hands of the mighty Titan Kottus coming down upon the people. The laughter of Cresphontes echoed behind him like an earthquake from Earth Shaker Poseidon.

Thrace awoke in a fury as if Fear had taken up residency within him. He looked around and witnessed dark-winged Night still embracing them. He stared up at the sparkling blanket of heroes upon the night sky and tried to catch his breath. Anthia was sitting beside him…watching. She handed him a damp woven towel to wipe his face and a water bottle from his back pack. He accepted it, wiped his face and drank greedily. He finished and noticed the fire was still ablaze. He could see Parker curled up with the bow of Atalanta as if loving her will allow him the ability to wield her. Aemon and Battus slept close to the tree line; each one snoring opposite the other as if a bad punk band. Sophos was nowhere to be seen.

"Sophos could not sleep. He is out for a walk." Anthia informed him as if reading his mind. "You had a dream?"

"More like an odd nightmare," he replied.

"You should tell Sophos about it."

"It's just a dream."

"It is never just a dream." Anthia replied getting up and offering her hand to Thrace. He took it. The warmth from it eased his nerves as he stood. She led him away from the fire and through the forest.

Thrace and Anthia walked alone in the woods, the sounds of Night echoed throughout the valley telling each of them they were not alone. He no longer felt fear as he had in his sleep and enjoyed this moment. Through all the present disaster and upcoming danger, he enjoyed walking alone with Anthia right now. He no longer felt fear of his mother's death, or the anguish of a half-brother who wished to kill him, just the softness of her touch and her hand within his. It felt like two young people walking alone one night, not the son of an Immortal and a Mountain Oread. He wondered if she has ever seen a movie or had pizza. He wondered if they made it out alive, if she would come and visit. Thrace looked over and saw Anthia smile at him. He silently hoped she was thinking the same thing.

"What do you think of this new world you have seen?" She asked.

Thrace mulled over what she had said, drinking in the softness of her voice. She had spoken very little since they had met. Only when it was needed. Yet, she played a vital role in the assistance of helping him save his mother. Now she asked a simple question, though thinking about it, it was not that simple, he thought.

"Well, it's put my mother in the hospital, my friend in a place he shouldn't be and now I have a half-brother who wants to kill me," Thrace replied. He noticed the sadness his comment brought to Anthia and added. "But, I will admit, walking here with you doesn't make it as scary as it's been."

She smiled at his response. She knew this world for it had been her life for centuries. For a mortal to be so immersed within it, it would always be difficult, especially for a son of an Immortal God, especially Ares. Not all tales and songs end in victory, just those that survive or those to teach mortals a lesson. Living forever for many Immortals makes them angry and bitter as if never appreciating anything; a perpetual child. The ancient Greeks understood this, this gift of life, of humanism that may end. Modern mortals, she thought, do not appreciate this short span of life that is their existence. They do not drink it in like nectar and ambrosia, the latter sustained the Gods, but life itself made the mortals immortal. She knew at least he would now. He was greater than even he realized, and she needed to help him in any way possible.

"There he is," Anthia pointed out.

At the valley edge, the sound of a river rippled along the land giving it the sensation of life. Sophos stood at its edge peering into the water in silence. He learned his father was spending eternity looking in a pond revealing all the worst of his life, starving and suffering. Thrace could not imagine the suffering Peirithous was going through and Sophos appeared to be try and understand as he peered at the water's surface. Sophos' head pulled back from the river at the coming sound of footsteps. He spoke without haste or fear.

"Many of our time believe water to be the soul, but I do not know if I believe that. I do believe it is a reflection of us, who we are, and what we are capable of."

"They say the human body is seventy percent water." Thrace responded not surprised Sophos the Clever knew they were near.

"Who are *they*?" Sophos asked.

"Ah, I don't know…scientists?"

"Tell me something you do know young Thrace."

"Ah, I just had a dream," Thrace replied trying to put a name or face to 'they', "…and Anthia suggested I tell you."

"She is correct. There is no such thing as 'just a dream'," Sophos said.

Anthia smiled at the mimic of her own words and turned to leave Sophos and Thrace alone to talk.

Thrace walked to the river's edge and stood beside Sophos. He gazed upon his reflection in the water with the assistance of White and Charismatic Selene the moon. He knew he was almost sixteen, but looking at himself, he appeared much older than he remembered. His pale blue eyes no longer appeared pale, but bright with experience, though he felt tired. Though he knew more than ever, he realized he still understood very little.

"Tell me of your dream young Thrace and please do not leave out anything." The Centaur said his eyes not leaving the rolling river.

Thrace took a breath and replayed the events that swam through his mind as he slept. He spoke trying to understand the meaning, but like the Oracle at Delphi, each could be interpreted as many different things. All but one, he thought. The double-sided axe splitting the golden eagle in half. As

148

he finished he turned to look for Anthia, but she was gone. He wanted to walk back with her, hand in hand again.

"Let us get back to camp. We have a few hours before Dawn awakes us, so let us rest."

"What does it mean though," Thrace asked. "I mean, is Anthia going to die."

"A dream may be a dream and not a prophecy if you act according to the signs," Sophos replied. "It can assist you in the coming events. It does not have to mean death."

Sophos turned and walked toward the camp. Thrace watched him walk away. He turned back toward the river and his reflection was gone. A young beautiful reflective face appeared in the water, her hair dancing in the river current. A water Naiad, he thought. He knelt down and whispered to the Naiad.

"Can you hear me?" he asked.

The water Naiad nodded and smiled as if glad to have someone speak to her.

"Can you do something for me? Can you tell Halia of the Sea that we, Sophos and Thrace, will be going to Crete soon, where Mighty Zeus was raised. We may need her help."

The water Naiad spun around in a circle like a trout, leapt from the river to give Thrace a wet kiss on the cheek and splashed back in the river.

Dawn's long red finger touched the morning sky as the sun chariot prepared Helios for his journey. Sophos awoke from a deep slumber of

149

concern as Sleep pressed hard upon him after he returned to camp. By the fire, he saw Parker still curled up with the bow of Atalanta. It brought a rare smile to the face of the Centaur. The sharp-tongue quick-witted young man, whom he believed should not even have come, was now the window to the Gods and continued them on the path to save Thrace's mother and his father's honor.

The noise of metal clashed in the distance. Sophos arose to all four in an instant. As his keen eyes panned the campground, Thrace or Anthia were nowhere to be found. The sound of metal clashed once again as if Echo reminded him of the upcoming battle.

"To your feet young Parker!" Sophos demanded.

"Five more minutes…" slurred from the mouth of sleepy Parker.

"NOW!" Sophos yelled. "And bring your bow." With that, Sophos gathered his bow and sword and galloped in haste toward the clanging of metal.

After the words 'bring your bow', Parker was up quicker than he had in a lifetime. With the bow in one hand, he grabbed his quiver and chased after the Centaur. He caught up to Sophos at the end of the oak-laden tree line upon a small valley opening near the river Sophos was only hours ago. Parker arrived with bow up reaching for an arrow from his quiver.

"What's up?" Parker asked still wrestling with the arrows in his quiver.

Sophos did not say a word. In the small valley Thrace with spear and sword in hand was battling Anthia, Battus and Aemon. They patiently took turns coming at him as he defended off each attack. He blocked Aemon's sword and swung the ashen spear of Achilles to put him on his back. Battus quickly came at Thrace with his sword high overhead coming down upon him. The latter stepped right to miss the sword blow and swung his blade broadside to Battus' back throwing him to his face. Anthia came next with her thick staff. She came strong, though it appeared she was only swinging a broom handle. Thrace blocked her first three attempts to bring him down and then brought his sword to the offensive, which like a mouse she dodged then swung the staff to the back of Thrace's knees. Thrace buckled as Anthia snapped her staff once more quickly to his chest sending him to his back.

Anthia stood over him with a smile, her dark blue-black hair dancing in the wind. Sophos then appeared beside her admiring his young pupil. Parker arrived next with his ear to ear grin.

"Ouch, she put you down hard."

"Thanks buddy," Thrace replied taking Anthia's hand as he got back to his feet. "Just thought I'd be ready. My half-brother is kind of a big guy."

"Half-brother?" Parker asked. "That just sounds wrong."

"Well then, you may need to remember when fighting with the ashen-spear of Achilles…its length. Holding at its center brings balance and allows you to use it like the staff Anthia uses. But also remember, holding it at its length, one can offer a sweeping blow or simply to bring distance from you and your opponent. It is being able to move the spear quickly between center and length that allows you to offer the deadly blow from the brazen point of Hephaestus."

"I guess I'll have to work on that." Thrace replied at his teacher with a smile, though it was not returned.

"On your feet you two." Sophos barked at Aemon and Battus who jumped like young Hoplite fighters in the Achaean army prepared to battle on the plains at Marathon against the Persians.

Parker, with bow and quiver in hand, let out a large yawn, stretched his arms and turned to head back to camp. A warm spot by the fire was in his mind.

"Where do you think you are going young one?" Sophos asked. "Is it not about time you learned to pull that bow and become Parker of the Atalantan bow, rather than Parker of the sharp tongue?"

"It does sound better," Parker said looking back at everyone. "But, I'm not really a morning person. Give me another hour and you'll see this bow sing."

In a single breath, Sophos was upon Parker as if to remove his head from his body. An arrow and a short sword were in each hand place firmly under the chin of Parker, whose eyes where as large as the great owl.

"Do you think Ares will wait until you get enough rest to send his Immortal seed upon you to remove that sharp tongue from your mouth? Do you believe Horned Cresphontes will wait until you awake and then ask permission to take your life?"

"Ah, no." Parker replied sheepishly.

Sophos lowered the arrow and sword, smiled at Parker and said, "Then I kindly suggest that you join Anthia and have her work on the finer points of archery."

"You know, I think that's a great idea." Parker said jogging quickly to Anthia. "Do you mind helping me out with this thing?"

"Do you think that was a little too much?" Thrace asked Sophos as he returned to his side.

"We all need a kick in ass once in a while." Sophos replied.

"And who said that?"

"I guess I did."

The sun-chariot closed in upon its long journey across the bright air, Aither, as the heroes prepared for the unforeseen. Thrace wielded the short sword well, but the ashen-spear of Achilles became an extension of his arm. He now could handle both Aemon and Battus simultaneously and Anthia, well, let us just say she was taken down once, but the guilt after said attack made it not possible for Thrace to aggressively attack her. This did not rest well with Sophos who quickly drew his sword and attacked Thrace. The ferocity of Sophos startled Thrace as his backside met Mother Gaia often and his mind was continually belittled by his teacher. As Rage took place within Thrace, the battle between the son of Ares and the Immortal Centaur became violent. All paused with concern that blood may be drawn as ancient weapons clamored with ferocity; then, there was a loud clang upon the shield of Perseus which did not come from the sword or spear of Thrace. The fighters stopped.

"Hey," Parker yelled. "You two are getting out of hand."

Sophos and Thrace stood in silence; each gasping for a breath; eyes still bearing down upon one another. Thrace turned his attention to Parker and started toward him as Sophos remained pondering his own anger.

"It appears Rage came and took control of each of us." Sophos said. "There is anger within us, and we need to control it; not let it control us."

"You know," Thrace replied out of breath. "I'm still amazed at the shot by Parker."

"Well, actually, I did not shoot an arrow. I threw a rock. I still can't get this freaking bow pulled back. It's made for a giant.

"Maybe we should get you started on some form of physical training." Sophos said.

"Like push-ups?" Parker asked with disgust. "How about a smaller bow?"

"I was glad you are with me because you're my best friend, and I didn't want to tackle this alone. It does not matter if you can pull a bow back or not. Though I am not a fan of Aphrodite, she does seem to like you. In the *Iliad*, having a God on your side was pretty handy. She pulled Paris out of trouble. Maybe you can get her to pull us out of trouble." Thrace stated at Parker's side, a look of comfort upon his face for his friend.

"I hope I can do more than be the Goddess whisperer." Parker answered.

"Do not underestimate the foresight from the deathless Gods young Parker. It has proven worthy and shall so again." Sophos added to give Parker confidence.

Parker smiled as he nodded to the immortal Centaur. "Hey, there's an olive Anthia hung at the center of that log that I can't hit, or couldn't attempt to hit. Maybe you can pierce it with a pencil?" Parker said to Thrace hoping to change the subject.

Thrace recognized his friend's demeanor and accepted the challenge. He grabbed his backpack and opened it looking for a pencil. A smile arose on his face as his pale blue eyes glistened.

"Well, I don't seem to have any pencils." Thrace said with a daring smile. "I do have these I found in Sophos' cave." Thrace pulled from his pack a glistening silver spear head.

"Those are adamantine spear heads forged by the Smith God Hephaestus." Sophos informed them. "It appears I have two thieves in my presence. I shall need to keep a better watch."

Parker eyes erupted revealing a more than usual 'how cool' look as he stepped back. Thrace targeted the olive upon the log and fired a single silver spear head. Like a thunderbolt from Olympian Zeus it stuck the log dead center of the small olive and the log exploded into a thousand pieces.

The heroes stood in silence but only for a moment.

"You gotta be kidding me! Parker exclaimed. "That was awesome!"

"I didn't think that would happen." Thrace stood amazed. He turned toward Sophos, whose eyes were transfixed upon the once resting log.

"Never have my eyes witness such destruction from the head of a spear." Sophos said with a hint of fear in his voice.

"Nor have I," sang out a voice from behind the training heroes.

They turned toward the voice to see a satyr reclining against a rock with a golden lyre in hand. He rolled his fingers across the strings of the lyre, a beautiful and elegant sound of joy sang from the strings, and laughter appeared to dance like leaves on the wind.

CHAPTER 15

"I have been sitting here watching most of the afternoon. I must admit, son of Ares, your skills have quite improved." The satyr said slipping off the rock that he now leaned against, crossing his hooves.

"It's the satyr Aemon and I saw before." Battus announced with his raspy lisp.

"Let me introduce myself," said the satyr proudly. "I am Pan, Son of Amaltheia, foster-brother to Olympian Zeus."

"It was said you died long ago, Pan, Son of Amaltheia." Sophos said.

Pan rolled his fingers along his lyre with a devilish smile. "Ah, yes…a most clever deception. I became tired of being the plaything to the Olympian Gods, and I did not have the physical prowess as my foster-brother to stop said pestering, I needed an out. I told a simple sailor, Thamus, in route to Italy of my death and was surprised it went over so well. Gossip on a ship with men alone at sea, too easy. I wish I would have done it years ago."

"So, how do you know who I am," Thrace asked.

"Many of us have heard of or watched the many sons of Ares, 'us' being the natural spirits and Immortals of the world. But, we know you, Thrace, killer of Stheno the Gorgon, who released the Immortal children of Ares, Cresphontes and Deinus." Pan said.

"Oh, yeah. Didn't see that coming." Thrace responded.

"Don't relish in it." Pan said with a goatish laugh. "Actually Stheno was getting quite haughty lately, ever since she picked up with Ares. With most of the Olympian Gods slumbering and Aphrodite jealously wandering about, she began to act like the Zeus' wife and sister, the Goddess Hera. Good riddance if you ask me."

"Yeah, but look what I unleashed."

"Look at it this way," the satyr said with a smile. "You were an only child. Now you have a brother and a sister. Maybe they won't pester you like mine did."

"No, mine only want to kill me." Thrace responded in dismay.

"What brings you here Pan?" inquired Sophos with caution.

"Ah, Sophos, son of Peirithous, grandson of Cheiron the Wise, it is nice to finally meet you as well. I knew your father you know. Sorry to hear about his fate. But, we know Ares, the Quarrelsome, without a leash is Ares, the Disastrous, and he has become so pompous as well, and those clothes…really?" Pan stated with another roll upon the strings. "Your father was a good man. Since your mother's death, he spent his life in pursuit of retribution. Many of us error in one way or another and fight to make amends."

"How well did you know him?" Sophos asked with a kinder tone.

"I know he buried those large ears of his in books and lost scrolls he had hidden away after the death of Theope the lovely. He spent days on end training with Naiads beside that cave by the sea preparing for some unforeseen battle. He was a better fighter than he was a scholar but a good

157

man with sharp common sense." Pan paused as he allowed Sophos to drink up all he said, and continued.

"You all look tired from a long day of training," he said as he played his lyre again as if the music itself was persuasion. "Why don't we go back to your camp, have some food, wine and music and celebrate your victory over Stheno and the upcoming journey."

"You may join us Pan, son of Amaltheia. Thrace and I will gather food." Sophos turned toward Thrace. "Gather your spear and come."

Sophos made his way toward the oak-laden forest. Thrace tossed his pack upon his shoulders, tucked his sword in its sheath, grabbed the ashen spear and followed Sophos in haste.

Parker approached Pan examining the first satyr he had ever seen as they stood eye to eye. His face was ruddy and his beard untamed, but Parker could not take his eyes from his hoofed feet. Anthia joined Parker hiding just off to his side. Pan smiled as the Oread approached.

"Well hello, Anthia. It has been a long time." Pan said with a smile.

Anthia transformed into a large golden eagle and flew away as quick as the adamantine spear flew from the hand of Thracian Ares.

"I guess you two don't get along?" Parker asked stating the obvious.

"You ever asked someone out, and they never say yes?"

"Actually, I haven't got to the asking part yet. I already know the answer."

"If you already know the answer, why not just ask?" Pan asked.

Parker shrugged his shoulders and offered the satyr a look of uncertainty. He knew he did not want to ask Helen out because imaging she might say 'yes' was scarier than hearing the words 'no'.

"Well my friend." Pan said walking toward camp, fingers upon the lyre as Parker followed with curiosity of his words and the sound of the music caressing his ears. "First, don't live life with regret; you will regret it. Second, if you never ask, you never know and if 'no' is only that...a 'no', you have your answer, and there is always tomorrow."

"So, you asked Anthia and she said no?" Parker asked changing the subject.

"Actually, each time I ask, she always flies away, like she did just then. I would rather get a no."

Parker laughed at the satyr's response as they walked toward the camp, the music of the lyre carrying them as if by ship careening by a soft breeze. He liked this being, this goat-person, Parker thought. He was straight forward, obvious and amusing.

"By the way, what's that thing called you're playing?" Parker asked pointing to the lyre.

"You are kidding...right?" Pan replied

Deep within the oak-laden forest, the sounds of nature imprinted themselves upon Thrace; the rustle of the leaves, the creaking of the trees, the pattering small steps of animals in the brush, and the noise from his own steps along the forest floor. Thrace watched as his teacher took each step with an elegant grace as if walking upon the clouds in the starry heavens above. The

Centaur's eyes scanned every leaf, every branch as if reserving the image for a painting. He tried to mimic his mentor, but the forest looked the same in all directions. He felt he could get lost here.

"Stop," Sophos whispered, as if reading his mind. "You are trying to see too much at one time. Catch a small scene with your eyes and drink it in. The way the tree grows from Mother Gaia, its shape and contours, the pattern of it branches, the turn of each leaf. Then watch how the land carves itself around said tree. You will notice a pattern with the life and how it focuses on Great Helios above. Once you recognize these distinctions, you can focus on smaller, more acute items."

Thrace heard his teacher's words and drew his attention to a large oak before him. Its thick trunk reached out to the starry heavens above and along its great hide, two large knots stood out resembling large dark buttons upon a long coat. Three strong branches reached from the trunk; two east, one north. Upon these dozens of branches stretched out toward the east as if wishing to kiss Helios as he awoke and began his journey across the azure blue sky above. He noticed the leaves on the morning side of the tree carried a deeper and fuller green and a rich neon green moss grew on the western side.

"On your guard." Sophos whispered raising his great bow.

Thrace raised his ashen spear keeping his eyes keen to the foliage that surrounded him. He heard the pounding of hooves upon the forest floor, but could not locate where it was from. It reminded him of a helicopter he heard as a child, the thumping of the blades, but did not know where it was coming from until it was right upon him, from the opposite direction he had expected.

A violent grunt resounded to his left. Thrace turned to see a giant wild boar barreling down on him as its powerful shoulders thrust it forward with great speed. The beast's large snout snorted violent grunts between two large ivory tusks that appeared to have been sharpened by the Smith God. Thrace could not get his spear around to face the wild beast and quickly dived out of the way. As the wild boar rampaged by, its tusk tore a gash in his calf. The boar continued on into the thick veiled foliage.

"Are you all right?" Sophos asked, bow with arrow still in hand.

"Yeah." Thrace replied wiping the blood from his leg. "I just couldn't tell where it was coming from."

"The sound of the hooves will bounce off of the trees, limbs and leaves. Sound travels at an extraordinary speed, so one must calm oneself and mentally record the sounds as it dances through the forest, then slowly play it back in one's mind."

Before Sophos could even finish, the pounding of hooves again echoed through the forest as if the wild boar had tasted blood of the son of an Immortal and wanted more. Thrace got to his knees, grabbed his spear and paused, his eyes transfixed as if looking through the forest. The sound of the hooves beat the dark soil like large drums. Within the trees he could almost see the thundering hooves galloping from tree to tree.

In a single breath, he turned to his left and with a violent thrust forward of the ashen spear of Achilles, he stabbed the wild boar just as it erupted from the brush. Thrace used all his strength to turn the giant beast as its momentum threw the boar at the son of Ares. They both fell side by side. The wild boar's eyes peered into the son of Ares as the beast took its last quick breaths of life with the spear piercing its throat.

Thrace watched the boar exhaled one final time as its eyes went lifeless. He heard the hooves of his mentor approach behind him. Finally taking a breath himself, he let go of the spear and sat up.

"Well done Thrace of the spear." Sophos said supporting a rare smile.

"Thanks for help." Thrace said staring up at his mentor.

"I did not believe you needed it."

Dark winged Night slowly broadened her black wings wide to blanket the land. Thrace and Sophos breached the oak-laden forest catching the final glimpse of Helios in retreat as he winked goodnight. The wild boar was stretched out upon branches strung together and pulled with rope by the mighty Centaur. Thrace walked beside him with a limp and the killing spear of Achilles had become a crutch. In the distance, the fire of Prometheus glimmered revealing the camp, but that is not what led the way. The sweet sound of music from a lyre swam through the trees as if caressing each and every leaf and the forest appeared to dance all around them.

Thrace could see Anthia, the beautiful Mountain Oread, as she danced around the fire. The light illuminated her like a goddess. His eyes followed every step of her foot, every movement of her hand. He felt a warmth blaze within his own chest as she moved, something more peaceful than the furious rage he felt with Stheno or Ares. With each step closer to the camp, the peaceful blaze made him feel nervous. He had just killed a giant wild boar, but approaching Anthia made him more fearful as his heart boiled like a warm spring.

Aemon and Battus bumbled by the flames attempting to imitate Anthia like two dancing bears. He focused his attention upon the actors and it dimmed the blaze within his chest and replaced it with amusement. It brought a smile upon his tired face. But the smile was extinguished as he saw the look of disappointment on his mentor's face as he watched the two large actors flounder around the fire.

"Come on Sophos, their just having fun."

"We have much work to do for Pan to be playing his games right now."

Just as Sophos spoke, Pan appeared beside the two dancing bears, spinning and dancing around them as natural and elegant as Anthia. Music was his forte, as was prophecy and troublemaking, and he obviously enjoyed good music. Thrace and Sophos looked at one another puzzled. They entered the campsite and Pan immediately stopped dancing and approached our hunters.

"By great Zeus, that's the biggest wild boar I have seen in a millennia." Pan said in awe. "Not since the great Calydonian Boar where Atalanta and another son of Ares, Meleager, competed to defeat the great beast."

The music stopped as Pan spoke. Parker stood from the rock he sat upon on the far side of the fire with Pan's golden lyre in hand and a mile-wide smile upon his face. Parker and Thrace both stood in awe of what each had accomplished. Anthia, seeing the blood dripping from the leg of Thrace, quickly ran to his aide.

163

He spoke to Parker trying to keep from staring at Anthia as she assisted him to the fire. "Heard you in the forest," Thrace said as Anthia led him by the fire to examine his wound. "That music was pretty amazing."

"He's a natural," Pan replied. "Rather poor with the bow, but a natural with the lyre. We have much in common, young Parker and me."

"Well, we probably wear different size shoes." Parker said humbly enjoying the praise. "So, you gotta tell me what happened." He finished moving to examine the giant boar.

"Yes, you both also entertain a quick tongue and an appetite for trouble." Sophos spate. "Aemon. Battus. You two get over here, clean this beast and prepare it for sacrifice and dinner."

The two large actors moved like soldiers in an old comedic black and white film, attempting their best, but with little agility and grace following their general's orders. They cut the fatty thighs and moved them away for sacrifice and prepared the meat for the fire. Pan stood patiently beside them.

"May I have the innards?" the satyr asked.

The two actors heard him, but turned to Sophos for direction. Their leader nodded and they handed the innards to Pan.

"So, how'd you get it?" Parker asked.

"Well, it's never as exciting as it looks." Thrace answered. "It charged me and knocked me over, gashed me; then, I got it the second time."

"Please," Sophos replied. "First he was unsure of the great beast's location, so when it charged, Thrace of the spear quickly dived to avoid being gutted by this beasts great ivory tusks, receiving only a slight scar upon his calf, similar to the one of crafty Odysseus in his youth. The sound of the hooves rumpled upon the land once again. Thrace of the spear calmed himself. Cautiously, he examined the land. Then, upon his knees he located the beast, quickly turned and holding the spear of mighty Achilles tightly in hand, thrust it confidently into the throat of the giant beast bringing an end to its life."

"You know it's safer to throw the spear at the beast son of Ares." Pan said.

"It sounds better than it was," Thrace said.

"Sounds exciting though," replied Parker. "And I think that's the most we've heard Sophos speak since the day we met him. He must be proud of you."

"I think I would rather be relaxing here being able to play the lyre like you, then getting gorged by a boar," Thrace responded watching Anthia clean his wound with the same delicate care and grace as was her dancing by the fire.

"Forever amusing," Sophos stated. "Each enjoys their life, their gift, but would always trade it for another's never truly understanding the purpose or reason of said gift. Never shun your gifts, but embrace them, for only then will you discover their purpose."

Anthia finished wrapping Thrace's wound with excessive care that caught Sophos' attention. He had noticed the glances between the son of Ares and the Oread, especially upon their return from the hunt. If feelings grew between these two, it would be difficult for his training and the task ahead of him, especially after his recent dream, the Centaur thought.

"Parker, of the lyre," Pan said. "Why don't you do the sacrifice? Though you all learned much today, you surprised many with your elegance upon the lyre."

"Ah," Parker stuttered. "Not really sure what to do."

"Just thank the deathless Immortals for what you are thankful and hopeful for. Though many are slumbering, they at times hear." Pan informed him.

"Let see." Parker said as he held the fatty thighs near the sacrificial altar. "To Aphrodite, I thank you for the continual guidance, though you did curse Thrace's mom. Oh, thanks to Artemis for the successful hunt and food tonight. And thanks to Apollo, God of music, for his new gift that I really like." He finished and tossed the fatty thighs upon the fire which lit ablaze in moments stretching smoke trails toward the starry heavens.

Parker looked around to see if he had done well. His friend Thrace nodded in approval. Sophos said nothing, his gaze consumed by the fire. The actors began roasting the meat for dinner. Pan filled goblets with wine and passed them around to all finishing with Parker last.

"You know young Parker, Apollo stole music and prophecy from me. Just letting you know." Pan informed him.

"Oh," Parker replied. "Should I have said something to you?"

"Maybe next time." Pan whispered and then addressed everyone. "Heroes, let us have a toast. May your quest against the villainous Immortals of the world be successful, and may the Gods be on your side in your attempt to save Cybele, mother of Thrace of the spear."

"We're not old enough to drink," Thrace said.

"Let me tell you something," Pan said. "You are on an adventure that you or your friends may not survive. So, why not? Plus, this isn't like your drinks of today. We mix wine with water, honey and grain to dilute it, so we may all enjoy it, relax, and it does not dim our thoughts or abilities, as Apollo himself learned after excessive behavior and latter had carved on the walls of Delphi, 'Nothing in Excess'."

Pan danced over toward Parker pausing only to smell the roasting meat by the fire. He poured honeyed wine over the meat, then held out his hand for his golden lyre. Parker regretfully released his new toy. Pan played his beautiful music which appeared to lift the spirits of all. Aemon and Battus passed out the roasted meat and all ate heartily after a full day of training. Anthia attempted to teach the unwilling Thrace how to dance. He was more willing after Sophos informed him that the movement of dance would help in battle, though with his present limp, Anthia's feet were in more trouble than Kottus, the Hundred-Handed. Sophos did not want the growing relationship to continue with unknowing consequences, but with his dream, he needed his warrior relaxed and ready, not fearful and protective of everyone around him. He would handle that later; he thought.

Pan returned to fill the wine goblets again and then retrieved the entrails he received from the actors. He moved toward the fire and placed the lyre at his side. Sophos stepped closer to the fire never taking his eyes off of the satyr. The heroes sipped their blended wine and watched as Pan took the entrails of the wild boar tucked within the beast's gutted stomach and poured them upon the ground. He eyes coursed over them as if reading a book. He mumbled words Thrace could not understand and sadness captured his face.

"What's he doing?" Parker asked.

"He's a soothsayer." Thrace answered. "He reads the innards of animals for prophecy."

"You're kidding?"

"At this point, I'm surprised you'd question anything we'd see."

"Very true." Parker replied and returned his attention to the satyr.

"There will be a great battle ahead for all, but it will take more than blood shed to win this conflict. One will die, one will grow stronger and a new friend will be made."

The prophecy sent Thrace's eyes toward Anthia as the dream unfolded once more in his mind.

"Who sent you Pan, son of Amaltheia?" Sophos asked.

Pan looked up from his prophecy and replied, "Let's just say a little bird sent me."

"Aphrodite?" Thrace asked.

"Did I say Aphrodite, Thrace of the spear?" Pan questioned.

The satyr picked up his lyre once again and gently played a soft quiet ballad that covered the heroes like a blanket. Sleep came with haste and consumed the heroes, one and all. Pan continued to play his lyre as gently as leaf on a stream as they all fell asleep by the fire. He walked around the fire admiring all of the sleeping heroes, smiled and poured out his wine upon the earth.

Chapter 16

Dawn's forever-reaching red finger etched out across the land sending gloomy Night back to her black marble palace upon the River Styx in Tartarus. Thrace and Parker, feeling tired and sore, ascended from Sleep's hold and tried to peer through sand filled eyes in confusion feeling as if they were climbing from their own beds far away in Colorado. The scent of herbs, spices and meat filled their senses and awaked their stomachs with vigor. This pleasure was disrupted by the bombardment of snoring from Aemon and Battus rumbling across the camp.

"I got a headache." Parker stated.

Thrace added attempting to stand and stretch. "Me too."

"It is the effects of the poison Pan put into the wine." Sophos informed them.

"Poison?" Parker asked.

"Not all poison's kill." Sophos stated, then as quick as the fury of Ares, Sophos swung his bow atop sleeping Might and Violence. They awoke and cowered together like sheep hiding from a wolf.

"Your snoring sounds like Poseidon himself is approaching. Up and begin to pack!"

"You knew this and let us drink it?" Thrace asked stunned by the quick change in temperament from his mentor.

Sophos toned down his anger and faced Thrace. "I assumed the wily satyr was up to something, and I myself did not drink the wine. But I did not witness him pour wine upon the roast, which Aemon said Pan did for flavor, after I ate some of course. I kept on eye on Pan as long as I could as he waited for us to sleep. I awoke after an hour, and he was gone. Though I do not trust the old satyr, he is not one for violence, just mischief. I felt the potion would allow you to sleep and rest. It is what both of you needed before we continue on."

"Hey, where's Anthia?" Thrace asked with a concern obvious even to the actors.

"She has taken the form of the great eagle and is scouting the area." Sophos informed with a cautious eye, which Thrace threw off and collected his gear.

"Hey, he left his lyre." Parker exclaimed.

"I watched him place it beside your pack," Sophos replied. "He must believe its purpose will be necessary for our success."

"I need to practice some more." Thrace said collecting his weapons.

"I admire your persistence, but we are running out of time." Sophos said. "First we will eat. If we are to continue on, we must devise a plan for retrieving the vial from Kottus with multiple back up plans. We also do not know the purpose of Cresphontes and Deinus and Ares' plans for them."

"We know he wants to rule the world," Parker said. "Probably run a big oil company or something."

"He will not wish to rule, but spread chaos from above and not just one country." Sophos stated. "His arrogance will need to be fed by followers."

"You know," Thrace jumped in. "I may have an idea about Kottus. I had it when I met you by the river, but I don't know the Titan well enough to know if it will work." Thrace got up and retrieved his backpack, pulling out a few books.

Parker pulled out his iPhone and again tried to search for information. "I still can't get any service or anything on this thing."

"Young sir," Aemon said as he packed, watching Sophos as he spoke. "Battus and I have realized that where the mist is strong, cell phones don't really work. Some kind of electrical disturbance or something."

Parker looked at his iPhone in dismay. It was always easy access to find anything he needed, no matter how trivial. Now it was worthless, since he figured they would be surrounded by mist until this was over. He shoved it in his pack, and dug around looking for a book though not sure what to look up.

Anthia landed beside the fire and transformed into her lovely Oread self. She looked at Sophos and shook her head as if she had seen nothing. She took a comfortable seat next to Thrace, though avoiding his gaze. Thrace smiled at her return as for her safety as the images of the dream and prophecy lingered in his mind.

"Oh, that smells good." Aemon said with hunger in his eyes.

"Yeah, can we have some?" Battus of the lisp asked.

"After you pour some for the others since you overslept as we prepare for the unforeseen." Sophos snapped at them.

Might and Violence cowered as they collected bowls to offer the stew to each of the heroes.

"Sophos," Parker asked quietly. "Why do you raze them so often?"

"Raze them? You say?" Sophos said with an admiring stare at Parker for defending Aemon and Battus. "They have the gift of sight, which as you know most of all Parker, is a wonderful gift to behold. They treat it as if at a constant celebration and the Immortals they see are celebrities not beings who live upon this world and have their own lives."

"We got a lot of that going on in the mortal world, and those they worship aren't even Immortal." Parker replied as he watched Battus hand Thrace a bowl of stew not taking his eyes from him following his stare with a quiet voice, "Here you are my lord".

"Ah, oh, thanks Battus," Thrace said and the actor smiled at the kind words he received. "Here. Hesiod said that Ouranus, Kottus' father, was struck by their stature and beauty and that's why he put them under they wide-wayed earth."

"Yeah, fifty heads, hundred arms…I can see why he thinks that's hot." Parker added.

"As you should know young Parker, each and all interpret beauty differently. I believe in your mortal realm, you are told what beauty is by your own type of Immortals…celebrities, did you not say?" Sophos said.

"O.K., you got me there," Parker said and added. "So, we tell him he's attractive?"

"A little more than that and we may need some help and may need to go to town." Thrace said.

"There is a small town just south of here, a day's journey." Anthia said.

"Sweet." Parker said with excitement. "I so need a vanilla caramel macchiato."

"Tell me your idea crafty young Thrace." Sophos said revealing his rare smile.

As dark-winged Night nestled above the weary travelers, and the trials before them lingered in their minds; the fire of Prometheus was their only comfort. This gift from the great Titan to the mortals led to his punishment, lashed with adamantine chains forged by the Smith God Hephaestus and chained high atop craggy Caucus Mountains under the order of Olympian Zeus. By day, blazing Helios would scorch his skin leading Prometheus to crave dark Night, but she brought ice cold freezing winds chilling his every bone. Each day upon the arrival of red-robed Dawn, a vulture arrived and greedily ate at his liver and departed at the arrival of Night, and each night his liver grew anew as the vulture returned every morning for another feast. His greatest torment was the eternal solitude atop the craggy mountain top, loneliness like a thirst that could never be quenched. This punishment was dealt to Prometheus for his kindness to mortals. It was his sacrifice to save mortals. For Mighty Zeus, son of Cronus wished to erase mortals from the earth to start anew, but Prometheus, a great and wise Titan, brought mortals fire from Helios and instilled mortals with their greatest asset…hope. Thrace

173

was riding this gift of hope along this long journey as he sat staring into the blazing fire before him along the sea coast. The tale of Prometheus lingered with him, especially as he watched Might and Violence embraced in Sleep. The red-orange fire danced before him and he searched for the small black eyes but did see not them. In his left hand, he twirled the gold coin of Ares around his neck, and in his right hand, he held the grey-eyed flower with auburn petals tight in his hand. The petals had dimmed, but the grey-eye shined bright. His mother was getting worse, but her inner strength was still holding strong. So must he, he thought.

The heroes sat in silence around the shimmering gold and red of the dancing flames before them. Each in their own minds rehearsed their upcoming roles of their plan, which Parker expressed, 'was holy as Swiss cheese.' They all knew it, understood it but found it impossible to prepare for so many variables. After a long journey of debate, and inquiry of 'what if this' and 'what if that', they could arrive at very few options against the Mighty Kottus who helped defeat the Ancient Titans.

Anthia sent word among her kin, the Dryads, who sent word to the river Naiads, along their journey through the valleys for information on Cresphontes and Deinus. The only word was of a giant pyre burning near the temple the heroes left days ago. The thought of killing an Immortal resurfaced in Thrace's mind. He took a life from one protecting the memory of her sister, so he could protect a friend all, to protect his mother from an Immortal God who bathes in death. He was in a world he loved and despised simultaneously, but as he watched the Dryads dance in the forest around him as others brought him food from the forest, he felt there was more good and beauty here than death.

His mind returned to the old tales for assistance and his eyes to the flames that danced like the bird-like daughters of Oceanus that visited Prometheus when he was chained atop the craggy mountain. He pondered over the sacrifice of Prometheus. He was a Titan and could not die and was later released by Zeus, but that did not demean the torture he endured, nor the punishment Prometheus knew he would endure for mortals. But, this was different. His mother was no Immortal and may die. Along with the prophecies that spoke of the death that lay before him. Was the death of a new friend worth saving his mother? A life for a life? Stheno for Parker. He did not know. Not because he did not love his mother, but because he did not want any more death. He began to feel that death may be out of our hands and in the hands of the Fates; Clothos, Lachesis and Atropos.

"Why are the Dryads being so nice to us?" Parker asked.

"They know the ancient prophecy has been revealed, spilled to mortal ears." Anthia answered quietly. "They believe Thrace is the true Seed of Destruction. They are hoping he can end the tyranny upon both the Immortal and mortal realms plagued by Ares, the Destroyer."

"No pressure there." Thrace said.

"Thrace," Sophos followed. "Though I have been training for many, many years, this is my first quest, and you are my first pupil. I know of my father's failures in the eyes of Ares, I believe his failures were intended to avoid not the battle which we now face but the battle that follows. He had more knowledge than we do going in. Fearful of the greater battle, he lost many lives along the way. Few lives sacrificed for a cure he did not wish to acquire to save the lives of many in the end. I believe he lost his own courage along his journey as if veering down a dark cave and the light before you getting smaller and smaller. All of us will learn something along this journey…about ourselves, about our past, about one other. This we must use wisely, this faith in each and all of us to accomplish this quest. Though we cannot know or predict the endgame, I believe neither can Ares, which places all of us on equal ground. But our advantage lies in our trust in one another."

Thrace acknowledged his mentor's wise words and added, "Our last plan didn't go as we expected, and I don't believe this one will either."

"You are correct," said Sophos. "We must be as malleable as bronze atop the Smith God's anvil. Especially if we accept that we cannot kill Kottus."

A lovely Dryad with straw-colored hair and milk white skin appeared from the trees and approached Anthia. She whispered in her ear and smiled at our young heroes and floated away like a butterfly into the trees. Thrace witnessed an acknowledgement of hope in her eyes. Was he the fire of Prometheus, he thought? He hoped not.

The empty sounds of Night surrounded them, in a steady calm of silence, as the Dryad's songs finished they vanished within the forest. They had traveled a few days now and the two young boys who rode into the mountains of Colorado upon their wheeled devises were long gone. Now, before the flames of Prometheus sat two young heroes. One with a talent of the lyre and the other, a demi-god, son of an Immortal with natural physical abilities far beyond any mortal upon Mother Gaia in many years and littered with compassion instilled within him by a god-like mother.

"The Dryads informed me that Cresphontes and Deinus are a top Mt. Olympus with Ares. Aphrodite is not there." Anthia said.

"I get the feeling she is always watching us." Parker added.

"It appears she has drawn a liking to you young Parker," Sophos said with smile no longer as rare attempting to ease the pressure upon the heroes. "Why don't you play us something upon your lyre? Allow to us to relax and acquire some sleep before we set out tomorrow."

Parker pulled the lyre from his pack and rolled his fingers across the strings. Music arose from Pan's gift that caressed the trees and would have calmed the wild boar Thrace had killed. At the sound of Parker's poetic strings, the Dryads returned and sang along with the music with voices that soothed the heroes like a warm blanket.

Thrace settled back against his pack and memories of his mother danced before him like the flames upon the fire. The last move from Virginia to Colorado panned before him like a silent movie. They spent three weeks getting there, camping, hiking and sightseeing along the way. They hiked the Appalachian Trail in West Virginia, drove to Chicago where she took him to a Cubs game, then a viewing of Mount Rushmore and one week of hiking and camping at Yellowstone National Park before arriving in Colorado. Under the stars at night, she told tales of mythical heroes, something he realized he missed. At a campsite near Mt. Rushmore, she spelled her longest rendition of the mighty Bellerophon, who after many trials placed upon him by a jealous king, captured the winged-horse Pegasus and battled the mighty fire-breathing

177

Chimaera with the head of a lion, the body of a great serpent and legs of a goat, as well as a great tribe of men and the mighty Amazon. In the end, Bellerophon in his hubris attempted to scale Mount Olympus atop Pegasus with the belief he belonged there after his many conquests and was stuck down by a thunderbolt from Olympian Zeus. His father carried such hubris, he thought.

The music ended, and Thrace was pulled from his memories. Echoes of Aemon and Battus' snoring rumbled the camp. The straw haired Dryad drifted toward the two actors and sprinkled dust upon their faces. The snoring was quickly hushed like a thought. Thrace mouthed a 'thanks' as she nodded and vanished into the forest once again. Sophos lay by the fire fast asleep, his four legs beneath him, and his arms crossed upon his chest. His eyes twitched as he appeared to be dreaming. Thrace hoped it was something wonderful to combat the thoughts of the enemies that stood before them. Maybe he was dreaming of Halia. With that thought, he looked beside him to see Anthia fast asleep. Her beautiful head of blue-black hair rested atop a pillow of leaves. Her loveliness beside her reminded him of his dream and the falling eagle.

"You all right bro?" Parker whispered.

Thrace rose not to awaken Anthia and sat beside his good friend.

"There's something I need to tell you. The other night, I had a dream. I told Sophos and he said it could be a forewarning, I guess. Anyway, I was at school on the track and field team. You and mom were in the crowd watching. I threw a javelin at a meet to win actually. Well, Cresphontes and Deinus showed up, flying above the field and struck the javelin in half. The

178

javelin turned into a golden eagle." Thrace sat quiet as the memory of the dream stood forefront in his mind and then continued. "You then led the band onto the field playing the lyre and mom was all excited. My half-brother and sister landed before me telling me it was all over and from behind the stands these serpentine like hands reached out for everyone."

"I was leading the band?" Parker asked and got a dark look from Thrace. "I'm kidding. So with your dream and Pan's reading of stomach guts, you think Anthia may die?"

"I don't know."

"It's just a dream."

"That's what I told Sophos, and he said it's never just a dream."

"What do you want to do?"

"I may ask her to leave."

As Thrace finished speaking, Anthia arose and turned toward them. Her pool blue eyes filled with tears, saddened from what he had said. Thrace and Parker froze, upset that she had heard their conversation. She walked into the forest alone.

"Wait!" Thrace yelled toward her, but she transformed into the golden eagle and flew off into the night sky.

"Well," Parker said. "At least she'll be safe."

"I hope so." Thrace said with uncertainty.

Chapter 17

Dawn's yellow finger stretched across the morning landscape awakening each leaf upon each tree limb, as they reached out to embrace the warmth. The heroes slept deep, except Thrace who watched Helios strike out from the east. The departure of Anthia hurt him more than he had expected. He wanted her safe; but she gave him courage, but was it false courage from the warmth injected into him? Right now, he didn't care. He couldn't care. The safety of those around him must take precedence.

Movement caught Thrace's attention as he turned to see Sophos approach the fire from the tree line. He was carrying fish upon a string. Thrace's mind was spinning in disarray. He did not even notice his mentor had left the fireside. He must have slept more than he realized.

"Thrace, stir the fire. I will awaken the actors to prepare this fish. We have much to do today."

"She's gone." Thrace stated.

Sophos stood over Aemon and Battus and rustled the two large soldiers with his front hoof. They awoke more alert than usual, nodded to Sophos and took the fish from him and went to work.

"I know."

"You know?" Thrace asked. "You heard?"

"Nights ago after your dream I thought of asking her to depart our company. Then after the prophecy from afar and the obvious fondness you two had for one another, I spoke to her about it. I was concerned you two would be a distraction toward one another. She agreed and said she would leave the night before we were to meet Kottus when Selene the Moon was high above, and you were fast asleep."

"After everyone fell asleep, I told Parker about my dream and the eagle getting killed. I told him I thought I should ask her to leave for her safety. I guess she wasn't asleep. She left."

"I guess you did not realize that Hamadryads do not sleep. They rest, but hear everything." Sophos informed him.

"I didn't know that." Thrace paused remember those pearl blue tears. "She looked upset."

Parker arose and attempted to clean away the residue of Sleep. His eyes scanned the camp to see the former thieves cleaning fish near the fire. He also saw Sophos and Thrace in a serious conversation. As he continued to look around, his eyes did not find Anthia.

"I guess she didn't come back?" Parker asked.

"I will admit I was nervous about her being here in the end." Sophos said approaching the boys. "You appeared too distracted and concerned for her safety. This is a good quality that many, Immortals and mortals, do not have, but now is not the time. In this upcoming battle this concern could lead away from the endgame and our purpose, which is to save your mother."

"Flipping through Hesiod I read that women were the bane of men." Thrace said.

"Do you really believe that?" Sophos asked.

"No." Thrace responded upset those words even touched his lips. "My mother spoke of how Plato stated women should have equal rights as men. In his perfect government, they would receive equal physical and mental training. She use to talk how Plato said that thousands of years ago, and how it's only recently happened."

"Women are better than me at most things." Parker added.

Sophos laughed not hiding his smile at Parker's response and added, "Not at the lyre my gifted young friend."

"Sophos?" Thrace asked his mind still drifting to the past and his mother. "I remember when mom used to tell me the old tales, like when one sees a prophecy they try to change the future, so it doesn't come true. In turn, they bring about the prophecy by changing something. Like, Oedipus's father was told he would be killed by his own son, so he sent his son away to be left to die. His son survived, and the latter unknowingly killed his own father."

"This is true. Prophecies tend to force one to act, in turn, doing something we may not have done or do something differently, in turn, bringing the prophecy to fruition."

So, because I mentioned asking her to leave..."

"Which she did." Parker finished.

"Thanks. Yeah, she did. I could have brought about my dream or the prophecy?"

"It is possible. Or it could change how or where it happens."

"Great." Thrace said with concern.

"But how or where can be very important. Right now we cannot concern ourselves with this; however, it does change our transportation plans to Crete. We need to eat then you shall take Parker, Aemon and Battus to town to acquire what we need, return here, and if I am not here you shall await my return."

"Where are you going?" Thrace asked.

"I shall find us a ship."

"As a horse?" Parker asked.

"As I have informed you before young Parker, mortals see what they want or need to see."

As Bright and All-Seeing Helios reached midday, the heroes approached the outskirts of town. It was more of a village outside a larger sea coast town, outside of a larger coastal city. All of which the boys hoped to avoid. As much as they missed the modern world, their actions needed to be focused in the ancient realm that still existed, especially since they did not have paperwork or travel plans to defend their little excursion in Greece.

Old stone and concrete homes staggered alongside an ancient dirt and stone road leading to the center of the village that appeared to have reached old age long ago. A few old cars were parked along the brick street and near a couple houses a dozen years shy a new coat of paint. An elderly couple made their along the brick street passing a withered man in a black coat sitting upon an old chair smoking a black cigar; the grey smoke drifting from the tip to the heavens. The younger generation had long since moved away. In the center of town a four points crossing divided the village, and at its center stood a worn and weathered statue of an Ancient Hoplite warrior wearing his greaves, corset, helmet with a large pike in one hand and a shield in the other.

These working warriors fought and defended Greece against the Persians in many great battles for freedom to only fight amongst themselves for power. The heroes stood before the statue as Thrace observed the sculpted warrior and admired the determination carved upon the Hoplite's face.

"I don't see a Starbucks anywhere or even a Euro-coffee shop." Parker stated.

"I don't think we'll find anything like that here." Thrace replied.

"Excuse me sir," Aemon said. "There is a café across the four points that has good coffee and an antique shop across the street."

"Thanks Aemon." Thrace said. "Parker why don't you grab us some coffee and I'll take the guys to get the mirrors. Oh, I need some of those gold coins."

"I can't believe you caught me taking those," Parker said digging out the coins from his pocket.

"I didn't, I just knew you'd take them. Especially when I saw you look at those gold coins Anthia held out."

"Am I that obvious?"

"As I said before, I'm glad you did."

"You wouldn't mind if we had a coin for our services?" Battus said with a cautious lisp.

Aemon looked at him and slapped him in the back of the head. "What are you thinking? We were born without the mist; we're supposed to be here."

"Sorry."

"No, it's ok." Thrace said to Battus. He handed Battus and Aemon each a gold coin. "Just this for now since I don't know how much the mirrors will cost."

"Thank you sir," Battus said slovenly. "Your kindness rivals that of the Nymphs of the forest who are so kind to us, no matter who we are."

"No problem…Might and Violence." Thrace said which made the actor beam with the light of Apollo. "Meet you out front of the coffee shop. And remember, we're in Greece." Thrace said to Parker.

"I don't know any Greek, or any language for that matter."

"Excuse me, Parker sir, just hold up fingers for how many and say 'café' and she'll understand. That's what we do." Aemon said as Battus nodded.

Parker of the Golden Lyre raced toward the coffee shop as Thrace of the Ashen Spear, Might and Violence entered the antique shop. It was besieged with what Thrace thought to be old trash engaged in battle. Faded paintings, worn chairs and tables and small multi-colored glass lamps filled the room allowing for little walking space. Might and Violence moved with bumbling inefficiency and with each and every step they had to pause to stop a lamp, or vase from being knocked over.

"You two just stop moving, and don't touch anything all right?" Thrace said feeling like his mother.

Aemon and Battus stood like the statues at the Gorgon's lair with only Aemon nodding his head in understanding. Thrace continued to the back of the shop and saw an elderly lady with ivory white hair pulled back into a bun and an olive green smock draped over her. Her eyes were a sea blue and filled with life. She saw Thrace and smiled which filled Thrace with warmth. His mother's grandparents died when he was young and never knew them. On his father's side, his grandparents would be Zeus and Hera, and he doubted, if he ever met them, they would be normal grandparents. This warm elderly lady he would love to visit with his mother on long weekends. He could spend the day helping her around the house and yard though she was the kind of woman that did not need it. At night, she would prepare a traditional style dinner that you dreamed of long after you left as you wore the beanie she knitted you didn't mind wearing just because she made it.

"May I help you young man?" The elderly lady said in a raspy voice with a crunchy undertone of a broken English accent.

"Wow, you speak English." Thrace said.

"One of my children moved to London years ago, and I spent some time there and learned a few things. How may I help you?"

"I am looking for mirrors, large ones."

"Mirrors?" The elderly lady said moving out from behind a desk revealing her five foot stature and broad shoulders. "Along this back wall." She pointed two rows away from Thrace.

He made his way through the antique debris to the far wall. He found two large identical mirrors trimmed in a gold wooden frame which stood over four feet in height and three feet across. These will be perfect, he thought.

"How much are they?"

"They are rather expensive. May I ask what you need them for?" She asked.

"Uh…" Thrace stuttered forgetting to prepare for any questions.

"We do theatre in various villages and are bound for Crete," Aemon spoke out. "I play Might and my brother plays Violence in *Prometheus Bound* and the young sir plays Hermes. We need the mirrors for set designs."

"Expensive mirrors for set designs." The elderly woman said making her way in front of Thrace. "How much money do you have on you?"

Thrace got the feeling he was all of the sudden about to get swindled as the old woman's sea blue eyes pierced into this soul. His hand fumbled in his pocket with the gold coins. He pulled out four thinking two for each. He did not know the price of gold or how much such an antique mirror should cost. But, deep down, he did not care, he needed those mirrors.

"I have these four ancient gold coins. I believe they are worth a lot. Probably much more than the mirrors."

The old woman stood silent in front of Thrace staring boldly into his eyes as if reading his mind. He felt desperately uncomfortable, and he no longer wished he had a grandmother like this woman. He would rather be in the woods with the Dryads, satyrs and centaurs.

The old woman took a deep breath as her sea blue eyes no longer stared deep into his, but now lingered upon him.

"Anything else?"

Thrace was shocked the old woman would not take the coins; unless, she believed they were fake. Why would a fifteen year old have gold coins in his pocket? He pulled out his wallet to find four American one dollar bills. Definitely not enough, he thought.

He turned to the former thieves for any ideas? Battus held up his coin given to him minutes ago as Aemon pulled out a credit card.

"You have a credit card?" Thrace asked.

"Just in case." Aemon responded.

"How about the necklace?" The old woman said, her crunchy English accent softened to a delicate tender tone.

Thrace fingered the coin about his neck. Why would this woman want his necklace? All he knew was that it had something to do with his mother and Ares, the God of War. It also had Ares' blood on it which took away his mist, but of a value or worth, he had no idea. No matter its value, it was not as much as his mother's life.

"Sure." Thrace replied. He pulled the necklace from around his neck and held it out to the old woman with the sea blue eyes.

She took the necklace from Thrace, her sea blue eyes not leaving the brazen coin of Ares as she held it up in the light peering from the window. She stood motionless as if watching a world pass before her eyes one frame at a time. Thrace instructed the two large actors to grab the mirrors and meet him outside. The did as instructed, but not without Battus knocking over a large aqua green vase that erupted into a thousand pieces as it hit the floor. Thrace turned back at the old lady, whom he thought may now ask for the gold coins for the vase. But she continued to stare at the bronze coin at the end of the necklace as tears welled up in her eyes.

"Where did you get this necklace?" She asked as tears choked her speech.

"My mother." Thrace replied and turned back toward the old woman.

Her tears did not stop as her gaze lifted from the necklace and once again her sea blue eyes met Thrace's pale blue.

"How is she doing?" She whispered.

"Not well." Thrace said. "How did you know?"

With her other hand, she pulled a similar bronze coin necklace hidden beneath her green smock. Her eyes peered back and forth between the coins, as her watered sea blue eyes churned in grief like a storm upon the Aegean.

It was an exact copy. Thrace stared in disbelief. She was a mother of a son or daughter of Ares, one who obviously died, though she lived on. He approached her and took a closer look at the coin around the neck. Ares, the Deceiver, must have these by the bushel as he played his games with the mortals.

"I survived...and he died." She whispered as tears rained from her sea blue eyes. "I wish it the other way." She finished as she looked upon Thrace once again. The old lady attempted a smile and appeared to drink in his features.

"So young..." she said as she turned and walked away.

Thrace found Parker, Aemon and Battus sitting on a bench in front to the café with coffee in one hand and a large fruit pasty in the other. A raspberry smile appeared upon Parker's face as he saw Thrace coming toward him.

"Here, I got you one too. It's not a low fat, vanilla and caramel macchiato with whip cream, but it's not bad. It's the pastry that's fantastic."

Thrace took a seat next to Parker and took his coffee. He hoped its warmth would shake off the chill from the old lady. He knew of the deaths of the other sons of Ares and assumed their mothers died as well, but this was a different revelation. His death would bring his mother's survival. Even if he failed, she would continue on. That is all he could ask for. But the words of the old woman lingered within his mind, 'I wish it the other way.'"

"You ok?" Parker asked. "The guys here tell me she took your necklace instead of the money. Is that a good thing?"

"I don't know. I'll tell you when we get back to Sophos."

"Well, you got the mirrors, and I bought a phone card inside since my cell is worthless, plus I don't think I can make international calls on it even if it did work. I was going to call my mom to let her know we're all right."

"That's a good idea."

Parker rose to seek out a phone and saw an old lady with ivory hair exit the shop and stare at Thrace sitting on the bench. Taking small, but direct steps she approached them. Parker kicked his friend, who was lost in thought. Thrace looked up to see the old woman standing before him. Her tearful sea blue eyes were different. They were a bright azure blue and shined like sapphires. Thrace leaned back trying to avoid her heavy gaze which felt like the weight of the world. He understood the burden of Atlas as his sat on the bench with café in hand.

"Remember the forgotten." She whispered as she held out both his and her gold coin necklaces.

"The forgotten?" Thrace replied accepting them.

The old woman did not respond. She turned and steadily returned back to her shop muttering in Greek.

"That was creepy." Parker said. "What do you think she meant by 'remember the forgotten'? How do you remember something you forgot anyway?"

"I don't know." Thrace said.

"Hey, guys," Parker said to Aemon and Battus. "Is there an ancient Titan or beast or something called the 'Forgotten'?"

"Not that I know of, but you may want to ask Sophos." Aemon replied.

"Let's get out of here. As much as I missed the city, I would rather be on a mountain or in the woods with the Immortals than here right now." Thrace said.

"Right on," Parker said. "Let me just call my parents."

"You can use my cell phone young sir. No mist here and mine makes international calls." Battus said, his lisp barely noticeable.

"It's so we can call our pop." Aemon finished, Battus nodding.

"Ah, thanks Battus." Parker replied looking at both of them differently. It was the first time they spoke of a parent, and he always saw them as part of the myth they had entered.

"Hello, Parker is that you?" He heard his mother shout upon the first ring with fear and concern.

"It's me mom."

"OH MY GOD! Where are you? What going on!"

"Mom, please calm down. I am fine. I am with Thrace. We're both all right."

"You scared your father and me to death. Tell me where you are, and I will come and get you."

"Mom, we're not done yet. We found a way to help Thrace's mother, and when we get what we're looking for, we'll be home."

"Parker, I love that you want to help your friend, but there is nothing you two can do for her. She is in a coma and getting worse. You both need to be here, now."

"Mom, you'll just have to trust me. I love you."

"Parker wait…"

Parker hung up the phone quickly.

"Everything all right?" Thrace asked.

"Well, she's not happy, but at least she knows we're still alive, for the time being." Parker said with a weak smile as he handed the phone back to Battus. "If she calls back, please don't answer." Battus nodded accepting the phone as Parker turned to Thrace. "She said your mom is getting worse."

"Let's get back and find Sophos and hope he got a boat. I should've never even thought of asking Anthia to leave."

"Hey, you like her and worry about her. It's not a bad thing."

"Yeah, first girl I like, and she's dozens of years older than me."

"She's older than that." Aemon said.

"Thanks Aemon. Let's go."

The foursome arrived back at camp to see Sophos waiting impatiently. The camp is packed with each individuals gear staged awaiting its personal carriage. Sophos had doused the fire, and circled the smoldered embers like a worried mother. Thrace noticed bones in the coals and realized Sophos had prayed to the gods. He wondered what he asked for.

"What took so long?" Sophos demanded.

"The town was further than we realized, and I had an incident with an old lady." Thrace replied.

"Please explain, 'incident'." Sophos inquired.

Parker jumped in. "This creepy old lady came out of the antique shop and eased in front of Thrace, stared at him, then said, 'remember the forgotten'. It was like some bad *SyFy* show."

"I don't understand many of your comments young Parker." Sophos replied. "Could it have been Aphrodite in disguise?"

"No way, she was old and ugly." Parker said knowingly.

"Actually," Aemon injected. "In many Greek myths the Gods played other individuals to advise or mislead. Ox-eyed Hera did with Jason. Lovely Athena did with Odysseus' son Telemachus as Mentor."

"The old lady who came out of the shop had these bright blue eyes. The same blue eyes I saw in my backyard with my mother, so yes, it was probably Aphrodite." Thrace said.

"Then we should be on our guard." Sophos stated.

"There is more," Thrace added. "In the shop, the old woman had these sea blue eyes like the morning Aegean in front of that cave. She also had the same necklace my mother had. Her son was a son of Ares. She said he died and she lived." He finished and held up both coin necklaces toward Sophos.

Sophos drank in this new information as Hephaestus drinks in the flames upon his forge to create magical weapons for mortals and immortals alike. His eyes turned to the bones still smoldering within the embers. His gaze turned toward Thrace who waited for him to speak. Sophos knew what was on his mind.

"This information does not change anything; no matter what you are thinking Thrace of the Spear."

"What? That if I fail, my mother is gonna be all right."

"What?" Parker jumped in, his eyes filled with concern for his friend.

"We must fight for more than that, more than the survival of one." Sophos stated.

"Really? But it's done. My mother will be safe. There will be no more sons of Ares, no more mother's cursed. He's got what he wants, those two Immortal children."

"Are you that naïve?" Sophos questioned and stood before the young son of Ares, his strong arms on Thrace's shoulders. "Do you think so many children died, just so he could have two immortal children? He already has a few; a few you have probably met, Fear and Panic to start. Ares will use these immortal children to wreak havoc upon this mortal realm and more than just sons, daughters and mothers of Ares will die. He will wage a worldwide war and carpet Mother Gaia with a blanket of mortal flesh and blood." Sophos released Thrace and turned toward the smoldering embers and added, "It is about more than you and your mother."

An uncomfortable silence rested upon the heroes as their eyes did not gaze upon one another, but within themselves. Much more is often asked of us, more than we can carry; the question is, are we willing to try?

"So, do we have a ship?" Thrace asked as he intertwined both necklaces and hung them around his neck.

"You know," Parker added to lighten the mood. "I've never been on a boat."

"We do." Sophos replied looking upon the young heroes who stood before them. More courage than men twice their age, he thought. "But we must make haste. Our departure depends upon our arrival and a few of those gold coins young Parker *borrowed* from my cave."

"Yeah, I just borrowed them *'cause they might come in handy.*"

Chapter 18

The wine dark sea stormed against the rocky shore proclaiming its prominence as if Poseidon's bronzed hoofed stallions stampeded beneath the white waves. Milky white clouds covered the journey of Helios across the blue heavens. The heroes made their way along an old Roman brick road through small villages that sprouted and grew in size the closer they got to the Aegean as flowers sprout brighter closer to a spring. Leering eyes of tourists and locals alike drew a flavor of curiosity toward the large and ragged former thieves, two young boys lugging a spear, bow and lyre and a regal gentleman in a corduroy brown suit also with bow and sword. They hastily arrived at a gated pier stretched out from the shore into the wine dark sea, a lone individual in a blue and black uniform stood guard, a modern hoplite warrior. As they attempted to cross the gate the guard stood before them restricting their passage.

"Με συγχωρείτε, μπορώ να σας βοηθήσω;" The guard asked.

"English?" Thrace asked.

"Yes. May I help you?"

"We are here to meet the Wilton's." Sophos said.

"One minute." The guard replied and entered a small wooden shed filled with a small desk, book, many keys and an old push button phone. He picked up the phone and dialed. He spoke to someone in Greek on the other end and then returned.

"Don't you speak Greek?" Parker asked Sophos.

"The only thing in common between ancient and modern Greek language are the letters young Parker." Sophos replied. "Hence why I picked up English."

"He is awaiting you, but you cannot go on the pier with those weapons." The guard informed them pointing at the spear and bows.

"Weapons? These are props," Aemon stepped in. "We are actors and in route to Crete for a performance. Sophos plays the Great Titan Prometheus in *Prometheus Bound*. Thrace here plays the Giant Killer Hermes and Parker plays lovely Io. My brother plays Violence as I play Might. *'This is the world's limit that we have come to; this is the Scythian country, an untrodden desolation. Hephaestus, it is you that must heed the commands the Father laid upon you to nail this malefactor to the high craggy rocks in fetters unbreakable of adamantine chain. For it was your flower...'.*"

"Fine, fine, just go." The guard said immediately bored and not wishing to be bothered. He unlocked the gate to allow the actors upon the pier, for he was no King Leonidas.

"Wow," Parker said. "That was good, but lovely Io?"

"Well, she is," Aemon said. "I can continue."

"Silence." Sophos commanded.

Along the pier small skiffs and aluminum boat smothered the edge of each wooden plank as if attempting to escape the horrors of the Aegean. At the end of the pier rested a large sailboat, white as ivory and trimmed in a blue that matched the eyes of lovely Aphrodite. Before the vessel stood a thin sun-weathered man in his early sixties wearing blue and white sailing attire that matched the ship. His soft brown eyes were hidden by glistening white teeth that shimmered in the afternoon sun against his sun bronzed skin.

"I thought you would never make it my friend." The sailor said through his smile with a deep Scottish accent.

"My companions were late getting the gear we required." Sophos said.

"If you don't mind, I would love to see those gold coins you mentioned." The kindly sailor said as he smiled again, but it was not the greedy smile of Battus, but a thirsty smile only quenched by knowledge.

Sophos looked toward Thrace, who stepped forward and pulled out two ancient gold Greek coins from his pocket and handed them to the sun-weathered sailor. The latter held out his calloused hands worn by far more than tying knots upon a ship.

"You keep them in your pocket?" The sailor asked and rolled the gold coins gently as if touching a delicate rose. His soft brown eyes sparkled rich with life. "These are in perfect condition. These stallions upon the coins almost resemble the coins found in Syracuse around 400 B.C."

"They have been in my family for generations. They are not from Syracuse, but were used during the reign of Pisistratus in Athens, which I believe is considered around 550 B.C." Sophos informed the sailor.

"Amazing," the sailor said in a whisper taking a handkerchief from his pocket and delicately wrapping the coins. "You must have to get to Crete in a jiffy to sacrifice those treasures."

"It is of the utmost importance." Sophos answered.

"Well gentlemen, let me introduce myself. I am Professor Charles Wilton, retired Classics professor from University of Edinburgh, hence my interest in the coins. My wife, Myrtle, is downstairs in our cabin sleeping. The waves of the Aegean are not kind to her."

"Professor, this is Thrace, Parker, Aemon and Battus." Sophos said.

"It is a pleasure to meet all of you. I love the ancient Greek names too. Where are you four from? I found out Sophos here is from Athens."

"He and I are American, from Colorado." Parker answered looking at Sophos in question.

"Wonderful. I taught some in Chicago, busy city, but never made it that far west. I hear its lovely country."

Aemon stepped forward, "My brother and I are originally from a small village north of Ipswich."

"Wonderful. I am originally from Glasgow, but lived most of my life in Edinburgh. Well good, let me introduce my lovely ship. She is called, *Amphitrite*, after the wife of Poseidon, Lord of the Sea. Come aboard gentlemen so we may set off."

The Professor Wilton led the way upon his thirty seven foot Hunter sailboat. He started the engine to pull away from the pier as the stench of the motor filled the skies until the sails were set with assistance from the actors. The professor pulled from the harbor and continued with his tale of Poseidon and Amphitrite and their three sons, Triton, Rhode and Benthesicyme.

Parker, Aemon and Battus sat entrenched by the tale spoken of with so much passion by the Professor. Thrace watched briefly as it reminded him of his mother and the intense passion she carried as she shared the ancient legends. He pulled the flower from his pocket. The petals were wilted and dim as the grey eye still stared back. She is strong; he thought. Sophos placed his hand on Thrace's shoulder and led him to the far end of the ship to speak with him alone.

"With no winds, it will take us much time to reach Crete from here." Sophos said. "We need to make a small sacrifice to Zephyrus the gentle and playful West Wind to hurry our journey. Do you have any equipment for a fire in you pack?"

"I do, one second."

Thrace moved to the side of the ship and caught Parker's attention. Parker saw Thrace; he rolled his finger over, and Parker nodded in acknowledgement. He knew he needed to keep the Professor's attention. Like many close friends, each nod, twitch or glance has a meaning and understanding. They were no different. Thrace pulled off his backpack and pulled out a small propane camping grille.

"So, what do we sacrifice?" Thrace asked.

"Check the cabin for flowers, Zephyrus escorts the coming of spring, he would appreciate that."

Thrace moved toward the stern of the boat where the Professor was deeply ingrained in Poseidon's attempt to overtake Zeus. Thrace climbed down into the cabin mouthing 'bathroom' to the professor, who smiled and pointed into the cabin, but did not leave pace with his tale. On top of a small table in the galley was a clear glass vase secured at its center with a bouquet of lilies. He pulled half the lilies from the vase and made his way topside. Hiding the flowers behind his back he quickly returned to Sophos.

"I found some lilies."

"Perfect," he replied. "This is your quest. You will need to make the proper sacrifice."

Thrace ignited the propane grille, clicked a red button at its side and a small blue flame erupted from the top. He knelt down beside the grille with the lilies in hand.

"I offer these lilies to Zephyrus, Son of Eos, the Great West wind. I offer these spring lilies to you for a quick journey to Crete along this wine dark Aegean."

Thrace held the lilies over the blue flame, and they began to quickly burn. He held them until the flame came close to his fingers and then released them as the ash danced into the air and drifted upon the ocean breeze.

"What are you doing?" a female voice barked behind them.

Thrace turned off the camping grille stood and turned to see a woman he could only imagine being Myrtle. She had sun bleached white grey hair, tan skin and white teeth though her eyes were a much darker and bolder brown than her husband. She wore a blue and white sailor suit that was the female version of what the Professor wore, which was even more obvious considering he was now standing behind her. Parker shrugged with a look of an apology.

"I asked you a question," she said again.

"It sounded like you were making a sacrifice to Zephyrus, the West wind." The Professor said.

Thrace thought, what the hell, he is a Classics professor. "I was."

"Honey, don't tell me you brought more crazy Greeky's on this ship." Myrtle said. "Can't we just enjoy the Aegean and not search for treasure and history. You're retired, remember."

"But honey, look at these gold coins…"

Just as the Professor attempted to defend himself, a large gust came from the East and caught the sails. The ship quickly picked up speed almost taking Myrtle off her feet as Parker reached and caught her. She regained her footing, straightened herself and nodded a thank you to Parker. The Professor ran to the wheel and Aemon and Battus rushed to follow him in assistance. Myrtle briskly joined her husband at the wheel. The Professor took control of the locked wheel and stared at his passengers in awe and confusion.

Parker laughed, tapped Thrace on the shoulder and pointed up to the sail. They both looked up to see the gentle face within the wind thrusting the sail south toward Crete.

"Let me introduce you to Zephyrus, the West wind." Parker said. "Be careful though, he likes to play jokes on you."

"Who are you?" The professor asked looking upon all of his travelers.

"Kind sir, we are just a few weary travelers who are in need of getting to Crete in haste." Sophos said.

"I need a drink." Myrtle said as she left the helm descended to the cabin.

"Excuse my wife," the Professor said. "She's a lovely woman, but thinks I take the world of history, especially ancient Greece, a bit too seriously."

"It's all right Professor," Thrace said. "My mom teaches Classics too. I don't believe I appreciated it until now."

"That's why I brought her here. I thought she'd learn to appreciate my passion."

"In any union, each must learn to appreciate one another's desires and passions as two river's flowing together to form the great sea." Sophos said.

"Who was that? Anixamenes? Aristotle, Diogenes?" Thrace asked.

"Halia of the sea." Sophos said staring out across the Aegean.

"Halia was a Naiad, she didn't write anything." The Professor stated.

"My parents are accountants. I don't think I could ever appreciate numbers, well, unless they dance like they dryads." Parker said attempting to change the subject.

The professor eyes turned from Sophos to Parker and his passionate expression turned puzzled. "So, tell me why you are going to Crete?"

Thrace watched Sophos walk to the bow of the ship alone. The thought of Halia was obviously on his mind. He turned to the Professor not wanting to answer his question and turned toward Aemon, who smiled as if his cue had been called.

"We are stage actors. I play Might in *Prometheus Bound.*" Aemon said.

Parker pulled the lyre from his pack to assist his new friend and began to play as Aemon began reciting the lines from the opening of *Prometheus Bound.* Battus stood beside Aemon as his role of Violence and began gloating over the invisible Prometheus. The Professor smiled a child-like grin watching with excitement. Thrace watched for a moment then left them to their theatrics. At the bow, Sophos continued to peer over the wine dark sea.

Along the side of the boat, Thrace stared deep into the wine dark Aegean and understood how it got its name. He wondered if the Earth Shaker Poseidon was asleep deep in his palace within a cave near the ocean's floor. Did Halia get his message from the river Naiad? Did he stand a chance against the Kottus, the Hundred-Handed? Retrieve the vial or not, his mother survives but at what cost? His mother had been to Delphi; she had seen Aphrodite. Somehow she knew something was coming, as she spoke 'you may need the practice'. The real problem was if he died upon this quest, his mother would go after whomever the cause. She would fight both Gods and Titans. And she would lose. They both would die. Sophos was right, much more was at stake, especially with the newborn fraternal Immortal twins. Right now, he just wanted to survive to see his mother.

Dolphins leapt and dived riding the waves breaking off the bow of the ship. He smiled as he watched the dolphins frolic along the white waves recalling a tale his mother once told him. They were music loving creatures, and once saved a man, Arion, who was thrown overboard by his countries tyrant leader because he was too rich. He rode a top a dolphin back to Syracuse. They were here for Parker's music. He did play magically. Even the West Wind Zephyrus gave thrust to the sails with a smile from the songs that sang out from the Golden Lyre.

The play at the stern ended as Dark winged Night stretched her arms across the sky and painted the black sky with the heroes and victims of old once more. The West wind Zephyrus took rest upon the mast drinking in the stars above. In the starry sky, the Professor pointed out Herakles, son of Zeus and the twins, Castor and Polydeuces, who were known as the Dioscuri, sons of Zeus. Castor was a great Spartan soldier and tamer of horses as Polydueces was the greatest boxer of his time and won honor at the Olympic Games. Thrace listened to the Professor as his words trailed far upon Night's wing. He knew Polydueces well, or Pollux, or at least his heart did from the endless pounding within his chest.

Night passed in silence as Sleep took the Professor to rest with his wife. Aemon and Battus curled up near the stern in blankets as if sleeping under the starry sky was their comfort, their home. Parker descended into the cabin for the cool Aegean night was too much for him. Sophos took the helm like Great Agamemnon leading the Greeks across the seas awaiting the first sight of land, the sight of Troy. Thrace curled up on top of the cabin under a warm blanket, admiring the beauty that sparkled across Night as her daughter Sleep attempting her best to bring him under her spell as he felt the rocking of the Aegean beneath him.

A voice whispered across the tail end of the West Wind. The sails fluttered as Zephyrus heard the voice himself and blew off in fear. Sophos' eyes scanned the ship then the horizon sensing danger. Thrace curled in Sleep's bosom heard a voice like a dream in which he was awake watching himself sleep atop the cabin.

"Wake up Thrace." The voice said.

Thrace saw himself sleeping atop the cabin warmly beneath a blanket under the starry night. He yelled at himself, though he had no voice. Across the sea, he heard the ripple of wings. A black winged stallion flew toward him, flames bubbling from its nostril for light. Deinus. But it was not Cresphontes upon her back, but his father Ares, God of blood lust.

"Wake up Thrace. It's coming for you." Ares spoke, not as the Destroyer, but as a father.

Thrace sat up in haste throwing the blanket from him. He panned the top of the ship and saw Sophos moving anxiously at the wheel.

"Sophos," Thrace said. "My father just woke me, and said 'it's coming for you'."

"Something has awoken the Old Man of the Sea." Sophos said, his eyes startled by this latest dream. "It has scared Zephyrus away. Quickly, wake the others and bring them topside. We must prepare for anything."

Thrace leapt from atop the cabin toward the stern sliding his pack upon his back. He kicked awake Aemon and Battus whose snoring would have silenced any screaming attempt to wake them. He descended downstairs to see Parker curled up with the Atalantan bow slung over his shoulder, and the lyre tightly wrapped within his arms. He shook Parker, who awoke with quickness pulling his bow from his shoulder and reaching for the quiver of arrows tucked between his legs.

"Wow," Thrace said. "Much different than I remember."

"Well, we're in a much different situation."

"True my friend. It looks like someone woke Proteus, the Old Man of the Sea; Zephyrus has fled, so Sophos wants us topside. We need to wake the Professor and his wife."

"I'll do it. He likes me or at least my music." Parker said with a knowing smile.

"You may want to grab some life preservers just in case."

"All right. And you'll have to tell me why the Old Man of the Sea doesn't like us."

"Right now, we don't know." Thrace answered.

Parker nodded an understanding and made his way toward the back cabin as Thrace returned topside. As his feet climbed the steps, the ship tilted up high on its side and rocked back down. He grabbed the rail for support and used it to pull himself to the deck.

The cloudless and once calm Night had changed as instantly as an Immortal's opinion. Dark black clouds filled the sky above as large temple sized waves rocked the ship back and forth. Aemon and Battus were pulling down the sails as Sophos turned the ship into the waves. Thrace joined Sophos at the wheel.

"I need you to turn on this motor to push the ship into the waves!" Sophos yelled above the crashing waves and howling wind.

Thrace found the engine button, pressed it and felt the vibration of the engine kick on beneath the ship and moved the throttle forward. Sophos turned the wheel to push the vessel head first into the giant waves. Parker, the Professor and Myrtle ascended topside, the latter two faces honeycombed with fear.

"Parker!" Thrace yelled above the storm. "I need you to play your lyre!"

"What? Why?" Parker yelled.

"In case we capsize!"

"Capsize?" Myrtle announced in fear.

"What's going on here?" The Professor yelled in confusion above the howling wind and thundering clouds.

"Well Professor," Sophos announced with his deep commanding baritone voice. "It appears you have rewarded passage to a couple of men and a centaur who are presently doing battle with the Gods of old. Thrace here is the Son of Ares. He was wakened by his father to warn him that the Old Man of the Sea was trying to do us harm. The question is, who awoke the Old Man?"

"You are all crazy!" Myrtle screamed at all who could hear.

A violent lightning bolt struck the metal rod atop the wooden mast as the ship lighted up in an instant. In that one instant, Professor Charles and Myrtle Wilton saw a Centaur at the helm of their ship. Myrtle went silent as she held her husband tightly unsure of what she saw. The Professor on the other hand...

"If the Old Man of the Sea was angered, it must have been one of his daughters or Poseidon himself." The Professor stated trying to help.

"Well Professor, most of the Gods are sleeping right now," Parker said catching him up. "So, I would guess his daughters."

"Halia?" Thrace asked Sophos.

"She would never hurt me." Sophos said without hesitation.

"Maybe she's just trying to stop you from going to Crete." Thrace said. "Maybe she's trying to save you."

"You know Halia of the Sea?" The Professor asked, but neither Sophos nor Thrace responded. The Professor approached Thrace with Myrtle in tow unable to take her eyes from Sophos nor her arms from her husband.

"It's a good thing your father woke you." The Professor said.

"Actually, we don't really get along. "

"STHOPHOS!!" Battus yelled over the churning sea.

Coming toward the bow of the ship was a wave as great and large as the Aloeids, sons of Poseidon. The Aloeids grew about two feet wide and six feet high each year and had once declared war on Olympus with Ares being the first God captured. It appeared this wave was the return of the Aloeids whose next capture would be the son of Ares.

Sophos thrust the ship forward hoping to reach its peak, but it was as if the wave itself was alive and grew as fast as the ship traveled. He saw the watered and angry eyes of the Old Man upon the wave. Sophos spun the wheel to port and attempted to ride the lip of the wave and curl down the face of the Old Man before it crashed.

"What are you doing!?!" The Professor yelled. "You can't ride it like a surfboard!"

"What's a surfboard?" Sophos asked. "I am trying to buy us time. We are going down and nothing will stop that. Grab a floatation device and some gear and prepare to enter the Aegean!"

Thrace tightened the straps of his pack and grabbed the ashen spear of Achilles. Parker followed his lead with bow and arrows slung and his arm slung through the Golden Lyre to not lose it. Myrtle dived toward a chest and tossed out life preserves to anyone she could see. Aemon and Battus took two each and wrapped themselves and a mirror with a life preserver. The Professor handed out light sticks that he cracked and lit neon orange in the dark night sky. This ship began to tilt on its side as the wave's tip prepared to crash down upon the thirty seven foot Hunter sail boat that appeared as a row boat upon the great ocean.

"Sophos!!" Thrace yelled.

Sophos turned toward Thrace at the sound of his name and leapt from the stern of the ship into the black waves of the Aegean. As obedient soldiers, Might and Violence followed his lead, life preserved wrapped mirrors held tight in one hand and the other holding their nose. The Wiltons held hands as the Professor gave his scared wife a confident smile for courage, and they leapt into the sea. Parker appeared like a thief at the ship's edge with gear wrapped around each appendage. Fear did not touch his face as he yelled at his best friend, 'Cannonball' and into the sea he went. Only a laugh could follow, and Thrace joined his friend into the abyss. Seconds later Proteus, The Old Man of the Sea's great wave crushed down upon the wooden sailboat shattering it like a house of cards.

Beneath the waves Thrace curled up like a ball with his pack against his back, the life jacket on backward on his chest, a neon light in one hand and the spear of Achilles in his other. He held his breath as he tumbled in circles as if riding an underwater rollercoaster with only a rumbling sound echoing in his ears. He opened his eyes to see a hint of orange glowing from his hand in a void of blackness. As the waves crashed above him, he noticed he was drifting the opposite direction. The weight of his pack and the adamantine spear heads was greater than his life preserver. He fought to swim to the surface, but the weight was too much and he continued to sink.

Thrace fought with all the strength his immortal father gave him to reach the surface as his lungs burned with the fire of Hephaestus. A force hit his thigh, and he spun in circles attempting to see what hit him. Once again he was struck on his side. Thrace swung the ashen spear of Achilles, but its movement was stagnant within the Aegean. Dullness filled his mind as the fire burned stronger in his lungs and his limbs went numb. He witnessed a dark object growing in size before him; its blackness amplified by the orange glow stick. The raking of teeth scraped his shoulder, and his mind envisioned the movie *Jaws*. He waited for the second bite and the sensation of teeth piercing his flesh. Instead, he felt pulled through the water, up or down he could not tell in the vast darkness.

His lungs burned as his face broke the surface of the wine dark Aegean, the salt air cooled his lungs like sweet ambrosia. The dull blur cleared before his eyes as he witnessed a dolphin at his side slapping the water with its nose. In the distance he could see other neon orange glow lights between the violent Aegean waves. He could not support his pack above the surface with the weight of gear and the adamantine spear heads as he gasped for a second breath. Beneath the surface of the wine dark sea the dolphin which pulled him to the surface skimmed between his legs and lifted Thrace to the surface again. He quickly grabbed the dorsal fin with both hands and held on with every morsel of his strength. The strength of the dolphin's tail thrust them toward the other neon sticks in the distance.

He approached Sophos whose large centaur body rode a giant white dolphin. Around him were his fellow comrades, along with Myrtle, who sat atop a dolphin in amazement and the Professor, who smiled like a schoolboy and yelled, 'Arion, I understand!'.

"Retain your strength," Sophos informed them all. "We still have a long journey to Crete, and it will be difficult. Halia will lead the way."

Halia, the giant white dolphin, splashed her massive tail upon the ravaging dark sea and headed south to the mainland of Crete. The other dolphins with their passengers followed. The raging black Aegean rumbled around them.

Thrace watched Parker with a look of exhilaration upon his face, similar to that of the Professor. The actors had no reason to pretend as they held on for their lives. Thrace himself had never favored the ocean, but riding a top this glorious creature rejuvenated his strength and his courage.

He believed his strength came from his mother, or for his mother. He was unsure, but he knew it also came from Parker and his trust in him. He did not join him or support him for who he was supposed to be, but for who he was. It was courage he needed to find. A courage initially given to him by Anthia in the mountains, who, he hoped, was safe. But that was not his own courage or strength. What he needed to find must come from within for his mother and his best friend. He needed courage from his mentor and trust in what he had taught him and finally, for those who he barely knew and worked with him and beside him to help him accomplish this goal. How could he not believe in himself if so many people already did?

Chapter 19

As red-robed Dawn stretched her finger out across the wine dark sea, the survivors of the *Amphitrite* arrived at the shores of Crete. The pod of dolphins circled around the break as the weary and tired travelers climbed their way from the Aegean Sea. Each collapsed upon the sand exhilarated and battle worn as their eyes watched Dawn step across the sky as Helios gave his morning wink.

"That was amazing." Myrtle said.

"What?" The Professor asked.

"When I saw…it, him, I mean the centaur when the lighting stuck, I was scared. When that giant wave took the ship, I was scared for my life. But riding a dolphin to shore…. I've never felt so alive." Myrtle said as she leaned over toward her husband and kissed him.

"Didn't see that coming." Parker said.

Halia of the sea stepped from the Aegean in her beautifully carved female form adorned in seaweed, not exhausted nor tired and sat beside Sophos, who rested upon the sand.

"Thank you Halia," Sophos said kindly.

"It is good that the son of Ares told Neis, the water Nymph in Argo that you would be traveling to Crete, or I might not have been there to help."

"Halia's here?" the Professor asked leaning toward the conversation that Sophos was having, though he could not hear nor see anyone upon the sand next to him. A conversation his wife was now interested in.

"She is, though with the mortal mist, you are unable to see or hear her." Sophos informed the Professor.

"Like the mist mentioned in Homer's *Iliad*?" He asked.

"The same," Thrace answered.

"This is amazing." The Professor replied as his schoolboy grin reappeared. "Thank you, Halia of the Sea for saving us."

"Yes, thank you," Myrtle follows.

"She says you are welcome," Sophos informed them though Halia did not speak as she was surprised they were talking openly to the clouded-eyed mortals.

"I must ask," the Professor continued. "You said you are battling the Gods. Which gods? And could you thank your father, Ares, for warning us of the upcoming danger."

Halia confused look turned puzzled as her oceanic eyes burned at Sophos, "Ares forewarned you?" He met her gaze and simply nodded.

"Well, not really fighting the gods, though we are...," Parker jumped in, "mainly fighting Kottus to get a cure to save his mother who was cursed by Aphrodite, who set us on this quest due to her jealousy of Ares and Stheno, which was Ares' plan all along, though Aphrodite may have known all about it all along."

"Wow, that's fantastic!" The Professor exclaimed. "Wait, did you say Kottus? One of the Hekantonkheires who helped Zeus defeat Cronus?"

"The same." Parker said. "Hundred hands…fifty heads. Good times."

"How do you plan to do that?" The Professor asked.

"Yes," Halia asked turning to Sophos. "How do you plan to do that?"

"First things first," Sophos asked. "Who set the Old Man of the Sea against us?"

"It was a daughter of Poseidon." Halia answered.

"Another daughter?" Thrace asked.

"He has many daughters young Thrace," Halia replied. "Would you like to meet one? A few would like to meet you."

"Another time." Thrace responded, blushing red as a rose.

"I would like to meet one." Parker added not wanting to miss the chance.

"They would like to meet you as well young Parker, especially the way you play the Golden Lyre of Pan. You rode Eurotas who thinks you rival that of the God of Music Apollo."

"Well, I was taught by Pan and Apollo stole it from…."

"Would you stop, this is not the time for frivolity." Sophos stated glaring at Halia who could only smile at his determination.

"Did you say you were taught by Pan?" The professor asked. "I thought he died?"

"Ah," But before Parker could speak he could feel Sophos' eyes upon him. "Another time."

"Sophos," the Professor said realizing his childish excitement was upsetting the Centaur and his task at hand. "Parker mentioned Stheno earlier. Could it be her?"

"No," Sophos said recognizing the obvious. "Thrace of the Spear killed Stheno in Argos, which means it was her sister Euryale, possibly 'the forgotten'."

"Great," Parker exclaimed. "Another Immortal that wants to kill us."

"You killed Stheno the Gorgon?" The Professor asked turning toward Thrace.

"Yeah, she tried to turn my friend over there to stone."

"May I ask how you killed her?"

"With the spear of Achilles," Thrace responded. "Which I dropped to the bottom of the Aegean."

"You did what?!" Sophos exclaimed.

"The spear of Achilles...amazing." The Professor said to himself.

"I see quick-witted Parker held on to Pan's lyre and the Atalantan bow." Sophos said chiding Thrace.

"Pan's lyre..." The Professor whispered to himself, mumbling all the items which he had only read about and now listened in their present day use with amazement.

"I was sinking like a rock because these spears of Hephaestus are so heavy. I tried to swim up, but couldn't fight the weight, then the dolphin hit me and I thought I was being attacked. I started to black out.... and dropped it." Thrace said more disappointed in himself than Sophos, which the Centaur saw and admired.

"So, how again did you plan to defeat Kottus," Halia asked once more.

"We plan to smother him with his own beauty." Parker said watching guilt consume Thrace at the loss of his best weapon. "By the way, did the mirrors make it to shore?"

Aemon and Battus were still on their backs exhausted from the trip across the sea aboard a dolphin. For them, it was not exciting at all. Aemon sat up and lifted his mirror. It was shattered with only shards of mirrored glass remaining. Battus raised his up in glory, unbroken, feeling he had offered little as of late and was proud he succeeded in bringing his mirror successfully to shore.

"One is better than none?" Parker mentioned as a question.

"If you are attempting to use beauty against the great Titan, maybe you could use the girdle of Aphrodite. That is if it exists." The Professor said.

Sophos and Thrace's eyes met in an instant and a small smile appeared from each of them shedding the anger from the loss of the spear.

"Why did we not arrive at this solution?" Sophos asked the group.

"Maybe with Stheno and Euryale, Ares and Aphrodite, Cresphontes and Deinus and, finally Kottus just in front of us, plus Thrace's mother and your father problems, we are having a difficult time focusing." Parker tossed out as a suggestion.

"Though you are correct young Parker, you might want to keep your ranting to a minimum." Sophos suggested more kindly than usual.

"Who is Cresphontes and Deinus," Myrtle said engaged in the conversation.

"They would be my half-brother and half-sister." Thrace informed Myrtle. "When I killed the Gorgon Stheno, they were born from her...blood."

"Like Pegasus and Chyrsaor were born from Medusa." The Professor muttered to himself in excitement and fear.

"Except Deinus is jet black with bat wings and throws fire from her nostrils and Cresphontes is muscled, bald and horned and they don't particularly like us." Parker added. "Sorry," he finished looking at Sophos.

"Amazing," the Professor stated to himself again.

"How can we get the girdle of Aphrodite?" Thrace asked.

"We will have to ask her," Sophos said.

"Aren't forgetting something?" Halia asked our weary travelers whose minds were working as quickly as rowers upon an ancient Greek trireme ship. "Only a woman can wear the girdle of Aphrodite, which means you will need me."

"If we are successful, it appears we will." Sophos said, his eyes not leaving Halia of the sea.

Silence befell the weary companions as if attempting to catch their last breath before they would have to call upon a Goddess and take on the Immortals. The silence was too much for an inquisitive professor who prefers the noise of the classroom.

"Excuse me Thrace, you said on the ship your mother taught Classics, I was wondering if I knew her?" The Professor asked.

"I doubt it, she taught for a little while in Virginia and before that a couple of colleges, but now at a college in Colorado. Cybele Kraft?"

The Professor paused as if running the name through a file folder in his mind, his finger pressed up against his lips. "Auburn hair, athletic, grey eyes, graduated from University of Texas I believe?" He asked. "A passion for femininity in Greece, particularly the difference between Spartan and Athenian women?"

"Ah, yeah, she did go to Texas. I don't know about what she use to study, but now she focuses on Greek literature and myth." Thrace responded curiously, which drew the attention of Sophos.

"Well, I don't particularly know her per say, but we worked together one summer in Thrace at a dig site. A couple of professor and I organized a dig for graduate students pursuing their PH.D. at a small site near a Temple of Ares which was a worship site for the God; it is considered his homeland. I believe she ran in the morning before spending all day at the site in the hot sun. I recall that because many thought it odd since we were so exhausted after just digging, so running first seemed crazy, but it didn't diminish her work. Near the end of the excavation we all got together to celebrate. We had found an array of vases, some broken weapons and armor. A good find. Well, no one could locate her the last two days. In the morning before we left, she arrived for breakfast. She said she meet a local who knew the ancient lay of the land well. Arieus, she said, which I recall because we were at the Temple of Ares. We simply assumed she met some local man who showed her Thrace and took advantage of her excitement for Thracian history. She showed us this coin on a necklace that was pristine and far from fake. She said it was a gift. That was, what fifteen or so years ago, I can't really recall."

"I'm fifteen. I found that necklace in a book, which it seems…" Thrace said cutting himself off as he handed the necklace to the professor to observe. He paused absorbing all the information he had just acquired. Coincidently, they had found transport to Crete from a retired professor who was in Thrace when his mother met his father. Almost too coincidental.

"Dude, how weird is that?" Parker said amazed.

"You said she was cursed by Aphrodite. May I ask how?" the Professor asked returning the necklace.

Thrace explained the events that had occurred the day he returned home from school, which now felt like years ago. The repeating it drove home the purpose that lay before him. From his pocket he retrieved the flower that fell from his mother with petals missing and the grey-eyed center beginning to fade. His mother deep down knew she had met Ares in Thrace all those years ago and held the secret deep with her, knowing no one would believe her, not even her own son. She even tried to warn him, 'to practice', she said.

"We need to build an altar and make a proper sacrifice to Aphrodite to acquire the girdle." Thrace said taking control of the scene. "Aemon and Battus, could you gather some wood for the altar? Parker, how about you create the sacrifice, since you appear to be the throughway to Aphrodite. We just need some fatty meats and flowers to sacrifice."

"I will gather some rich and fatty fish from the sea." Halia said as she rose making her way to the Aegean.

"We would like to help," Myrtle said. "I will gather some flowers if that will work?"

"Thank you," Thrace said with a smile.

"I'll go with you," the Professor said as he and his wife arose, brushed off the gritty sand of Crete and made their way inland.

Sophos watched his pupil put everyone into action. He was impressed and proud. He was unsure of his ability to train the young man, one who was older than Herakles or Achilles when they were trained, but younger than the last sons of Ares who were trained by his father. His purpose was to train Thrace, and prepare him for what befell him, so he may save his mother, though he was never informed what to prepare him for. Personally, he also wished to save the honor of his father, who did all he could to stop Ares the Cunning from bringing forth his progeny. He did not know if his book knowledge or his practice fighting with Oceanids, would be enough to train anyone. What he did know was that this young man who stood before him, with a variety of enemies at his heels, was more a man of courage and strength that ever he was a boy whom he met in his own backyard.

Sophos galloped up and down the beach stretching his legs as Thrace organized the building of the altar with Aemon and Battus. Parker paced by the wine dark Aegean with his mind trying to create a sacrifice to the beautiful goddess who has influenced his thoughts along this journey. A journey, in the beginning he felt he should go to help his friend, then he thought he might be in the way, but with his talent of his new found gift, he had a greater purpose and, though nervous, would want to be nowhere else.

Halia stepped from the foam white waves of the Aegean with a large sea bass she carried toward the altar. Dropping the bass by the wooden altar, she watched Sophos race along the beach maneuvering his sword as if defending attacks. She admired his continual determination despite the odds that were greater than his father had encountered. He was different than his father as well, she noticed. Peirithous fought to redeem a reckless youth that led to the death of his wife. Sophos fought to regain honor of his father, but there was more…he cared deeply for this son of Ares, as if he were his own son. He would be a good father, she thought.

The Professor and Myrtle appeared on the beach from inland hand-in-hand and carrying roses in the other. They appeared more youthful, more alive than when they embarked upon the seaward trip south. It is said near death experiences awaken those to tackle life with more vigor, but this was different. Originally, it was something she had difficulty understanding, and he thought only tales. Now they were a part of something magical and wondrous, and though they could not see it, they knew it be real, as the wind upon one's skin. They had their own faith.

"There's a town just up the beach. We're in some park right now." Myrtle informed them.

"Then we better hurry things along before someone arrives," Thrace said.

A fire was lit in the middle of the wooden cubicle altar and smoke stretched it arms toward the heavens. The sea bass and roses were placed atop the altar and the flames began to tickle the roses until it engulfed both sending the smoldering black smoke toward the heavens. The Professor and Myrtle knelt before the altar, and Parker smiled as he approached to make his offer.

"They're not Catholic you know." He said.

The Professor laughed realizing what he was doing and stood taking his wife's hand lifting her to her feet.

"Beautiful Aphrodite," Parker started. "Goddess of Love. I have appreciated your guidance during our journey and am now humbly requesting your further assistance to finish this journey and help Thrace's mother and bring honor to Sophos' family. Please golden-haired Goddess, grant us your assistance…"

He was cut off as the sea bass and roses were violently consumed by a single engulfing flame erupting from the altar. Smoldering embers lingered where the flame once blazed, except for a single red rose. Aemon pointed to the heavens and high above a large golden eagle circled the rising smoke. Thrace's heart pounded as he saw Anthia flying high above. The eagle flashed like a dart toward them and just before the altar her wings opened to slow her pace and with its great sharp talon grasped the single red rose. The great golden eagle then morphed into the beautiful and elegant Goddess, Aphrodite with the red rose in hand.

Thrace's initial hope that Anthia was flying high above was quickly dashed. He felt a rage begin to boil within him as Pollux, long rested, had taken up arms within his chest once again. Now before him stood the very woman, Immortal, Goddess, who had cursed his mother and placed his friends in danger. Rage and Anger consumed him as his journey replayed page by page in his mind. His mother was bed of flowers, his friend almost turned to stone, his killing of a mythical being and the thought of Anthia the Mountain Oread dying at the hands of his step-brother because of a Goddess' petty jealousy. Part of him wanted to fire one of her husband Hephaestus' adamantine spear head's toward her and watch her golden ichor drip from her to the sand. But is that who he is? Will it bring back his mother? Is he more like his father than he was willing to admit? His mind stormed like Boreas the terrible North Wind. He needed to be calm. Right now, he needed Aphrodite, just as she needed him.

Aemon and Battus quickly dropped to their knees as if the Professor had the correct idea. The Professor and his wife watched as the eagle, still clutching the rose in its talon, move away from the altar. It moved unlike any eagle they had seen before. The professor cursed the mortal mist before his eyes.

Aphrodite stood before Parker, smiled and caressed his face. He almost melted at the tingling sensation of her touch, his eyes unable to maintain the gaze from her bright blue eyes. She leaned in and gently kissed his forehead. A blazing shade of red appeared upon his face. She moved before Thrace and could feel Rage move within him and witnessed the flaming anger in his eyes. He was not the same boy she glanced in his back yard as she set this play into motion so far away, yet only a short time ago.

"I know how angry you must be Thrace, son of Cybele." She said, her voice dancing on the breeze.

Thrace's anger ebbed after the sound of his mother's name. She addressed him as the 'son of Cybele'. Throughout this journey the constant reminder of the importance of being the son of an Immortal was thrust upon him. He was the son of the God of War and capable of wonderful or horrible things, but what drove and defined him was his mother, Cybele the great athlete, teacher and mother.

"We Gods, though Immortal, tend to be weak and petty," She said looking at the heavens for answers. "I have seen much, but these years alone with Ares have awakened me. Our youth-like passion we once had living among the other Immortals was playful and exciting, but when you are the only two, it changes things."

Aphrodite was caught up in her own thoughts. Her solitude and loneliness was evident to all. The idea of a romantic and passionate relationship with her adulterous lover forever without the other Gods intervening as they slumber was just as fictional as the world believed the ancient immortals to be. Power had consumed Ares and everyone else, mortal or immortal was inessential.

Thrace was getting impatient, but he knew he must control it. Did he care about the petty wants of this Immortal Goddess? Not really. He saw his companion's eyes (except for Sophos) transfixed upon the beauty of Aphrodite as if to quench an insatiable thirst. Without question she was flawless, but that was her greatest flaw, he thought. He must let her rant. He will be her ear if she needs to rationalize her decisions as long as he can acquire the girdle to save his mother.

"You see here Thracian Ares," Aphrodite continued. "There is more at stake here than saving your mother. The other Gods need to be awakened."

"Or you and Ares could be put to sleep." Sophos stated matter-of-factly.

"That is not an option Centaur," the Goddess stated, a tinge of anger in her tone. "You would once again have the Titans rule? They do not even recognize these mortals." She glided toward Sophos holding his gaze. Sophos did not turn away from the beautiful, yet hot-tempered Goddess.

"One thing at a time Aphrodite," Thrace said respectfully. "The odds are stacked against us already. Let us attempt to acquire the vial to save my mother, then we may discuss what I can do for you."

"I have your word Thracian Ares Kraft, Son of Cybele and Ares, the God of War that after you acquire the vial to awaken your mother, you will come when I call?" Crowned and Flowered Aphrodite was immediately upon Thrace, her tone stern yet gentle.

"You do." He responded.

She studied him carefully as if reading his mind and a smile arose upon her face, the gentle and caring smile of a lover. She leaned in and kissed young Thrace Ares where he stood, and he was filled with enchanted warmth. Thrace felt a tingling sensation that ran throughout his body and eased the Rage though his blood remained heated like embers of coal. It was more than courage she infused him with but enduring confidence.

From beneath her ivory white garment, she revealed the Girdle of Aphrodite and handed it to Halia of the Sea who accepted it with grace as she stood quietly before the Goddess of Love.

"Halia of the Sea," the Goddess said, "you are a daughter of Poseidon and goddess of the vast ocean and one of his greatest daughters. I entrust you with my girdle. Any woman who wears is has the power to woo any man. You need only to think of the desired effect, and the individual you wish to seduce."

Halia accepted the girdle and nodded in acknowledgement. Her green eyes sparkled as she took a delicate glance at Sophos the Centaur, who caught her glance and unknowingly blushed.

"But you shall not use the girdle for personal gain," The Goddess of Love added returning to Thrace once more.

"An ingenious plan Thrace of the Spear…a non-violent plan. The first against the mighty Kottus. I wish you well on your quest."

Aphrodite smiled her blinding smile once more at the young son of Cybele, stretched out her arms wide and morphed into the golden eagle once more and still clutching the red rose, she took to the skies.

Except for Thrace and Sophos, this was the first encounter with the Goddess of Love for the heroes. They stood staring into the heavens as if she floated above them showering them with love and beauty. Aemon and Battus, still kneeling, their eyes stretched wide glistening with tears and their mouths agape could not move. Parker stood quietly with a small smile as if he had been given a personal gift. And he had, for he was her communiqué. The Professor and Myrtle's eyes followed the eagle as it left, not understanding what happened, but knowing something amazing had occurred.

"What happened?" Myrtle asked with excitement.

"We have the girdle," Thrace informed her. "That's what counts."

Sophos said approaching Thrace. "You are bound by your word to the Goddess as all Gods are bound by their oaths over the River Styx."

"I know." He replied.

"What is she like…Aphrodite?" The Professor asked with his school boy tone.

"She's beautiful." Aemon said.

"She's perfect." Battus added.

227

"She's kinda like a spoiled celebrity…Lohan or Kardashian." Parker said.

"Didn't see that coming?" Thrace said in response to his friend's comments.

"Don't get me wrong, she is hot, but so are those celebrities. Did you hear her whine?" Parker said amusing himself.

"You have matured quick-witted Parker of the Lyre." Sophos said happy with the growth of his comrades, then changed his tone. "It is a long journey to Mt. Dicte and we have much preparation." Sophos said to the heroes.

"How about we eat, pack and rest here today and set out early in the morning?" Thrace suggested.

"Wise words once again Son of Cybele." Sophos said noticing the appeal it had on him earlier and it was matched once again.

"There must be a town nearby. We can get some food and stay at a hotel. It's on us, as long as one of you tells us of your journey so far." The Professor asked.

"It's probably the safest decision since we are no longer hidden in the mountains." Thrace agreed. "You probably need to report you boat being lost too."

"We can call that in at the hotel." The Professor added. "I will help you gather your gear."

The companions, new and old, gathered their remaining gear and made their way inland. A jogger passed along the shoreline watching the heroes curiously. Parker smiled and wave. Crossing the sands of Crete to its manmade pavement they passed a few tourists who looked at them with question. Their clothes were old and worn, weapons at their side, and they were still covered with salt of the wine dark Aegean. But as tourists do, they pulled out cameras and took pictures assuming it was part of the show. At least they could not see Halia in her seaweed outfit, Parker thought.

The Professor and his wife took the lead into town asking for information and the closest hotel explaining their boat had capsized in the Aegean. They found out they were south of Heraklion (which Aemon and Battus thought to be a sign) and there was a small hotel just in town. The Professor acquired rooms, and Myrtle went to gather food as the remaining attempted to get comfortable in the new surroundings. Aemon and Battus joined the Professor and began telling their version of the adventure with great enthusiasm. Thrace figured Parker would crave a warm soft bed, but before they slept he said he missed seeing the stars at night.

He understood. Living lives as if they had in an Ancient Greek lifestyle, by the fire at night, beneath the starry sky with food caught by their own hand prepared them for the upcoming battle. Staying in a hotel, made it seem a bit more surreal or unreal, he was not sure. He curled up with the white milky sheets hoping Sleep would allow him to pass the night away quickly in a long silent, dreamless sleep.

Chapter 20

A metallic clanking of fallen brass chalices echoed throughout the dull grey room. Both Thrace and Parker erupted from their beds as if Mount Vesuvius in the Bay of Naples had awakened once again gurgling its molten hot sludge upon the land. Parker reached out with a newfound quickness as if loading his bow, though still unable to fire it, and pushed the phone on to the floor bringing silence back into the fold.

"Man, I never thought I'd hate that sound." Parker said stretching across the motel bed. "Rather be swat with Sophos' bow," he added with a smile.

"What time is it?" Thrace asked looking upon the end table that used to support the phone/alarm clock and now only supported a lamp and the once auburn flower with only three petals remaining with its center a dull grey that matched the room. It was as if the entire room was telling him that time was running out.

Just as he spoke there was a rap upon their door. Thrace rose from bed and answered. Sophos stood on the other side with an anxious look upon his face.

"Are you ready Thrace of the Spear?" He asked.

"I guess," Thrace responded. "Though 'Thrace of the Spear' may no longer be appropriate."

Sophos pulled his left hand from beyond the doorframe and revealed the Spear of Achilles. Thrace slowly reached out to take the spear; his face radiated excitement. He was not only pleased for the return of the weapon, but for this great treasure not being lost forever by his own hands, though by his own hands it may lost nonetheless.

"Where did you find it?" He asked.

"You should thank Halia of the Sea for this act. She returned to the Aegean last night and with a little help from her friends who assisted us to shore, it was located."

"I will definitely thank her."

"Now, you and Parker gather your belongings. The Professor has acquired what he refers to as 'a good reliable truck' and is taking us to Mt. Dicte. You may also tell Parker that Myrtle has acquired some coffee for him."

"He'll appreciate that. We'll be right there."

"I also believe today is your sixteenth year." Sophos added with less confidence, yet with more emotion as this act was new to him. "I offer you the Shield of Perseus as a gift for the upcoming battle."

Sophos held out the glimmering shield that appeared to have been recently cleaned and polished and looked as if it was just created by the Smith God Hephaestus himself for this day. Thrace hesitantly accepted the gift, more in awe than anything else.

"Wow. Ah, thanks Sophos. It really means a lot to me. Not just the gift, though thanks, but all that you've taught me."

"Let us hope that in the short time together we both have learned enough to succeed." Sophos replied with a kind smile which was not as rare as it was when the journey began.

Thrace watched his mentor shed his regal nature and was humbled by his kindness. His heart was filled with hope at Sophos' presence. He had never known his father nor had a father figure growing up, and his mother rarely dated over the years. Her sacrifice toward her own solitude for his growth and education appeared ever so selfless. Now, unusual as it would have been to him years ago, over these last couple of days, this Centaur, the magical and wise being had been the closest person to a father figure in his life. And though his mother had given him all he could have asked for in life, Sophos had given him a few things more. Not a father, but a mentor, and he could not have asked for anyone better.

"Ah, man," Parker said pulling Thrace from his thoughts. "How am I going to compete with the Shield of Perseus?"

"Don't worry about it. Just think, we would've been in Steamboat hiking and camping by the hot springs, and surrounded by girls on summer vacation, and you would have broken your arm again or maybe this time your leg. Instead, we're about to battle an ancient Titan, and we may not survive."

"Yeah, this is much more fun."

"Wow," Thrace responded. "That didn't even sound sarcastic."

"It wasn't," Parker said surprising himself. "I believe I'd actually rather be here with you and our new friends going off to save your mother."

"Me too."

"I mean, who needs hot springs and girls in bikinis? Plus, that broken arm really hurt." Parker added.

"Let's go men!" Sophos yelled across the parking lot.

"Did he just call us 'men'?" Parker asked.

"I believe he did."

"Wow, I think he likes us."

Thrace and Parker gathered their packs and weapons as Thrace stowed the flower in his pocket once again quickly leaving the dull grey room. Across the parking lot was an old white and blue pick-up truck that had as much rust as it did paint. The Professor at the helm reminded him of an old farmer just stopping in town picking up supplies; he was much smarter than he appeared. Aemon and Battus sat in the back with the remaining mirror between them wrapped in a hotel towel for protection. Halia, wearing the girdle of Aphrodite, sat on the tire well with the look of a child about to ride in a truck for the first time. Then again, it probably was her first time. Sophos climbed aboard and nestled into the remaining space in the back of the truck. Thrace and Parker placed their gear with Aemon and Battus; the latter informing them he would protect their weapons with all the energy he could summon.

"Halia," Thrace said. "Thanks for finding the Spear of Achilles."

"You are welcome, Thracian Ares. Just use it as well as its forbearer."

"I will try." Thrace said smiling to Halia. He was glad she was with them, especially with the girdle of Aphrodite, but her presence revealed to him his longing for Anthia, and though he missed her, he was glad she was not here for her own safety.

"Here you go boys," Myrtle said handing Thrace and Parker a cup of coffee and a pastry.

The young heroes thanked Myrtle and climbed into the front of the pickup where the Professor sat behind the wheel with a youthful smile upon his face. He had a difficult time taking his eyes from Thrace, a son of an Immortal Greek god. He looked like an old man who had found out Santa Claus was real. Myrtle climbed in and saw her husband staring and gave him the wifely glance that every couple had and understood. The Professor acknowledged her glare with a smile and pulled up a map from the dashboard looking for the correct route he already knew. The four sat tightly in the front seat as the Professor started the old truck with a vibrant rumble and drove out of the parking lot.

"Is that really the shield of Perseus?" asked the Professor.

"Did you boys sleep well?" Myrtle asked, interrupting her husband.

"Yes," Thrace replied answering both.

"You know," Parker said. "I started sleeping better outside than in a room or in the bed. I never thought I'd say that."

"Well you boys get some rest on the ride for it'll be close to midday by the time we arrive at Mt. Dicte." The Professor stated and drove on feeling like a young college freshman first reading the adventure of Odysseus and Achilles as new heroes sat beside him.

Along the trip south to Mt. Dicte, the Professor spoke of the nearby Minoan palace of Malia that the French excavated in the early nineteen-hundreds, and the elaborate frescos that were discovered. This led him into the tale of Theseus and the Minotaur until Myrtle asked him to refrain from his lecture until another time. She reminded him that these boys have much more to concern themselves with, she stated very motherly. Her husband acknowledged stating that his lecture was more to alleviate his own excitement and nervousness.

Thrace watched as cars, shopping plazas, fast food restaurants, towns turned to countryside as they rolled along the Lassithi plateau adorned with stone windmills with sails spinning in the wind with Mt. Dicte in the distance. His mind replayed all they had occurred over so much time to bring him to this moment. This quest, which started centuries ago, and has continued to unfold with old and new actors taking the stage all for ego, pride and a simple cure created so long ago. A recipe he needed to save his mother. Thrace pondered all the events his mind could summon through history his mother had told him over the years, it appeared they all spawned from similar purposes as all did who challenged the ancient Immortals; their continual pursuit for power and their child-like insecurities and petty jealousies. Though so much time passed from the birth of Zeus within this mountain to this quest thousands of years later, so little had changed with the Immortal gods. Then again, without death in site, how can one change or appreciate life, he thought?

Parker looked out the back window to see Battus securely holding the Atalantan bow and his pack containing Pan's lyre. He felt naked without them, especially the lyre. Like Thrace's spear, it had become an extension of himself. His mind spun like a spider's web with all that had occurred to him over such a short period of time. His fear of being in the way and not assisting his best friend had changed. He was more than quick-witted Parker, he thought. He would help his best friend in this final battle, but his mind also evoked a second thought. He wanted to get home to his family. He never saw a similarity with himself and his parents and in the end, it did not matter. They always allowed and understood his various passions or as they called them 'trends', no matter how obscure. His insect farm he started in the garage, his growing train set and his present video game collection. They even took him camping, twice, though they did not enjoy it themselves and were excited when Cybele and her son moved next door and enjoyed the outdoors. They were indoors and numbers people, and he loved them and looked forward to seeing his mother and father again. He even looked forward to cleaning his room.

Battus grinned at Parker who looked back through the window at his fellow adventurers and Parker returned the smile. He liked the witty one, he thought as he held his gear tightly. He would let no one touch them, just as his brother Aemon held the mirror snug like a puppy he wanted close, but did not wish to hurt. He felt like a soldier in his first campaign, excited and nervous. But this was not a play that he and Aemon performed on stage, one in which they knew the outcome. This was a great ancient battle in modern times with glory to be won. No matter what happened, he and his brother would be on the ancient field of battle as his brother always felt they were destined never having the mortal mist.

"Aemon," Battus said fighting back his lisp to sound brave. "If anything happens to us, it has been my honor to be your brother, for we are now actually Might and Violence."

"You as well," Aemon replied. "If either or both of our end comes, it will be in a great battle and not upon the stages we've spent so many years."

"I agree. And if the Fate Atropos decides to cut our thread, it will be an honorable death."

"It shall," Aemon agreed. "My brother, we were destined to be here, together."

Sophos listened as the two actors spoke with such ancient grandeur as if on the beaches by the hollowed Greek ships preparing to fight Hector and the Trojans. It would be less adventurous and more dangerous then they imagined, but this was not theatrical rhetoric they had spoken, but true courage in their voices and led him to feel they would play their parts true. They had become more than just bumbling actors. Then again, he himself never imagined such a final battle. His father always left preparing for such combat and coming home tired and worn, but then later having a craving for it, like Spartan warriors missing combat. But this was different. They were not going in aggressively with violent war cries and weapons clanking against shields, but more theatrical, with more wisdom than strength. This was the plan of the son of Ares, and it was crafty like Odysseus. Did he really believe they had a chance? Deep down, he was unsure. If the theatrics did not work, were they capable of handling the great Titan Kottus? They were playing the odds that Euryale, Cresphontes, Deinus and Ares would not be there since no son of Ares had survived said battle. It was a dangerous gamble. All he could do is hope he had taught these men well enough over the past week. If his life ended here, he would join his father in the depths of the Underworld, and he could accept that if they acquired the vial, and Thrace and Parker returned to their homes and saved his mother. A deeper sensation wrestled within him as he turned to see Halia sitting close beside him enjoying her first ride in a truck. He had always cared for her but held his feelings at a distance for concern for his father and now, his pupil. He not only wanted to succeed but to survive; for his father, for Thrace, who had become closer to him than he was prepared, but also to see Halia outside of battle and on the shores of Greece once more.

The rusty blue and white truck came to a halt along a dirt road with Mt. Dicte stretching up to the blue heavens. The companions exited the truck, strapped on their packs and grabbed their weapons to prepare for the journey to what Sophos informed them was a cave along a small plain near the top of this historical mountain. Thrace imagined the mountain would be bigger, especially compared to the fourteeners he and his mother hiked in Colorado, but the historical imagery and imposing nature of this mountain gave it greater strength. The image of Mighty Zeus staring back at him and throwing him back was still embedded in his mind. He knew the hike up Mt. Dicte would be the easiest part of this entire journey. He felt nervous, but he was filled with more confidence than the first night he and Parker met Sophos on the road in the forests of Colorado. He knew he was only sixteen today and no matter the maturity level of teenagers in ancient Greece, he was still young in any time. He still had two years of high school; he did not have a driver's license, or a job, or a car, or even a girlfriend he could get in trouble sneaking out to see. Those were events of tomorrow, not today. Today his thoughts were with his mother, and his desire for her to be with him through all of those events and more. Today, no matter his age, he had to be a man.

"Let's go," the Professor spoke up first.

"I'm sorry Professor," Sophos said. "We appreciate your help, but you will not be going with us."

"What? But this is a legendary tale, just like the ones I spent years teaching. I can't miss this."

"But you can't see it either." Parker reminded him.

"How about we hike up with you," Myrtle added. "We can help out if anything happens. I was a nurse."

"What if one or both of you get hurt?" Thrace asked her. "We've had a few prophetic forewarnings."

"About what?" The Professor jumped in with eager ears.

His wife interrupted. "Well, all the more reason you may need a nurse."

"Let them come." Halia said.

"So be it," Sophos said taking control of the group. "Halia of the sea said you should join us, but, you will not enter the cave and must stay hidden within the rocky crag along the plain near the top of the mountain. Understood?"

"Sure," the Professor and Myrtle simultaneously.

Sophos led the array of mortals and natural beings along a small path leading along the mountainside. They saw a few tourists along the trails making their way to and fro, and all kept silent ignoring all and focusing on the final conflict. Halia looked back at the Aegean from time to time as if ensuring it was still there. The Professor turned in various directions to try to take in the ancient sites of Crete and the movement all around him as if mentally writing his own book but was pressed forward by his wife. Thrace and Parker did not speak, just trekked on deep in thought about the task at hand. Aemon received odd glances from tourists and quietly whispered that they were actors, as if that made it all right to carry ancient weapons hiking.

Sophos paused by an old misshapen pale brown ash tree with only a few branches each carrying a dozen leaves as if it was all it could bear. It appeared as if it should not be there, but had been for hundreds of years. He turned through the brush as if following an invisible trail.

"Excuse me," the Professor spoke up. "I believe the Dikteon cave is this way, along the path."

"It is not." Sophos answered without stopping. "The cave of Zeus is not along that mortal path, for it was hidden by the mist many years ago from mortals, who would exploit it, as you have done."

"Probably good idea." Parker said. "It would be funny if tourists took pictures of us talking or even fighting with things they couldn't see. We'd probably get arrested and thrown in the loony bin."

"I am surprised you have not been there already?" Sophos stated briskly.

"Did you just make a joke?" Thrace asked.

"I believe he did?" Parker replied.

Sophos stopped at a small rocky crag stretching out from Mt. Dicte like a shoulder. Over the rocky crag a small plain about half the size of a football field that resembled the one Thrace dreamed about with the mountain continuing up another hundred yards or so at the south end of the pitch. The rocky crags encircled the small field and a small cave appeared visible along the mountain side.

"So, this was Mighty Zeus' playground as a kid?" Thrace said breaking the silence.

"Needs a swing set." Parker added also feeling the tension of the silence.

"Professor, this is where you and your wife will wait." Sophos said.

Chapter 21

Bright and All-Seeing Helios stretched his journey across a cloudless sky as if the sky had been cleared so the gods could watch without interruption. If the Immortal gods were physically watching, it would be only two on this day. The minds of the slumbering Immortal Gods were strong, as Apollo, the God of Light, penetrated a prophesizing Pythia, and the son of Cronus entered the mind of the mortal son of Ares revealing his youth as Olympian King when he placed his hand atop the navel of the earth before the temple of Apollo at Delphi. In their way, they were watching.

The heroes removed their packs and gathered the necessary gear needed. Besides his Ashen spear of Achilles and the Shield of Perseus, Thrace took a small satchel filled with the two remaining adamantine spears, which he hoped he would not have to use. The one they used at the stadium, where remnants of the shattered log remained, could not be located. Parker slung the Atalantan bow and quivers over his shoulder, though he felt it was more of a burden, since he could not wield the bow, and held the Golden lyre of Pan tight in hand. Myrtle arranged the packs in a row along the rocky crags as if tidying her grandson's room. Sophos donned his father's ancient brazen armor and appeared like a god in the light of Helios. Might and Violence strapped on the quilted armor they wore on stage with care; as if it were made of gold from the Smith God.

Thrace looked upon is friend, adjusting the bow, so it would not interfere with his lyre. This is where the trip upon their bicycles into the mountain had led each of them. Thrace realized this quest began long before either of them was born, but he knew it needed to end on this day, not only for himself and his mother, but for future sons and daughters of Ares and their mothers. He was glad he was not alone and his best friend was here to assist him to whatever end lay before them.

"Parker, I'm glad you decided to come along."

"You say that as if we're not going home." Parker replied. "I'm going home. My mom's already pissed at me. She'd be really pissed if I didn't come home." Parker added, "By the way." He found his pack in line next to Myrtle and dug through it. "It's no Shield of Perseus, but I figured since you were kinda battling an ancient Greek battle, you needed some ancient Greek armor."

Parker pulled out a dark leather corset with circular bronze shoulder pads sewn in for protection and an olive tree embroidered upon the chest. He also pulled out a set of bronze greaves with silver clasps to tie up behind the calf. Thrace took the armaments gingerly as if accepting delicate crystal.

"Wow, thanks Parker. I can't believe you've been lugging this around since Sophos' cave."

"There was this really cool all bronze one with what look liked gold in it, but it wouldn't fit in my pack."

"I must keep a closer eye upon our lyre playing thief," Sophos said watching Thrace strap on the armor over his shirt and the greaves over his jeans. "But, a wise decision and a good choice, Parker of the Lyre. That was my armor when I first started training, as it was my father's and his, Cheiron the Wise."

"Your grandfather is Cheiron, teacher of Herakles and Achilles?" The professor stated more than asked in awe.

"Stop." Myrtle chided her husband like a child at an amusement park, and the Professor closed his mouth and simply stared in excitement.

"To the skies." Sophos said. He raised his strong arms pointing to the sky blue heavens.

Soaring through the heavens upon a backdrop of blue was a large golden eagle. It circled twice then dived quickly toward the mountain top. It approached the mountain surface with its sharp talons stretched out. The great bird brushed the mountain side and the sharp talons snatched up a large snake. The eagle again soared into the sky, but the snake was not dead. The heroes watched as it fought and squirmed within the claws of the eagle and then tried to strike its attacker. The eagle dropped the snake and flew off into the blue sky.

"What do you think Halia?" Sophos asked.

"I am not the soothsayer Sophos." She said turning away as if hiding something.

"Bird signs?" the Professor asked.

"What are you thinking Sophos," Thrace asked. "We're the eagle and the snake is Kottus, and we both go away alive?"

"It is a possibility."

"Yeah, but that doesn't say whether we get the vial or not." Parker added.

"I am tired of all these prophecies and signs and reading of guts." Thrace said disgruntled with the guess work.

"May I ask the prophecy?" The Professor asked.

"*Within the one-hundred lies the one, born of a god, painted in red, will return the love and forgo the dead.*" Thrace said instinctively, for it ran through his mind as if upon a never-ending Ferris wheel, and he was unable to get off.

"Painted in red...what is painted in red?" Myrtle asked.

"We're not sure." Parker said.

"Sophos as you are well aware, prophecies can mean a variety of things. Since you are unsure of the 'red', it may be wise to keep an eye out for whatever 'red' may be." The Professor said.

"Yeah, no problem." Parker said sarcastically. "Because the hundred-handed Titan won't keep us busy. At least your half-brother and sister aren't here."

"Hold your tongue young Parker," Sophos barked. "The Professor is correct. We must attempt to be aware of many things. When in battle one's eyes and mind must stay attune not only to the action but to the surroundings."

"Can you repeat the second prophecy?" Halia asked which drew silence from the heroes, a silence the Professor noticed without hearing Halia's voice.

Thrace stood his ground wishing not to repeat it. The revealing of it brought forth the death of an immortal Pythia and placed hope in various beings, many of which he only recently met and most he did not know. He did not care what it meant. He simply wanted acquire the cure and get home to help his mother.

"The seed of destruction shall calm the savage wine dark sea. But beware his strength, for it does not lie in the spear, and it will rival the lightning of the son of Cronus." Thrace said looking at Halia who stared at him in amazement.

"Are you the 'seed of destruction'?" Myrtle asked.

"I believe so." Thrace said.

"Enough." Sophos said ending this prophetic debate. "We know Thrace had a dream in which Anthia was injured. We know Pan read the entrails of the giant boar saying someone will die. We saw a bird sign that may be read that each shall leave unharmed. All we truly know is that the Mighty Hundred-Handed Kottus is chained inside that mountain and guarding a sacred vial with the cure of Asclepius for Cybele, the mother of Thrace. No matter the signs nor the prophecies, we have a...creative plan that we need to execute with detail."

"You know, that's a lot of chains." Parker said and was quickly dismissed by Sophos.

"Before we go," Thrace said calmly. "I believe we need to make a sacrifice to my father."

"What?" Parker exclaimed. "You're kidding, right?"

"No." Thrace moved to the center of his companions. "He orchestrated this entire event. All of us know a little more about ourselves because of it. From my mother's teaching and what I've read, I remember that Ares, at times, tried to protect his sons as well as their companions."

"Except his most recent sons." Parker reminded him.

"True. But he did awaken me on the ship to prepare us for Proteus, the Old Man in the Sea. He didn't have to."

"Wise decision young Thrace, your wisdom and understanding have grown much in such a short time," Sophos stated with honor.

"Kinda like brown-nosing the teacher before the big test. I get it," Parker said with a humorous smile.

"We will collect wood for a fire," Aemon said as he and Battus scurried off to gather branches and limbs along the mountain's craggy slopes.

Halia of the Sea moved in front of Thrace and took a long and admiring look upon the young son of Ares. She placed her fingers upon his face. "Peirethous, son of Cheiron spoke often of the children of Ares in his quests; some were strong, some pompous, some wise and some apathetic. I believe you are truly the Seed of Destruction; for in our world, the Seed of Destruction is hope. This is not because of your father, but for your wisdom and courage, and though Ares should be proud to have you as a son; your mother would be even prouder."

"Thanks." Thrace responded and drank in the winged-words from Halia of the Sea. The kind words touched him as only a mother's words can.

Thrace breathed in the moment. A moment that would be his last calm moment before the great storm of Boreas rocked the mountain with a terror unlike anything anyone had witnessed in a millennia. If all worked as planned, there would be no storm, but Thrace read many great ancient myths and legends, which he understood now as tales of history, and he knew there would be a thunderous storm once again atop Mt. Dicte.

Aemon and Battus arranged the wood for the altar and quietly stepped back unsure of what to expect recalling the last time the God of War appeared through the burning fire in a suit looking as impressively dangerous and arrogant as they would have expected. They understood their roles as sidekicks upon this quest as was their role in *Prometheus Bound*, but this surpassed the theatres they had played for years. If their lives were to end, they each hoped it would be upon the battlefield, not at the quick and impatient hands of an angry and petty god.

"Thrace, what are we gonna sacrifice?" Parker asked.

"I have an idea, maybe not a good one though. Let's get this fire started."

Halia of the Sea reached in and like Anthia, sparked a flame that quickly caught in the timber. All of the heroes stepped back as Thrace stepped forward. He took a quick glance at Sophos. He no longer saw his stern gaze, but a look of pride upon his mentor. It was the look he had hoped for from a father he had never known.

"Father, Ares, God of War, son of Olympian Zeus, it is I, Thracian Ares Kraft, your son. In this final act which you have orchestrated so well I offer you the spear of Achilles, son of Peleus with a staff forged by the Athena, Goddess of Wisdom, with an adamantine spear head forged by the Hephaestus, Smith God of Fire. May this weapon offered upon this altar in your name give us courage and fortune against Kottus, the great Hundred-Handed, and guardian of the dungeons in Tartarus."

Thrace, holding the spear above the fire smoldering high to the heavens above, dropped the ancient spear upon the bright red flames. The Professor let out a sharp squeak like a small mouse losing a piece of cheese. Sophos, the Centaur stood silent, though his face was riddled with concern. The flames blessed to Ares the Destroyer consumed the ashen spear with a ravenous hunger.

The flames appeared to pause in a hungry blood red blaze. Then, in an instant, a small remaining orange flame vomited up a single bright flaming spear head. It glimmered and shined in a golden hue as bright as Helios. Thrace caught it in the air by the neck avoiding the blades that appeared sharp enough to filet the fine hairs of the Fates themselves.

"Now that was awesome!" Parker exclaimed.

"I can't believe what I just saw," the Professor spoke in awe. "I witness the destruction of the ancient ashen spear of Achilles in return, a gift from the gods; a new beautiful weapon from the God of War himself." The Professor stood stunned and added, "Do we need to make a shaft?"

"My boy needs no stinking shaft," Parker stated amusingly taking a closer step to admire the new golden spear head.

"Thrace," Sophos said with wisdom. "This is no longer the spear head of Achilles' ashen spear. It has been touched by Ares, the Deceiver. I am suggesting caution in its use until we know more."

Thrace recognized these wise words as he examined the new weapon, dubbed by Parker the golden spearhead of Thrace. He placed the golden spear head in the satchel over his back which held the other adamantine spear heads he had acquired from the cave of Sophos. Thrace moved beside Sophos at the front of the trail which lead to the cave along the small hidden plain before Mt. Dicte. Sophos nodded and turned back to the heroes.

"Prepare for battle!"

Parker tightened the small corset around his waist, adjusted the Atalantan bow over his shoulder and gripped Pan's Golden lyre tight in his hand. Aemon and Battus checked each other's quilted armor, clasped one another's forearms and clanged foreheads as if football players preparing for the Superbowl. Halia of the Sea, with the girdle of Aphrodite sensuously clasped around her creamy soft skin, lifted the large mirror with grace and ease. Sophos watched as each prepared. He donned his helmet with his bow and quiver across his shoulders, and his short sword at his side. He took a long look at his army. Not the traditional army he had read about or imagined, but this rag-tag group of heroes had a gigantic battle before them.

Chapter 22

There was calm upon the afternoon as if All-Seeing Helios paused in the blue sky above to witness the battle. The four Great Winds; Notos, Eurus, Zephyrus and Boreas had taken a seat along the edge of the rocky crags around the plain atop Mt. Dicte. Beside the Great winds sat hundreds of Oreads, Hyamadryads, Oceanids and Naiads along the rocky crags that circled the small plain. Rumors stretched across the lands that before them walked The Seed of Destruction; hope from oppression. Even two of the ancient children of Ares; Phobus, Deimus sat at the far edge of the plain to watch the events unfold.

The heroes reached the plain atop Mt. Dicte and the calm enveloped each of them. Sophos and Halia saw the audience viewing atop the rocky crags of legendary Mt. Dicte. Thrace stood at his mentor's side and also felt the unusual calm. He noticed the stillness atop the crags of Mt. Dicte and realized he had a viewing audience. At the far end, he saw the dark and shadowy sons of Ares.

"I believe I have seen those two before, or at least one of them." Thrace pointed out to Sophos.

"That is Fear and Panic, Immortal sons from the union of Ares and Aphrodite. Where?"

"After my mother was cursed. Once I thought I saw one of them before we went against Stheno and Euryale, and I think again in the village where I saw Aphrodite."

"It appears they also have a part to play in all of this but on whose side? Let us not bother with those two; we have bigger issues before us."

"Yep, and it's like we're the only show in town." Parker added.

Hidden in the rocky crags of Mt. Dicte, Professor Charles and Myrtle Wilkins watched them walk the grassy plain below. The professor observed these modern heroes pause and view the rocky crags that surrounded them with a cautious eye. Quietly, he passed the binoculars to his wife.

"What are they looking at?" Myrtle asked taking the binoculars and panning the area.

"I am unsure," the Professor replied.

The vibrant sound of a ram bleated at them from behind. Myrtle dropped the binoculars as each observer turned in fear. A large black ram with curled golden horns approached them inching ever so closer. Its eyes blazed with coal hot flames.

"That's no ordinary ram, is it?" Myrtle whispered quietly.

"Whoever you are, we simply assisted the travelers here on their journey and are hoping to make sure they make it home safe." The Professor attempted to say with confidence, though it may have lacked a full effect.

The black ram stood fast, but somehow appeared to be moving. Myrtle was the first to respond that her eyes began to burn. As the professor turned to assist her, he recognized the same sensation. He reached for a water bottle to rinse their eyes, but realized the packs were tucked together, out of reach. Before he could do anything, Myrtle spoke.

"Oh my god?!"

"Your God? Soon enough. But you are correct Myrtle, for a God I am, Ares as a matter of fact."

The Professor heard the words, but did not see until he blinked the tears from his eyes. Before him stood a tall man with statuesque features and shoulder length black hair donned in ancient Greek armor as if preparing for battle. The gold of the corset, greaves and helmet glimmered off the brightness of Helios and was trimmed in a deathly black. He wore a blood red cape of a Spartan and the blood red plume atop his golden helmet stood tall upon this windless day.

The Professor stared in amazement as the God of War stood before him. He turned quickly to see his new friends along the plain. He could actually see Sophos the Centaur leading them toward the ancient cave of Zeus, and he saw the lovely Halia of the Sea adorned in the Girdle of Aphrodite. He spun back toward Ares who watched the Professor gather all he had witnessed.

Ares the Cunning knelt down to speak to the crouching mortals eye to eye.

"I am not here to harm you Professor. But since you are a professor of Ancient Greece I believe, I have cleared the mortal mist from your eyes so that you may tell this tale of the Great God of War, his rule over Mt. Olympus and his magnificent progeny that will rule beside him."

"You speak of your son, Thrace?" The Professor asked.

"I said magnificent, so no. I will admit, the young mortal has surprised even me, then again, he does have a slice of me within him. I speak of Cresphontes and Deinus whom you have not met. Thrace's fate on the other hand is in the hands of the Fates and all depends on this day. No mortal children of mine have been successful over the centuries against Kottus, the Hundred-Handed. Nor will any."

"No one's been successful against the Hundred-Handed, not even the great Titans, how do you expect him to win." The Professor asked with the concern of a parent.

"I don't." Ares responded with a dark smile and proceeded past the Professor and his wife down the trail toward our heroes.

"I don't like that man," Myrtle said.

"Well no one really liked him in Ancient Greece, not until the Romans, who loved war." The Professor responded.

"He's kind of like a spoiled kid." Myrtle replied. "What are we going to do?"

"What do you mean, 'What are 'we' going to do?'" The Professor said in shock. "He is the God of War, and we are just mortals."

"Yes, but you are a retired Classics Professor, you must have some way to stop him."

"The Aloeids captured him as did Hephaestus, but the Aloeids were gigantic and Hephaestus had a magical net." The Professor paused trying to focus on too many myths and legends he had taught and apply them to the present situation. "What we need is some help."

"What kind of help?" Myrtle asked.

Parker eyes spanned the rocky crag. "Got a bit of a crowd." He said turning in amazement toward Thrace. His nerves trembled like an earthquake at the Olympic size crowd.

"Many of the Immortals," Sophos replied. "Many know of Thrace's victory over Stheno, and Pan would have also spoken of the killing of the giant boar."

"But it was just a boar." Thrace responded defensively.

"It is not that it is 'only a boar', but the parallel between your killing the boar and other ancient heroes such as Meleager, Theseus and Herakles. As Aphrodite said, there is much more at stake here than your mother."

"Right now, I really don't care what else is at stake. I just want to get that vial and go home."

"Then let's do this." Parker said clapping the armor upon his friend's back.

"All right everyone," Sophos stated firmly, "though the plan of Thrace's is far from fool proof, it is the best we have to offer. Aemon and Battus you will lead the way with torches held high as heralds for Halia of the Sea. The three of us will move in the shadows of the light until we find Kottus, then Halia will proceed with her...portion of the plan."

"Why Sophos," Halia replied. "Is that a tone of jealousy I hear?"

"No, it is not." Sophos replied quickly. "Let us go."

Halia of the Sea lit the torches held by Aemon and Battus who had difficulty taking their eyes off the beautiful Halia, which was magnified with the girdle of Aphrodite and the flickering light of the flame. She gave them a stern glare and the thieves became actors once more. They played their greatest role upon the cave of Mt. Dicte and took position before Halia as escorts, armed for her protection. As they approached the cave, it opened larger feeling the presence of an immortal. Halia of the Sea, with mirror in hand, followed close behind.

"Now men," Sophos said addressing Thrace and Parker. "Parker, you will follow behind Halia with Lyre singing throughout the cave to ease the Titan. We will proceed in with two spears distance between each of us in case one is spotted, the other may assist in defensive positions or in withdrawal."

"I will not withdraw until I get the vial." Thrace replied.

"I'm with him." Parker added.

"Understood, I am with both of you, but if we must, we may have to withdraw to try again for you cannot save your mother if you are dead. Remember what the Professor said also, we must keep an eye out for anything red for the completion of the prophecy."

"As long as it's not blood." Parker replied, which caught an eerie silence between the three. "Sorry."

Thrace clasped Parker and nodded in understanding. He was nervous; they both were. There was no more to be said. Words seemed inappropriate at this point. The three stood looking at one another. This was quite different than when Thrace and Sophos saw one another for the first time in his back yard, or when Parker saw the Centaur in the mountains when the Immortal Hamadryad pulled away his mortal mist. Now, the three stood as comrades, friends with great admiration and respect which wove them together like a giant tapestry. There was trust now when originally there was uncertainty. Trust is what was needed in these dark depths against the Hundred-Handed.

Without a word, Parker struck a chord upon his golden lyre, and the music sang upon the plain. A sigh echoed from the on-looking Immortals as Parker proceeded into the cave. He looked back at his best friend and teacher and offered a crooked and confident smile, then was gone in the darkness.

Thrace and Sophos stood alone outside the cave. The student and the teacher clasped forearms in the traditional manner with obvious care for one another. Sophos calmly spoke to his pupil.

"Odysseus's teacher, Mentor, said, *'Few sons are equals to their fathers; most fall short; all too few surpass them.'* I believe you have already surpassed your father." Sophos turned after he spoke and departed into the darkness following the music ringing off the cave walls from the Golden Lyre of Parker.

Thrace stood alone outside the cave waiting momentarily before entering, the words of his teacher echoing in his mind. Now he needed to think of the task at hand, as his mother taught him. He pulled the flower petal from his pocket. The petals were all but gone and the bright eye in the center was fading. His time was short, and he could not fail. In this final moment of solitude before he entered, he gazed upon the rocky crag and saw dozens of Immortals standing and watching. He wondered if Anthia was there among them. Part of him wished she was, for now he knew it was not her magic that gave him courage, but simply her. A movement along the plain caught his eye. He turned to see his father, the God of War, in full armor regalia proceeding toward him.

"Hello son."

CHAPTER 23

"What are you doing here?" Thrace asked knowing he should just turn and run into the cave. He needed to be inside assisting his friends who were risking their lives for him and his mother, not out here with The Deceiver…his father.

"Your offering was very generous and I felt, as a father, to come down and wish you well," spoke Ares with a flavor of sarcasm.

"You don't want or expect me to succeed."

"True," The God of War stated honestly. "But by some chance you do, you would have proved yourself greater than any of my mortal sons over many of years. It would be said that you may be greater than I; and, well, I can't allow that."

"I do not wish to be greater than you; I am not seeking glory! I just want to save my mother!" Thrace stated sternly. "Now, if you will excuse me."

Thrace turned to enter the cave and heard the blade of Ares being drawn from his sheath. His own hand went quickly to the hilt of his own sword. Though he felt he had little chance against the God of War, he would not give up without a fight.

"Honorable son, very honorable." Ares said. "You may have made a great Spartan, but I cannot let you enter that cave. I know the prophecy of Apollo has been spilt; if you truly are the Seed of Destruction, I cannot give you even the most remote chance of success. As Zeus replaced his father

Cronus, I shall replace my father. My reign as king of the Gods is far from over and with my new and greatest son at my side, we will rule the Heaven and Earth for all eternity."

"Not if I can help it." Thrace replied pulling his short sword from his sheath and charged his father.

Ares, Stormer of Strong Walls, brushed away his hasty attack and brought down his sword against his son. Thrace raised the shield of Perseus and blocked the attack from his father, then spun broadly swinging his sword towards his father's stomach. The God of War was quick and had fought many battles. He deflected his son's counter and again brought his sword down on the shield of Perseus. He repeated this attack bringing his son to his knees. Thrace held up the shield with all his might.

"I will admit son, you are masterful with the spear; hence, the reason my flames devoured Achilles' spear. But I have seen you fight with the sword, and you are a long way from ready to battle me!" Ares exclaimed, then paused as two glimmering lights reflected at him from the light of bright Helios just as Thrace raised his shield once again. Ares the Cunning saw two of his Greek ram coins around his son's neck.

Quickly, Ares pulled the shield of Perseus toward him. Thrace, not expected the change in tactic, raised his sword, but just as swift, Ares swatted it back. He released the shield and grabbed Thrace around the neck and sheathed his own sword.

"Where did you get these?" Ares asked, grasping both coins and rubbing them between his thumb and index finger.

Thrace did not say a word, but fought and wrestled to get free. He recalled Parker being held by Stheno, unable to free himself. But this time, there was no one to save him as he saved Parker at this moment.

"Ay, this belonged to Alexandra. She was almost as beautiful as Aphrodite herself. The son she bore, as beautiful as Adonis with a heart as cold as the peaks of the Caucus Mountains." Ares said with smile as if his son's cold heart was his most beloved feature.

Thrace needed to move fast. His father was reminiscing about another dead son and broken mother. A move from the video game he and Parker played came to mind. Quickly, he brought his knees to his chest, then, with all his strength, he sprang them forward into the God of War's lower abdomen and spun, swinging his shield to hit Ares…anywhere.

The Stormer of Strong Walls, buckled as he quickly went to his knees with a gasp. Though only for a moment. Through his brilliant brazen helmet, Thrace could see his eyes burn like smoldering coals.

"You will pay for that son." Ares stated slowly catching his breathe.

Thrace's mind raced. Should he run, he thought? He was too close and probably too fast to out run. He was a God. Could he use the adamantine spear head? No, he was too close, and there was no time to grab it from his pack. He needed a distraction, a way to get into the cave. As if by request, a howl erupted in the background. A familiar howl, he had heard before.

Ares had heard it also, as he got to his feet and grasped his sword tight to attack his son. Thrace quickly peered out from behind the golden shield to see the face on the wind he had seen in the sails upon the wine dark Aegean.

It was Zephyrus, the West Wind who had given his friend Parker so much trouble.

Zephyrus, howling like a crazed man, raced between the God of War and his son pushing them both back. Ares looked stunned to see this ancient Immortal disturb him, the King of the Gods, the new ruler of the Immortals.

"How dare you interfere with my affairs Zephyrus!!" Ares exclaimed. "I will have you chained and bound for this insolence!!"

With that response, Zephyrus took a second pass around Ares knocking him to his back. Thrace watched as his father fell in anger. Far beyond Ares, Thrace saw the Professor and Myrtle cheering him on. He realized they could now see beyond the mortal mist. More of Ares doing he assumed. His father's own arrogance.

Knowing he would only get a moment, Thrace ran into the darkness of the cave. His father would pursue, so the plan, no matter how far along would have to be altered. Thrace was concerned about fighting the Hundred-handed and Cresphontes or Euryale, but now it's a Titan and the God of War. Great, he thought racing through the darkness.

Moving in haste through the darkness, he edged his way along the cave walls. The cave path widened, but there was no sign of his friends. He hoped he was not too late. Then as the cave wall abruptly turned right, he saw a flicker of light in the distance. He proceeded with caution not wanting to be seen. Behind him he heard a vicious roar, which could only be his father. He turned and his foot caught something in the dark, and he fell face forward; but not upon the dirt surface of the cave.

He rolled to sit up, and the room was dimly lit from a torch at the near end of the cave hall. Battus held the fire closer to Thrace for his assistance. Thrace looked down to see himself atop a bloody corpse. He had fallen upon the bloodied and mangled body he had seen in his painful images. A bronze helmet still incased the bloody skull and his hand still held an eighteen foot Macedonian pike. Thrace saw a necklace around his neck bearing the symbol of the ram. It was another son of Ares who had died at their father's hand for the birth of the perfect son to rule by his side.

Thrace grabbed the pike and ran into the chamber toward Battus. What stood before him is an image that will be burnt in his memory for all eternity.

The chamber stretched over a hundred feet high as did the height of Kottus, the Great Titan. Two giant legs supported a massive body stretching fifty feet wide with fifty serpentine arms reaching out from his colossal and majestic chest. Atop his broad shoulders extended short serpentine necks each supporting fifty brutish heads with eyes of white from years in Tartarus guarding the barren gates of the Great Titans whom Zeus defeated. Curled up beside him was Halia of the Sea morphed to his height and adorned in the sensuous girdle of Aphrodite holding the mirror before the Great Titan wooing him and all his exquisite beauty. Kottus' many arms slowly caressed the beautiful Sea Goddess.

The music pulled Thrace's eyes toward Parker sitting upon a rock playing his lyre as beautifully as he had ever heard, calming his own raging heart within himself. At the other end of the cave Sophos stood in the shadows his bow pulled tight to strike the Titan if he attempted any aggressive move toward Halia. Thrace turned to Halia who was caressing each of his serpentine arms without hands, but small suctions like that of the giant octopus laced with razor sharp claws. Halia's hand slide along one of Kottus's arm and Thrace saw her touch the vial, and with elegance and grace she slipped it from his arm.

Kottus did not react to the removal of the vial, but Thrace saw a few of the fifty heads watch as she removed it. The head followed her hand as she tossed it gently to the far end of the cave, and the hand of Halia was quickly in place again caressing the great Titan.

Thrace understood. Kottus did not want to be here anymore than any of them did. He had been forced or tricked here against his will and like himself, he just wanted this to end.

A giant roar again echoed throughout the cave. The music from Parker's lyre stuttered for a second, then continued on. Sophos did not draw his attention from the protection of Halia of the Sea. Ares would be here any second and provoke violence that could get all of them killed. He needed to do something before that happened. Thrace stepped from the shadows into the light and stood before the Great Titan and stuck the Macedonian Pike into the earth. All the heroes saw him, and the eyes of Sophos exploded in fear. His saw his pupil covered in blood, not knowing it was the blood of his dead step-brother.

"Painted in red." Parker let out in a gasp.

"Kottus, the great Hundred-Handed." Thrace yelled at the Titan.

Kottus turned his attention as all fifty heads turned down toward Thrace in anger.

"Have you come to fight me? Are you another son of Ares?" Kottus' heads asked in unison. "You did not have to enter, the vial was yours. But like Ares, your arrogance shall be your death."

Kottus stretched out his serpentine arms as if to quickly bring them down upon the next son of Ares, all but four. The four chained to the cave wall.

"No Great Kottus," Thrace replied. "I did not come to do battle with you. For OUR fight is not with one another, but with the same Immortal, Ares the Cunning, Ares the Deceiver. He deceived you to bring you here. He has punished my mother to bring me here; so we may fight for his amusement. So I may die for his amusement, and you shall be trapped here for all eternity for his amusement. We are not enemies Great Kottus, though Ares pits us against one another. He alone is our enemy."

"Winged-words young son of Ares, and what you speak is truth. The God of War brought me here centuries ago with the promise of being able to alter my form, to walk among this new world. His words were far from the truth as the potion he gave me made me slumber, and I awoke in the dark, chained to these walls. Since then, he sends his children to their death against me, for no mere mortal can defeat me. All for a vial that is empty."

"Empty?" Thrace replied as if his world had just ended. He walked over to the vial and picked it up. It was a ceramic vial painted gold, withered and cracked. Thrace removed the string-corked cap to reveal nothing at all. Thrace stood stunned in dismay.

"That is correct my son."

The God of War stepped from the darkness, his golden armor drinking in the light from the torches and reflecting it throughout the cave. The son of Zeus carried a glow of arrogance. His eyes sparked in victory at this final meeting; one in which in the past he only watched from afar, and now he watched the end up close.

Halia of the Sea shrank her giant Titan form to that of Ares and slowly approached him in the Girdle of Aphrodite that had brought him to submission so many times in the past. As she stepped toward him, her beauty radiated like Helios in the bright blue on a cloudless sky. The light from the torches dimmed as Aemon and Battus lowered their torches unknowingly transfixed by her beauty. She seductively eased up beside him. The God of War laughed.

"Please Halia," Ares said in jest. "Hephaestus built this armor for me eons ago to keep his wife's girdle from seducing me. You have been enough of a hindrance in something you should not have been involved." Ares drew his sword with a sociopath's glare.

"NO!!" Aemon yelled throwing his torch in the direction of Ares and rushing forward pushing Halia to the ground.

Sophos turned and fired an arrow at Ares. Ares, the Cunning, caught Aemon and pulled him in front of the arrow. It struck his shoulder, where once a pencil had struck. Bloodthirsty Ares glared into the pale eyes of Aemon.

"You two are abominations of this world and should not be allowed to live." Ares said thrusting his sword into Aemon, then dropping the large actor to the cave floor.

"AEMON!!" Battus yelled.

In a frantic rage Battus ran toward Ares, his sword high above his head. Parker dropped his lyre, and the cave went silent except for the echoes of terror at a brother lost. Parker came at Battus and tackled Might.

"Stop or he will kill you!" Parker yelled holding on to his legs like a small safety trying to tackle a three hundred pound full back.

Kottus, the Hundred-Handed let out a roar that was said to have been heard across the wine dark Aegean as Halia of the Sea was almost slain. Sophos pulled his sword from his sheath, let out a fierce battle cry and charged the God of War.

The cave was in disarray as Battus was crawling his way to get a hold of Ares as Parker held his ankles with all his might. The serpentine arms of the Hundred-handed were swimming throughout the cave. Halia in fear got to her feet and tried to stop the rushing Centaur with blood rage in his eyes. Ares, Slaughter of men, raised his sword welcoming the battle.

As Kottus attempted to pull himself from the cave wall to get at Ares, Thrace saw a stack of ancient Greek ceramic vases in a corner near the Titan's thunderous feet. One large vase to the side reminded him of his vision at Delphi. A black vase, painted in orange, detailed a scene of Olympian Zeus placing the stone that his mother, Rhea, fed Cronus, into the earth at Delphi. Zeus had giving him this image to reveal where he hid the vial so long ago.

"STOP!" Thrace yelled with the voice of an Immortal that even amazed himself. Sophos the Clever, pulled back his charge as if commanded by Mighty Zeus. The Mighty Hundred-Handed turned in amazement at the young son of Ares, who had stood before him earlier and sang truth and now commanded obedience. Ares, stunned and impressed, turned toward his son.

"You have more Immortal in you than I would have never imagined." Ares said with pride. "You may actually deserve a place by my side. It is too bad I cannot offer it."

"Why? Because you fear the prophecy?" Thrace asked calmly.

"I fear nothing!" Ares barked with anger. "I am king of the Gods!"

"You? Whose life is consumed by fear father? You fear the prophecy and the Seed of Destruction if you wish my death."

Ares wiped the blood of Aemon from his sword upon his blood red cape as he approached his son. "Let us say in my experience, prophecies tend to reveal themselves unless unable, and those prophecies are then forgotten. I shall make sure this one is as you shall be."

"What I have learned is that the more you attempt to stop a prophecy, the more likely you are to make it come true." Thrace stated standing steadfast before his approaching father.

Thrace reached into his satchel and pulled out an adamantine spear head he had acquired from the cave of Sophos. He held it high in the air like a torch before his father.

"You plan to defeat me with just a spear head? You are not as wise as I might have imagined son." Ares said with an arrogant smile continuing his approach.

"No, I do not. For I am Thrace of spear, son of Cybele of the Javelin!" Thrace turned toward Kottus and fired the spear head as he did on the plains of Delphi at the wooden log. In a single breathe and like a lightning bolt from

Zeus it struck the cave wall and exploded. Two adamantine chains which held Kottus the Hundred-Handed to the wall snapped free. Kottus and his fifty mouths let out a murderous roar.

"Son, what are you doing?" Ares said stopping his movement and for the first time his face was stricken with fear. "He will kill us all!"

"I have no battle with this great Titan, and he has no battle with me." Thrace said as he pulled a second adamantine spear head from his satchel.

"You don't want to do this!!" Ares yelled. "I am your father, and I demand you to stop!!"

"To quote a poet of my time, 'I know all the rules, but the rules do not know me." Thrace sang out. "And Ares, you are no father of mine."

Thrace looked up at Kottus, whose many heads looked back, though as many kept an equal eye on Ares. Kottus nodded as the great Titan understood and was as wise as his enormous size.

Thrace fired the second spear head and again, in a single breathe and like a lightning bolt from Zeus, it stuck the cave wall between the two adamantine chains and exploded. Kottus once again let out a murderous roar and stretched out all of his serpentine arms for the first time in a millennia.

"Thank you Thrace, son of Cybele." Kottus said in unison with his fifty heads to young Thrace.

Ares, the Deceitful, became Ares, the Cowardly, as he turned with the speed of an Immortal and fled the cave. The Great Titan followed, his thundering footsteps echoed upon the island of Crete as they pounded the cave floor in pursuit.

The pounding of his footsteps fell silent as Kottus' pursuit took him from the cave. Battus shed Parker and quickly ran to Aemon's side. The remaining heroes slowly gathered around him. Battus wept as he held his brother in his arms.

"He saved my life," Halia said kneeling next to him and gently kissing him on his forehead.

"He will receive a heroes' burial." Sophos said.

"This is how he wanted to go." Battus said pulling back his tears, his lisp gone. "He will be in the Elysian fields soon with other great heroes like himself."

"You were quite brave against Kottus and your father Thracian Ares." Sophos said with pride to his pupil.

"Sometimes you don't always have to fight." Thrace replied.

"Sorry about the vial." Parker added.

"Let's not be so sure." Thrace said as he walked to the cave wall where the Great Titan was chained. Near a pile of cave debris that had fallen from the exploding spears, ancient Greek vases lined against the wall.

"I noticed a vase with the same painting in the vision I had at Delphi." Thrace said moving the debris of rock and vase chards.

"You mean the one where Zeus threw you on your ass?" Parker asked.

"The same."

From the debris, Thrace pulled out a large vase with a black figure of Zeus, Olympian King forcing a large stone into the earth.

"I bet Ares never knew where the vial was." Thrace said as he reached inside the vase and pulled out a golden vial glimmering in gold as if it gave off light.

"Only metal made from the hands of the God of Fire would glimmer like that after many centuries." said Halia of the Sea.

"You have completed the prophecy. More than that you have saved your mother. Congratulations Thrace of the Spear, son of Cybele." Sophos the Clever said.

A howl echoed throughout the cave, its wail sounded familiar to the heroes. Thrace slipped the vial into his pocket for protection and grabbed the Macedonian Pike. Parker reached for the torch Aemon had dropped and held it high in the air, then retrieved his lyre. Sophos gripped his blade in hand and handed Halia of the Sea his bow and quiver. Battus lifted his brother to take him from the darkness; a howl again rang out and came in their direction. It entered the chamber and a dark face in the wind circled them sweeping dust in the air.

"Oh, it's Zephyrus." Parker sighed in relief.

"He saved my life outside the cave against Ares," Thrace said. "Thank you Zephyrus, the Great West Wind." He yelled out to the circling wind.

The West Wind stopped beside our heroes, a dirt clouded whirlwind covered his form, though his warm lovely face shone through with his wings spread high in the air. Zephyrus appeared to be speaking. The words 'follow me' trailed like a soft note on a breeze singing through the cave.

The heroes followed as the West Wind spread his wings and exited the cave. Sophos instructed Battus to place Aemon on his back. Battus would have nothing of it not wanting to let go of his heroic brother and carried him from the cave. Halia followed beside Sophos as Parker, still with torch in hand walked beside Thrace as they exited the cave.

Upon the small plain of Mt. Dicte the heroes stood once again under the bright light of Helios. On the rocky crags the Immortal spirits sang a song for the ages that filled the air with a sound of victory. Zephyrus danced and played like a dolphin in mid-air among and between the Oreads and Hamadryads. It was a joyous celebration of victory and freedom.

In one instance when Helios and the Immortal's music warmed the heroes after many tribulations, it stopped. A large dark cloud quickly moved in and blocked the long golden arms stretching down from All-Seeing Helios. An eerie cold sensation crept over the small plain of Mt. Dicte.

"What now?" Parker asked.

At the far end of the plain Euryale stepped out from a rocky crag in full armament. Her beauty masked the hidden Gorgon within fighting to reveal itself. Euryale let out a wail. It was the same crying wail that echoed from the Temple of Argos just days before.

"Thrace, son of Ares. You killed my sister Stheno and now I demand retribution." Euryale wailed in anger approaching the heroes, her sword held high in the air.

"Euryale the Gorgon," Sophos yelled. "Are you sure you wish to do battle with the one who forced both the Great Titan Kottus and the Immortal God Ares running from the Cave of Zeus?"

Sophos' winged-words stopped the Gorgon in her tracks, but not the anger she held in her eyes. She waved her sword in the air and from the rocky

271

crag to the east, Phobus, son of Ares appeared with blade in hand. Beside the blade were the Professor and his wife Myrtle.

"You will pay for the death of my sister!" Yelled the Gorgon.

"You wish me to pay for the death of Stheno, though it was orchestrated by her lover Ares, the Cunning," explained Thrace with a cautious tongue.

You lie!" Euryale barked. "Ares loved Stheno more than Aphrodite!"

"I am sorry Euryale, but you both were deceived. Ares, the Cunning, wished her death for the arrival of his immortal children, Cresphontes and Deinus. He did not care for her, and I am sorry for her death."

"Again you lie! It appears you have become the deceiver in these present times." Euryale spat at Thrace, though the latter recognized the hesitation on her voice.

"And now," she added. "Your friends will die as will you."

Thrace gripped the Macedonian spear tight in his hand. It was longer than any spear he had thrown and was not intended for throwing. Could he hit the Gorgon from such a distance? He did not know, nor could he risk the life of his friends. If he did, her death would lead to the quick death of the Professor and Myrtle at the hands of Phobus, Fear himself. If he did not act, it would surely be their death. He also knew if the Professor and Myrtle died, his fellow comrades in arms would slaughter Euryale, which it appeared she desired, glorious death in battle.

Thrace glanced ever so slightly to his side to notice Halia with a quiver taut in the Atalantan bow. Sophos' grip upon his blade was so tight, Thrace thought the hilt would break. Battus appeared to be breathing fire from his nostrils in rage like the Giant Cretan Bull. He did not need death here, not his new friends nor Euryale's.

"I know you Phobus, my half-brother, and know you have followed my journey." Thrace said hoping his words might help lower the blade and attempted to slow down these events to devise a plan. His brother's eyes quivered at the sound of 'half-brother', but Thrace could not tell whether it upset him or not; his stance did not change.

A lightning bolt from the heavens struck the center of the plain between the heroes and their adversaries. In its stead stood in all her beauty and glory, the Goddess of Love and Desire, Aphrodite adorned in her white robes with golden trim.

"STOP!" The Goddess yelled echoing so loud the top of Mt. Dicte itself trembled. "There will be no more death on this day. The Fates have not ordained it."

"But Goddess," Euryale begged. "I demand retribution!"

"You will demand nothing!" Aphrodite bellowed. The Goddess walked patiently toward the Gorgon and stopped directly before her. Her lovely white arm stretched out as her fingers caressed the face of Euryale. The Gorgon fighting to reveal itself was placed at bay by the hand of the beautiful goddess, and all the comely appeal that was Euryale, daughter of Poseidon, was revealed to all.

"I am sorry for Stheno, but what the young son of Ares said is correct. She was betrayed by the God of War as was I."

Euryale, the last of the Gorgons, cowered by the touch of Aphrodite, bowed and accepted her statement. She turned toward the rocky crags along the plain of Mt. Dicte. Her anguish and loss still burned in her eyes as she glanced back at the heroes for one long last look. A look Thrace would not forget.

Aphrodite's attention turned to her son, Phobus. "Son, why are you here?" Aphrodite asked. "This is not your fight."

Phobus, the face of Fear, became fear itself at his mother's words. "Yes mother," was all he replied and quickly disappeared within a wisp of grey smoke.

The Professor and Myrtle recognized their freedom as their assailant were no longer at their sides. Their movement was dispelled by the awe of Crowned and Flowered Aphrodite. The Professor stared at a loss for words, which his wife fixed by bowing and thanking the Goddess and pulled her husband quickly across the plain toward their new friends. Even at their age, their nimble steps appeared as youthful as the young heroes. Myrtle took Thrace into her arms the way a mother is proud of her own son. The Professor stood before the heroes as if looking at them for the first time.

Aphrodite crossed the plain toward the heroes with all the patience of an Immortal, who knows little of time. She drank in one long look at each them as would a proud painter admiring her work. "You have all done well, and putting all of you in this situation was needed in order to end this game of Ares," The Goddess of Love stated simply and her eyes moved upon Thrace. "I am very proud of you, son of Cybele, for she has given birth to an extraordinary man; she will be very proud."

Aphrodite stepped forward and kissed young Thrace upon the forehead, and the young hero, even after all of his battles, still blushed.

Recognizing his embarrassment, the Goddess of Love smiled and raised her lovely white arms to the heavens and smiled. The dark clouds dispersed to allow the golden arms of Helios to embrace Mother Gaia once more.

In the blue skies above a golden eagle circled overhead, then swooped down toward the plain atop Mt. Dicte and just before reaching the surface, she morphed into the mountain Oread, Anthia. As her feet graced the plains she did not stop, but proceeded toward Thrace and stopped before him.

"I am very proud of you." Anthia said. She leaned in and gently kissed the son of Cybele. And once again, despite all his endeavors, his blood boiled once again, but this time not in anger.

"Now," Crowned and Flowered Aphrodite said. "Anthia will lead Thrace and Parker home to the mountains in the west to heal his mother."

"What about my friends?" Thrace asked turning toward Sophos the Centaur.

"We must remain," Sophos said. "Here we will build a pyre for Aemon and place two coins upon his eyes for Charon the Boatman."

"Yes, he will receive a hero's burial." Battus added with tears falling from his eyes as he held his brother. Aphrodite approached Battus and brushed the hair from his eyes and smiled at Battus. He felt courage surge through him once again and nodded and thanked to the Goddess.

"We must remain as well," the Professor added. "Nothing ancient, though I would love to stay and assist with Aemon's funeral procession, but our boat did sink in the Aegean, which means we have much paperwork to do."

"What about Euryale?" Parker asked.

"You have changed quickly from the wise cracking youngster only days ago." Aphrodite said with a smile as she placed her hand on Parker's cheek filling him with strength with her touch. "The Fates have decided it is not her time to die today, for her journey is not yet complete." Aphrodite informed Parker of the lyre. "But when you get home young Parker, strike the cords upon your lyre at night, for I love to listen to you play."

"I will." Parker said quietly, but with more confidence than their first encounter.

"Now, Halia of the Sea, I shall need my girdle back."

"Oh, I was hoping you would forget," Halia replied. "I wanted to put it to use." She finished with a coy smile.

"You will not need it," Sophos said quietly, though all heard.

"I will need it to get Kottus back with his brothers guarding the dark gates in Tartarus where the remaining Titans are imprisoned." Aphrodite said taking the girdle back from Halia then stepped before Sophos the Centaur.

"I wish to thank you. I put you on this journey with little information, and you carried the burden of your father that was not yours to carry. Your father did what he did to protect the world in which he lived. He sacrificed much, and many mortals died to save even more. I forced you to do what he would not to end this present game of Ares. But all is not over," Aphrodite said stepping back from the heroes.

"Thracian Ares, you made a promise to me, and I shall hold you to it when the time comes." Aphrodite said as she stepped away from our heroes stretching her arms to the heavens.

"Excuse me…Goddess?" Thrace asked quickly and quietly.

The Goddess of Love paused and her eyes took a long offensive look at Thrace, which quickly changed to a smile while lowering her arms. She stood patiently, awaiting Thrace to continue.

"Sorry, but I was wondering why you came to us in the village as the old woman? Why not whisper through Parker as you did during the journey?" Thrace inquired witnessing the quick temper she revealed as he interrupted her.

The stunning Goddess stared at Thrace for what felt like an hour, her eyes puzzled as she studied every feature of his face. "Young Thrace, I have not portrayed a mortal in many years." Quickly, she stretched out her arms reaching for the heavens, then transformed into a lovely white dove and took to the skies toward Helios who was making his way home in the west.

Thrace and Parker exchanged puzzled glances then both turned to Sophos who was watching both of them. Their eyes asked the same question. 'Then who was the old woman?' This thought was vanquished quickly as Thrace felt Anthia take his hand and watched as Halia of the Sea stepped before Sophos and commented on his last statement, which caused the stern Centaur to be nervous.

The heroes exchanged goodbyes and wishes of seeing one another once more, though next time, hopefully over better circumstances. Battus walked away from the plains to acquire timber for the pyre. Oreads and Hamadryads along the mountain ridge joined him. Anthia made her way toward the tree line at the plains edge to lead the two heroes homeward. Sophos joined them. Thrace, Parker and Sophos stood in silence.

"Thanks for helping me out and putting up with my antics Sophos." Parker said quickly to break the silence.

"It has been an honor and a privilege to know you young Parker of the lyre. You may continue on with your wise-cracking humor, for great comedies are just as wise as great dramas or tragedies."

Parker embraced forearms with the great Centaur and left the latter and Thrace alone as he joined Anthia's side. He watched as the two admired one another as father and son. He looked forward to getting home and seeing his own parents.

"I must ask who this poet was you spoke of who mentioned the rules not knowing you?" Sophos asked.

"Oh, ah…Eddie Vedder." Thrace said. "Mom's favorite."

"Unusual words of wisdom, but useful. I shall search for more of his winged-words." Sophos replied and added. "Thrace, I can only imagine how my father trained other sons of Ares and watched them die and attempted to try again. For I could not have done so upon your death. You have become like a son to me, and no father could have been any prouder than I am of you at this moment. You have shown great leadership and poise, and I hope what you have learned will help you in your world."

"I doubt what I have learned will help me get through high school." Thrace said with an awkward smile. "I want to thank you as well. You have taught me more about myself than I ever could ever imagined, things a father teaches a son. You will always have a place in my heart Sophos the Clever."

The young son of Cybele and the wise son of Peirithous embraced like father and son, not as teacher and student.

Thrace left his mentor and joined Parker. The Professor brought them their packs, which they reloaded with their armor and weapons.

"Will I see you again?" Thrace called back to his mentor.

"I believe you will." Sophos responded with a smile. "And if Aphrodite calls upon you." Sophos grasped the ivory horn he received from Halia of the Sea and tossed it to Thrace. "Just give me a call, and I will join you once again."

Thrace nodded to his mentor. Soon he would see his mother, and though it had only been a week, it felt like a lifetime. It had been a lifetime of an adventure he wished to share with her. One she would truly understand. He turned and clasped Anthia's hand as she clasped Parker's, and they proceeded toward a lonely ash tree atop Mt. Dicte.

CHAPTER 24

The heroes exited the large doorway knot they had entered a week ago, though with more confidence and agility, and set foot upon a mountain they had not seen in what felt like a lifetime. No longer the adventurous, yet scared young teens, but courageous and open-minded young men knowing great mysteries of the world and themselves.

Dark-winged Night stretched across the heavens, and the heroes of old took their position upon her wings. Anthia fixed two torches for Thrace and Parker to guide their way. Thrace accepted the torch from the beautiful Mountain Oread, and as their hands touched, he paused and gazed into her deep blue eyes. He was glad she was safe, and at least one prophecy had not come true. His gaze was distracted as Parker hit his shoulder to point out the dozens of tree nymphs drifting through the forest. They witnessed them sing on that first day where Parker lost the mortal mist. But now the singing was not to assist the forest growth, but a song of praise to the boys on their journey home.

They returned to the brush where their bikes were hidden, but they were no longer there. The searched around the forest to see if they had been moved or stolen, but found nothing. Thrace asked Anthia to check with the tree nymphs, but they had witnessed nothing, only seeing the natural world and not noticing the objects made my mortals.

"Thrace, look at this." Parker called out.

A sign upon the tree only twenty yards from where they hid their bikes read: "MISSING", with pictures of both Thrace and Parker with their names, ages and addresses printed below.

"I always hated that picture." Parker said as he pulled the sign down from the tree. "I bet my parents posted these signs all over town. I guess I wasn't that convincing when I talked to mom in Greece."

"I wonder if your parents called the police and traced the phone call to Greece. That would be fun to explain." Thrace replied in amusement. "Let's get to the hospital, so we can clear all this up."

"Not so fast." Barked a deep baritone voice from above.

The black reptilian wings of Deinus beat above them as their eyes only caught their movement as their width hid the heroes etched upon Night's wing. On her back sat the horned and muscled Cresphontes with a massive double-sided battle axe in one hand and a long ash Pike in the other. No shield for the Immortal son of Ares. Deinus' hooves settled upon the forest floor and, Cresphontes dismounted with an earth-shaking rumble, his brazen armor and sharp horns greedily absorbed the moonlight. The forest went silent as Thrace watched his dream come to life.

"Well my little half-brother," Cresphontes growled from his sharp teeth. "It appears you were successful after all with the help of Zephyrus as you mimicked him by running like the wind away from our father. Such cowardess."

"Cowardess?" Thrace replied. "How about Ares sending sons to a certain death for amusement?"

"Mortals are mere toys. Ants on a playground." Cresphontes stated. "If it wasn't for Zephyrus, that interfering winged beast, our father would have killed you. Now I shall overcome his failure."

"He would not have killed me." Thrace felt inside this was true, as he attempted to continue the monologue and figure a way out of this and to his mother.

Parker slowly edged his pack from his shoulder to retrieve the Golden Lyre knowing the Atalantan bow was slung across the back. A weapon he had yet to use. He needed to read his friend to prepare for his next move. There was just the three of them against these giant immortal children of Ares who wished their death greater than any other mythical creatures they had come against. He felt there would be no Immortal Goddess' assistance this time, and Sophos was on the other side of the world.

"Is your arrogance or pride so immense that you believe he would not have destroyed you?" Cresphontes asked. "Your only task was to kill my mother and release us and for that, we thank you. But for you being the 'Seed of Destruction', amusing. It is not you, but I. I will calm the Mighty Aegean and be greater than my father and my Grandfather, Olympian Zeus."

Cresphontes blazed a large fanged smile as his green eyes blazed red. He stared for a moment not saying a word. His straight-forwardness in killing them was replaced with the attitude of a cat playing with a mouse. "I stopped by to see your mother." He stood silently waiting for his words to reach Thrace. He watched as Rage made his way through his step-brother and fed off it like the hunger of the Cretan Minotaur craving his next sacrifice.

Thrace's blood boiled as he was consumed by Rage who flooded every vein of his body. Pollux once again took up arms against his heart. Thrace wanted to destroy this beast. For the first time upon this quest, he sought to intentionally end a life. Not for survival. Not to save a friend. He wanted to kill his half-brother and watch the life force fade from his eyes. His hand slid into his pack and his fingers slid around the stem of the Golden spear head that was revealed to him on the altar of Ares atop Mt. Dicte.

"She makes a beautiful flower bed. Then again, her room is more of a garden then a flower bed. I shall plant her in front of my mother's temple in Argos. A temple to her death, and my birth." Cresphontes gloated, holding the battle axe tight in hand, the long ash pike at his side.

What would this Golden spear head do, Thrace thought? It was given to him by Ares; and his father wanted him to fail. This could backfire, but he had no more of Hephaestus' adamantine spears to destroy Cresphontes.

"Enough of these games." Cresphontes stated getting bored with the lack of response from Thrace, or his friends.

With his mighty left hand, the Horned and Immortal son of Ares raised the long ash pike. He quickly offered a fanged smile and fired the pike at Thrace.

Thrace was not expecting this quick and far flung attack. He assumed his brother would want to take his life up close. He tried to pull the shield of Perseus from atop his pack. The straps from his pack were laced within the shields handles and he could not release them. He could see the sharp iron pike head closing upon him. He would not have time.

CLANK!!!

Thrace shuddered at the noise that erupted before him. The ash pike was not driven deep into his mortal flesh. He looked around to see what had just occurred. He saw the ash pike against a tree; the iron spear head was pinned to a tree just beneath the blade by an arrow.

He turned toward Anthia, who held no bow. Beside her, Parker stood with the Atalantan bow in hand; his fingers that released the string were still up beneath his eyes. Wide eyes filled with shock and amazement at his own accomplishment.

"I thought the bow was a better idea than the lyre." Parker stated in one exhale.

"That was amazing!" Thrace replied.

"It appears Aphrodite breathed strength into you little one." Cresphontes said impressed by the shot himself. "No matter. I should not have wasted time attempting to kill you from afar brother. I wish to spill your blood upon Mother Gia."

Cresphontes raised his giant double-sided battle axe and let out a war cry that echoed across the mountains and awoke All-Seeing Helios from his nightly slumber.

Thrace pulled from his pack the Golden spear head of Ares and held it up before his eyes. Its golden hue shinned bright even under the dark wings of Night. Parker watched wondering if his friend was going to throw it at this massive immortal before them. If so, what would happen, and how do they deal with the fire-breathing winged horse next? He questioned whether he could fire an arrow at this black winged beast.

Cresphontes' war cry stopped abruptly and the golden hue of the spear head sparkled upon Night's wing. "What is that?" He asked impatiently.

"I was given this by our father atop Mt. Dicte on an altar when I sacrificed the ashen spear of Swift-footed Achilles, son of the Goddess Thetis to him before I faced the Mighty Titan Kottus." Thrace informed him and kept his eyes upon his step-brother attempting to read every movement, every reaction.

Cresphontes took a long dark look at the Golden spear head, the gift from his father. Then he appraised his own brazen armor. He was wearing greaves and armor from other ancient sons of Ares that had fought on the fields of battle in ancient Greece, but he was the son his father Ares had been patiently waiting for, an Immortal son. He was the Seed of Destruction, not this mortal. Yet, he was given no new golden armor, nor magical weaponry. This mortal son of Ares, this human, was awarded a Golden spear head.

"Mortal son of Ares," Cresphontes said with his deep growl. "If you give me the Golden spear head of our father, I will make your death quick and painless. I shall even allow your mortal friend and little Oread to live."

Thrace stood absorbing all the words Cresphontes had to say. As Rage consumed him with the thoughts of killing, he had forgotten about the consequences to Parker and Anthia. His own impetuous anger may have led not only to his own death, but to their deaths as well, and finally the death of his mother, which meant the whole journey would have been for nothing. If Parker and Anthia lived, Parker could take the vial to save his mother, and she would live knowing he knew the truth. He did not believe he could defeat these massive children of Ares with a Golden spear, a small short sword and

Parker's bow. They had lost a good friend in Aemon, and no one else needed to die.

"Don't even think about it." Parker whispered.

Without hesitation, Anthia yelled, "RUN" and transformed into a golden eagle in the blink of an eye and shot like an arrow at Cresphontes. Her talons sparkled in the night sky from the glowing Golden spear head as they stretched out toward the giant horned head of the Immortal son of Ares.

"NO!!" Thrace yelled, but it was too late.

Cresphontes swatted the broadside of his battle axe at the golden eagle. It struck Anthia sending her to the forest floor. Cresphontes stepped beside her and gloated over her body as she slowly transformed back to her human form. She gasped for each breath as blood tricked slowly from her lips.

"I guess then that all of you shall die." Cresphontes barked as Deinus reared up on her back legs shooting fire from her nostrils.

Thrace saw his dream unfold before his eyes. The prophecies continued to come true. The golden eagle that was Anthia was struck down by Horned Cresphontes and now lay upon the forest floor dying. Rage took a second offensive surge within him and danced without control like drunken devotees at the festival of Dionysus. Everything was different. This journey and all the trials did not matter. High school, and all it offers one did not matter. His father did not matter. This Immortal beast was going to kill Anthia, kill Parker and himself, just as his father had killed Aemon, a good man. Then this being would use his dying mother as an offering to Stheno. The hell he was; Thrace thought. Not now, not after all this.

In a single breath, he raised the Golden Spear of Thrace.

Cresphontes roared in a barbaric laughter that echoed upon the mountainside. He raised his giant battle axe high in the air, showing his great strength as his horns glimmered like the last light of life before death.

A swift warm breeze ran through the forest and caressed both Thrace and Parker. A sensation Parker had felt only twice before. The warm breath raised the hairs on the nape of his neck. An idea struck him once again as he rolled his fingers across the strings of his lyre. A delicate and warming tune danced gently across the breeze touching every sliver of life around them.

The trees did not shiver upon the roar of Cresphontes as their leaves appeared to dance upon each note. Deinus, the black-winged Syrian mare settled upon the forest floor. She no longer blazed roaring flames from her nostrils. Her black reptilian wings calmed against her strong glossy onyx frame. Her blazing red eyes turned the soft green of her mother, and she gazed upon Parker and her half-brother.

"What are you doing sister?" Cresphontes bellowed.

But neither his roar, nor his anger could alleviate the calm that consumed the Mighty Immortal winged mare. She left her brother's side and moved within the trees as if to dance.

"A lyre settling my sister will not save you, little boy," Cresphontes thundered. He whirled his great axe and proceeded toward the boys.

"Thrace, aim for the axe." Parker said with his fingers never leaving the lyre.

Hearing his friend's words after recognizing wisdom upon a breeze, Thrace, in single breathe, fired the Golden Spear head of Thrace like a lightning bolt from Mighty Zeus. Cresphontes hesitated as he watched

Thrace fire the Golden spear head. Its speed was so quick that the Horned Immortal knew if he blinked, he would miss it.

The Golden spear struck the giant battle axe of Cresphontes and unlike any spear or spear head Thrace had thrown before, it was absorbed into the great axe as if the axe's broad blade had drank it like a glass of mead wine.

Cresphontes stopped and stared at his axe waiting for something to happen. When nothing did, he roared in laughter. A mighty roar so violent and vast it shook Parker's fingers from the Golden Lyre.

"So, this is the great weapon our father gave you!!" Cresphontes howled at Thrace and Parker, whose finger reached to continue playing the lyre. "A weapon of false confidence to bring you to your death. How wise our father is. Think of this now brother, upon your death, you will get to meet that Centaur's father suffering in Tartarus. And your mentor will spend his days in anguish of another failure. Like father, like son."

Cresphontes raised the great battle axe once more and began swinging it in the air. He moved toward Thrace and Parker with a murderous look raging in his brazen red eyes. The weight of the axe became a burden to his immense arms and shoulders and his large steps slowly began to falter. Cresphontes, in all his might and strength, could barely hold the massive axe waist high. He stumbled as a puzzled look replaced his murderous glare. Feeling like he was running out of time, the mighty Immortal son of Ares and Stheno, muscled the great battle axe with the last of his strength once more above his head and ran toward the heroes.

"LOOK!" Parker yelled.

Cresphontes thundered forward with all the energy he could summon to move and hold the massive axe above his head toward Thrace and Parker. The axe began to shimmer and as quick as a warming breathe from the Immortal goddess Aphrodite, the shiny brazen broad blade of the axe was consumed in gold. The gold spread like the great River Styx flowing rapidly through the depths of Tartarus as it drowned the handle of the axe and continued to the hands of Cresphontes.

"What sort of magic is this?!" The Immortal son of Ares bellowed trying to let go of the axe, but it was too late. It was as if King Midas of the golden touch had reached out from the Underworld himself.

Within minutes, the golden river streamed its way along his arms to his broad and massive shoulders to his wide chest and strong legs. Cresphontes attempted to yell. But again, it was too late. Inches before Thrace and Parker stood a chiseled golden statue of the giant horned and muscled Cresphontes with his giant battle axe held high above his head as if in a great battle with a look up anger and pain carved upon his face, a work that would rival the Greek bronze sculptor Myron known for his famous disc thrower.

"Wow. That was cool." Parker said reaching out to touch the golden statue.

"That was too close is more like it." Thrace responded. "I guess we owe Aphrodite once more."

"That doesn't sound like a good thing."

Thrace took his attention from the golden statue of Cresphontes to the bat-winged Deinus. Another image from his dream spawned in his mind. His dark-winged half-sister stepped forward as he stretched out his hand. Deinus cautiously proceeded forward. Her nose nuzzled his fingers and then slide to his palm as if hoping to be scratched. Deinus *neighed* with a gentle kindness as Thrace scratched her head.

"Thrace," Parker whispered.

Thrace turned toward his friend who was knelt beside Anthia, who was still bleeding. Her eyes barely open. Thrace quickly went to her side.

"I tried to keep her away from the battle, but I kept her away from the wrong one." Thrace spoke softly. His words filled with sadness.

"You yourself told Ares you can't alter the prophecies." Parker reminded him.

"WAIT!" Thrace exclaimed as he pulled the golden vial of Asclepius from his pocket.

"But Thrace, it's for your mother."

"Sophos said we would only need a drop." Thrace pulled from his memory. "It depends on how much we have."

"Are you willing to take that risk?" His friend asked.

"We wouldn't be here with this vial without her."

Thrace removed the lid from the golden vial of Asclepius. He peered in with thoughts of hope for enough elixir to save both his mother and Anthia. His eyes looked into the vial to gaze upon the elixir, an elixir to stop death for all, except that of its creator.

"It's empty." Thrace said once again, defeated.

"What?!" Parker exclaimed.

Behind the heroes, Deinus *neighed* once, then twice and began nudging Thrace upon his shoulder. He turned toward his half-sister with a destroyed look upon his face. His heart accepting the fact his new friend, this beautiful Immortal who rattled his heart, and his mother, the woman whose courage and wisdom had prepared him for this journey, were not to survive. They were not to survive because he did. His eyes met those soft jade eyes of his Immortal sister. They were warm and wise. As if through her eyes his sister spoke and he understood.

"Of course, The God of Fire!" Thrace exclaimed.

"What?" Parker asked.

"This vial was forged by Hephaestus, the Smith God, the God of Fire. It needs to be heated to reveal its content."

"Did your half-sister, the winged horse, tell you that?"

"Actually, in some weird way, she did."

Thrace held the vial of Asclepius out toward his half-sister Deinus. She snorted out a low funneled blaze of fire from her nostrils torching the vial.

"Is it getting hot?" Parker asked.

"No...colder." Thrace replied.

Deinus stopped her nasal blaze. Thrace looked inside the golden vial to see a creamy white elixir bubbling slowly. He thanked Deinus as he scratched her nose and then returned his attention to Anthia. He tilted the vial allowing a single drop of the white elixir to fall upon Anthia's lips.

Moments passed. The two waited, each scanning from one another to Anthia questioning whether or not to give her more. They agreed to give her one more drop. As he tilted Asclepius's vial, she took a deep breath and her bright blue eyes sparkled brightly upon Night. The large wound along her arm and abdomen slowly healed leaving a long battle scar. Anthia, the

291

beautiful Mountain Oread sat up and with great strength, hugged both Thrace and Parker.

"That's how you alter a prophecy." She said.

CHAPTER 25

Red robed Dawn stretched her lovely finger across the sky sending black-winged Night home to her dark palace deep within the realm of Tartarus. With her reptilian wings stretched out wide, Deinus soared through the ruby red Colorado sky with Thrace and Parker upon her back. No matter whether each was good with the spear or the lyre, both glowed as they drifted through the morning sunrise. Anthia, once again the beautiful golden eagle, glided gracefully beside them. The heroes escaped the forest terrain of the Colorado Rockies as the quiet urban sprawl of Bemus stretched out below them. The temples and caves littered with mythical creatures that had consumed them for the past week were replaced by modern sketches of house, malls, designer parks, shops and hospitals.

Thrace saw the hospital up ahead but didn't have to inform Deinus; since, his now golden step brother told him they had already been there. Deinus stretched out her leathery black wings wide and glided downward toward the hospital.

Deinus' glossy black hooves hit the parking lot in stride, and she continued toward the front door. Anthia settled beside them morphing back to her human form as Thrace and Parker quickly dismounted. Thrace, remembering to reignite the elixir, pulled the golden vial of Asclepius from his pocket and held it before his half-sister once more. With a second fiery nasal blaze, Deinus ignited the vial. The vial felt cold once again. Thrace thanked his sister and scratched her nose as she neighed once more. The heroes sprinted toward the hospital's front entrance.

The three of them entered the hospital with angst. Thrace spun around attempting to remember where his mother was, but he had been gone awhile, and she could have been moved. He ran up to the information desk where an elderly woman with a patient face watched them in amusement, her name tag read Minerva.

"Excuse me, Minerva. I am looking for what room my mother is in. Cybele Kraft?"

"Let me check," Minerva replied flipping through the hospital book before her. "Room 215. Wait, aren't you her son? There's a search party…"

"Yeah, we found ourselves." Parker interjected.

With haste, Thrace, Parker and Anthia raced down the hallway and to the stairwell. Bounding the steps with urgency, the trio barreled through the second level doorway, paused to get their bearings, found a sign pointing directions for rooms and took two quick corners. At the end of the next hallway, Mr. and Mrs. Wells stood in active conversation with Dr. Sheridan beside the door. The mother sensed her son. Mrs. Wells looked down the hallway and saw her son running toward her.

"OH MY GOD!!" She yelled.

Without saying a word Parker of the Golden Lyre, the Quick-witted one, was now just a boy, a son of Mr. and Mrs. Wells. A son who missed his mother. He embraced his mother as if he had not seen her in years.

"Where have you been!?" Mrs. Parker asked as tears cascaded from her eyes. "You've had me, us, so worried."

"I told you we were in Greece." Parker replied quickly without thinking.

"Where?" She said holding her son in front of her.

"Doc," Thrace said watching his friend's reunion with his parents turn awkward, but still wishing for the same. "How is she?"

"Not well, her condition has worsened each day. I can't believe you have not been here at your mother's side." Doctor Sheridan said in contempt.

"Parker, who is she?" Mr. Wells asked looking oddly at Anthia.

"You can see her?" Thrace asked.

"Of course we can see her." Mr. Wells replied.

Anthia gently smiled at Thrace. He realized she was allowing herself to be seen. She wanted to meet his mother.

"She's my friend, Anthia." Thrace answered.

"So son," Mr. Wells asked. "Where did you say you were?"

"Ah…I told mom," Parker stuttered. "We were getting a cure for Thrace's mom."

"Is she into herbal medicine or something like that?" Mrs. Parker asked not taking her eyes off of Anthia.

"You think some herbal cure will help your mother?" The doctor asked as his large owl-like eyes opened wider than appeared possible.

"Not really." Thrace brushed past the doctor and stepped toward the door to room 215 and peered through the window.

"Parker." Thrace said.

Parker let go of his parents and peered through the same window. Inside the room was a jungle of strong brown roots which entangled the furniture. Auburn petals with grey eyed centers sprouted from all curves and turns of the strong brown roots and filled the room like a terrarium.

"Wow. She does make a beautiful flower." Parker said.

"What are you talking about?" Mrs. Wells asked.

Thrace entered room 215 and Parker, through the entire journey, was at his side. They fought through the tough root and vines of his mother's flowers. He could only make out the rise of her shape upon the bed in the room. His mother produced a strong vine, he thought.

Mr. and Mrs. Wells and Dr. Sheridan entered the room and watched. They appeared puzzled as they watched the boys wrestle their way through an unseen maze.

"What are they doing?" The doctor asked.

"They are saving her life." Anthia quietly stated not taking her eyes from Thrace fighting his way through the strong brown thicket.

Parker turned back to his parents who stood watching him with a bewildered look he had seen so often and now realized he missed so much. They appeared to be standing in a thicket of vines and flowers. Without realizing it, all three of them kept brushing their arms and faces as invisible flowers continued to tickle them. Parker could only giggle.

Thrace fought his way past the strong vine to the bed. He could barely see her face through the immense growth of auburn petals. He reached the bed frame and used it to pull himself closer though the thickest of the vines. He brushed away the flowers to see his mother lying calmly. Her breath was short as if Death was in the room with him. His hand touched her face, and he could still feel warmth trickling through her. Thrace held up the vial of Asclepius which he held tightly in his hand.

"Hold on mom." Thrace whispered removing the cap from the golden vial.

"What do you think you are doing?" Dr. Sheridan asked approaching the bed.

"Stop right there doc!" Parker barked at the doctor with an authority his parents have never witnessed.

"Parker," his mother asked. "What are you doing?"

"Trying to help my friend save his mother's life." He replied. "Trust me mom." He smiled at her as only a son could do; she paused and watched.

Thrace looked at his friend and smiled. From start to finish they stood side by side and now, not against mythical creatures, Immortals or Titans, but this time the most difficult of opponents to stand up against, one's parents, especially when he had missed them so much.

Parker nodded. Thrace removed the cap from the vial of Asclepius to reveal the creamy white elixir still bubbling within. Once again, Thrace tilted the golden vial to release a single drop of the white elixir upon his mother's lips.

Thrace stood and waited.

"Mom," he asked. "Can you hear me?" Moments passed like hours.

"There's so much to tell you," he whispered. "I met my father. We don't actually get along, and well, he saved my life and then tried to kill me. He knows I may be more to deal with than he originally realized. I got that from you."

In the room the auburn petals began to whither, and the roots and vines turned black and crippled as if unquenched by water for days on end. The living water of life that appeared to be feeding the flowers was returning to his mother.

"It's working!" Parker exclaimed.

Cybele blinked her bright grey eyes and looked upon the pale blue eyes of her son. A son's features she remembered, but a strength and wisdom in his eyes she was unfamiliar with, yet proud to see. The remaining flowers fell from her shoulders to the hospital room floor. Slowly, Cybele Kraft sat up, reached out and touched her son's face.

"Welcome back mom," Thrace said.

"I knew you'd save me." She replied as mother and son embraced.

"What just happened here?" Doctor Sheridan asked puzzled and confused his large owl eyes spinning toward everyone. "What's in that vial?"

Thrace peering over his mother's shoulder replied, "The ancient cure from Asclepius that you said wouldn't work."

"Now doc, if you don't mind," Parker said. "Why don't we leave these nice folks alone? Oh, and can you bring me a broom?"

Chapter 26

All-Seeing and Bright Helios struck across the sky blue heavens with vigor not seen since he witnessed the ancient plays of Aristophanes and Sophocles. Helios swam as if reawakened, a dolphin free from captivity that had returned to the sea. His golden arms stretched out long and far caressing the greenery of the land and warming the dark and craggy skin of the Rocky Mountains.

The meandering trail carved though the mountains with switch-backs and steep grades. Cybele, Thrace, Parker, and his parents, Bill and Jenn Wells worked their way tirelessly along the trail with determination in their eyes and a smile of calm, peace and camaraderie upon their face (though Parker's parents were more riddled with sweat). This was no journey for prophetic guidance or against some mythical creatures or a dangerous quest, but a journey with family and friends for companionship and serenity.

His mother, fully recovered, marched on hard and strong as if trying to reclaim time that had been taken from her. The soft, yet confident smile upon her face, he witnessed when she knelt before Aphrodite, or the sigh of relief upon seeing him in the hospital was reclaimed by that of a strong woman of determination he knew his whole life, who had trained him without his even realizing it. Thrace could see how his arrogant father was impressed by her.

"I don't see anything." Parker said quietly to Thrace.

Thrace knew to what he was referring, the Hamadryads. All along this hike the two had kept their eyes peeled for any Immortals along the way. They were in a similar part of the forest they had been before with Sophos and Anthia, so they expected an Immortal presence or at least their songs drifting upon the leaves. Thrace was beginning to wonder if it even happened at all.

After his mother awoke and thanked her son, she did not say a word, but held him tightly in her arms. It took a full day before he could explain his entire tale, as Dr. Sheridan took Parker's 'request to leave them be' for only a few minutes before he came in to examine her and the contents of the vial. Thrace, concerned with what the vial might offer in the wrong hands, quickly tossed it to Parker, who stepped out of the room and tossed it to Anthia. She understood the benefit and consequences of the vial of Asclepius and left as if she was never there. He was asked to leave as his mother insisted for that he go home and get some rest; he appeared to need it more than she needed it. She was not wrong. For the adventure was physically catching up to him now that his mother was awake. Outside the hospital Deinus was gone. Thrace looked around to see if she had wandered off, but she was neither on the grass nor in the sky. Mr. and Mrs. Wells watched him without question as he wandered about, before offering him a ride home.

The next morning Thrace, with Parker at his side, told his mother their adventure like young athletes who had won their first victory, and then told it again to make sure she heard correctly. She did not speak nor interrupt but listened as tenderly as a leaf drinks in the sun on a cloudless afternoon filling herself with strength and life. Her confident smile, her trusting eyes were a greater reward to Thrace than all the glory or gold in ancient Greece, and all he could ask for. Upon coming home, she replaced her prize vase from the Temple of Ares with the armor he wore to retrieve the vial. She honored him as she had once honored a man, an Immortal who gave her a son.

Fortunately, their return to school to finish their exams was welcomed with the assistance of his mother's healthy return, the adamant request of Mr. Wells, who they came to find out did taxes for most of the teachers and the principle at the school, and a quiet suggestion from Mr. Grissom with the principle. Later they were informed that they had done well on their in class essays and tests as Mr. Grissom asked why both where riddled with an ancient Greek influence and simultaneously they both shrugged.

His mother asked him questions about the Immortals they met, and the places they had traveled. Thrace realized he relished talking about it. Parker did not have as much luck. His parents nodded kindly at his tales, though he knew they did not believe a word of it and were more excited he was home and even more surprised he cleaned his room. The hardest part for Thrace was not seeing a single Immortal since his mother's awakening. They had ridden out along the path they rode that first night they met Sophos and hiked to where they had seen the Hamadryad, but no one. Many days, he thought of blowing the ivory horn, but he did not. He was in no danger, no need of help, he just wanted to know it was real.

During the hike, his eyes scanned the forest as Sophos taught him, eyeing a central point and allowing his focus to expand all around him, but still he saw no one. More than anything, Thrace wanted to see Sophos once more. His mother was safe; he had met his father, but it was his Immortal teacher, his stern instructor who had become his friend, his mentor. He wished to thank him once again and introduce him to his mother. This hike was deemed unsuccessful as his eyes stretched out across the forest in the distance and to the skies above.

The trail weaved before Thrace and the more he hiked, the more he saw around him, and the less he saw before him. A root reached out as if alive and caught his foot. Thrace's eyes quickly met the trail beneath him, as did his hands and chest.

"You all right?" Parker asked as he reached out to give his friend a hand.

"Yeah."

"You know," Cybele said. "For someone who fought gorgons and Immortals, you have little balance."

"Thanks mom."

She smiled at her son as he appeared more embarrassed than she would have expected. "What were you looking for?"

"A golden eagle or maybe a horse."

"I don't believe there are golden eagles in this mountain range." Mr. Wells stated.

"Dad, you'd be surprised what's in this mountain range." Parker said. "Hey, I think we're close."

Parker jogged off trail toward a small clearing where he and Thrace were only days ago. Parker stopped in the clearing, and Thrace appeared quickly at his side. The image of Cresphontes barreling down on them with his double-sided great axe was still vivid in their minds. The spot where the muscled and horned Immortal son of Ares was turned in to a golden statue stood empty.

Thrace and Parker knelt down to where the large golden statue once stood. There were two deep footprints upon the rich forest soil. Cybele knelt down beside her son and examined the soil with expertise of one who had studied the earth and its contents many times.

"There was something here recently that was very heavy to leave such a deep impression upon the soil." Cybele stated professionally.

"What could it have been?" Mrs. Wells asked as her and her husband finally caught up, both leaning against a tree catching their breath. This hiking was much different than the car camping they preferred.

"With this much weight, a lead or golden statue." She replied with a smile from ear to ear. "What's confusing is who could have moved something that weighed that much. There are no other tracks."

"Ares." Thrace said.

Mr. Wells smirked at his response but pulled it back quickly as his wife gave him a dark stare. Neither believed the tale their son told and allowed it without punishment due to the fact that Cybele was now out of her coma (which they suspected was due to the fact her son had returned) and for some reason, their son was more mature.

"You are correct Thrace of the Spear."

Thrace turned toward the familiar baritone sound of his name as his eyes gravitated toward a familiar face. To his left stood the great Centaur, Sophos the Clever, who appeared from behind a group of trees. His usual firm and confident glare was replaced by the look of compassion for one who missed a long lost friend.

Thrace raced to his mentor and paused before him as Sophos stood, his strong arms bent with hands upon his waist, and smiled. Thrace embraced him, much to the surprise of Sophos. Parker too ran to his side ever pleased to see the 'wily' centaur, which Parker now referred to him. Sophos caught off guard by such affection embraced both of the boys, his heart had softened since the first time they had met.

"Why are they hugging a horse?" Mr. Wells asked.

"It is good to see you up around Cybele, mother of Thrace." Sophos said gazing upon the woman he recognized at once behind the boys from her auburn hair and grey eyes that matched the flower Thrace peered at each night along the journey.

"Thank you, and it is a pleasure to meet you Sophos, son of Peirithous." Cybele said. "And thank you for bringing my son home."

"It was my honor to fight alongside him. You are a wise teacher and mother."

"Sophos didn't you say Thrace's mother was at Delphi once." Parker reminded him, a hint of mischief in his tone.

"That's right," Thrace replied turning toward his mother. "What did the Pythia tell you?"

"She told me beauty would need my son's help." She said looking upon her son. "When I first met your father, he told me his name was Arieus. He spoke of the ancient world, and it was alive to him, all of it, myth, philosophy, even the simple lives of the people he spoke of so intimately. I was mesmerized. I spent two days with him, and he showed me hidden treasures of ancient Greece and spoke of the ancient wonders as if he lived them. I will

304

admit, I was smitten. The second night at his cottage, we talked and drank ancient Greek wine with grain and honey. He told me he was Ares, the God of War. Of course I didn't believe him. I was a grad student in Greece enamored with the past, but he said it so passionately, without doubt and with such confidence. The next day he was gone, except for a necklace. I looked and couldn't find him. I couldn't even find the little cottage again. I soon noticed I could see things and later realized, I no longer had the mortal mist."

"How did you know?" Thrace asked.

"I meet back up with our grad class, and we were supposed to leave. I walked out to the Aegean one last time and saw a white dolphin close to shore that turned into a woman and came ashore. She looked up at me knowing I was staring are her, and we both just watched one another. She smiled and nodded and returned to the sea and back into a dolphin. Instead of leaving, I decided to go to Delphi once more. I met a girl, a mountain Oread she told me, who assisted me and the Pythia gave me a parchment about 'beauty needing my son's help'. When Aphrodite came and told me she needed your help, and that she would protect you, I volunteered."

His eyes drank in every word she said. She was not shy, nor bashful of her experience, just honest. An unimaginable tale he would have never believed, until now. "You sacrificed yourself?" Thrace asked.

"From what you have told me, it was coming whether I called for it or not. And, I knew you wouldn't fail."

"You knew much more than I did." Thrace replied.

"That is why I'm your mother." She said with a smile and embraced her son.

"Could someone please tell us what's going on?" Mrs. Parker asked puzzled.

"Well mom, that's Sophos the Centaur, though you and dad only see a horse. You know, the mortal mist and all, and you see what you want to see."

"You expect us to believe a horse is a centaur?" Parker's father asked in a stern tone of one fed up with such farce.

"Come with me," Sophos said. "There is more that lies ahead."

Sophos led Cybele, Thrace and Parker into the forest. Mr. and Mrs. Wells stood puzzled as they watched their neighbors and their son follow a horse into the woods. Mrs. Wells shrugged her shoulders and proceeded after them. Her husband followed.

They hiked for another mile through the woods, and the woods themselves began to feel alive. Thrace and Parker's heads snapped right and left as they witnessed shadows of movement within the forest, and a voice upon the wind appeared to sing through the leaves. A large clearing opened near a valley floor between a pair of mountain peaks. In the clearing a group of individuals stood awaiting the coming party. Thrace's keen eyesight spotted Battus in the distance along with the Professor, Myrtle and Halia of the Sea.

"Look who it is!" Thrace yelled at Parker and the both of them rushed off.

There were hugs and warm embraces all around with light hearted laughter when Cybele, along with Mr. and Mrs. Wells arrived. Thrace made introductions as Mr. and Mrs. Wells were pleased to see a couple they could see and talk to; that is until Mr. and Mrs. Wilton spoke of all the mythical creatures they had seen along their journey with Parker. Battus energetically shook Parker's parent's hands and ranted on about how well he played the lyre. His mother looked at Parker surprised. After they did not believe the story he and Thrace told them, he did not wish to prove anything for his proof lived within the Golden Lyre of Pan. He waited until they went to bed at night to play the lyre on the roof as Aphrodite requested. Thrace's mother immediately remembered Professor Wilton, and they were amused how the Fates had allowed their paths to cross once again.

"So, these people we are talking too… are they mythical in any way?" Mr. Wells quietly asked his son.

"No," the Professor said overhearing with a chuckle. "I am a retired professor; Myrtle is my wife, and Battus here is an actor who battles Titans on the side; yet Halia of the Sea is a goddess."

"Who?" Mr. Parker asked.

"They still have the mortal mist." Parker informed the Professor.

"Trust me parents of Parker of the Lyre, there is more than meets the eye here," the Professor said.

As he spoke, Halia of the Sea stepped forward and reached out her elegant white arms; her left hand before Mr. Parker and her right before Mrs. Parker, with a whisper from her lips and as gently as pulling a cord, she removed the mortal mist from their eyes. Each took a step back as a burning sensation tickled their eyes. They blinked the tears from their eyes and as the tears subsided, they saw a beautiful woman who appeared miraculously before them.

"Mom, dad, this is Halia of the Sea." Parker said. His parents stumbled through their hellos, just as Parker turned them to their right, "And this is Sophos the Centaur."

Mr. and Mrs. Wells stood silently staring with a bewildered look at a Centaur that only moments ago had been a large horse.

"It is a pleasure to meet the parents of the quick-witted Parker, master of the lyre." Sophos said.

"Hello, I am Jenn and this is my husband Bill." Mrs. Parker replied.

"I know you." Cybele simply stated as she watched the young woman remove the mist before the Wells.

Halia smiled at Thrace's mother and gracefully approached her and embraced Cybele Kraft. "Years ago, I came ashore and you stood upon the beach watching me. You were not frightened, just observant. It is no wonder you gave birth to the Seed of Destruction."

"The Seed of Destruction?" Cybele asked.

Thrace heard his mother's question as he watched her eyes widened with concern. He had left some parts out of the journey, just a few parts, so his mother would not be overly concerned. Though concern was the first thing he saw in her eyes when she heard those words.

"LOOK," Parker called out.

High above a golden eagle soared above the open field gently gliding in perfect circles over the company of friends. Behind her, Deinus, her large black reptilian wings stretched wide, followed as their circling brought them closer to the valley floor.

"What's that?" Mr. Parker asked.

"Ah, that's Anthia, a Mountain Oread, and behind her my half-sister, Deinus." Thrace said matter-of-factly, and he watched Mr. Wells formerly stern face transform into a puzzled stare as his mind attempted arrange and categorize everything around him.

Just as the talons of the golden eagle touch the open plains, she transformed into the beautiful blue eyed Mountain Oread, Anthia. As her feet gripped the soil, her progress took her directly to Thrace, who without hesitation embraced her as someone who has missed a lost love. He felt her warmth that he had missed as he felt the warmth within his heart, not the violence of the Immortal boxer, but the warmth of a fire. A fire he hoped would bring him courage as he witnessed his mother watching this embrace.

"Ah mom, this is Anthia." Thrace said nervously. "Mom, Anthia."

"It's a pleasure to meet you Anthia." Cybele said.

"It's an honor to meet she who gave birth to the Seed of Destruction, the mother of Thrace of the Spear, who freed the hundred handed Titan Kottus." Anthia said calmly as she bowed before Cybele.

Cybele, embarrassed by the honor, reached forward to grasp her hand. Anthia smiled at the honor bestowed upon her, and Cybele surprised her and her son by embracing the Mountain Oread. "Thank you for watching over my son."

Thrace and Parker exchanged surprised looks at her response. Anthia had been helpful, yet quiet during the adventure. The nervous flirting between Thrace and Anthia was quickly diminished when she overheard them whisper about her departure to keep her safe. But her actions in the Colorado Mountains to save them revealed her affections for both of them. This present showing of affection, and the honor bestowed upon his mother caught him off guard. He realized how little he knew about Anthia. Thrace watched the interaction between Anthia and his mother, and he felt a nudge on his shoulder. He turned to see his half-sister Deinus beside him.

"It is very good to see you too Deinus," Thrace said reaching out and scratching her nose, which she had admitted to Thrace she liked so much.

"Mother, this is my half-sister Deinus." Thrace said.

"Uhm, nice to meet you Deinus," Cybele said in awe of the beautiful black winged Syrian mare, who nudged up for another scratch upon her nose.

"Sophos, what is everyone doing here?" Parker asked.

"After the death of Aemon, we built a giant Pyre on the plain of Mt. Dicte. In tradition of a hero's death, funeral games must follow. We are here along with other friends to compete in the funeral games, and this quest taken up by Thrace and Parker will be replayed on stage by Battus, the Professor and an array of mountain Hamadryads for entertainment."

From the woods dozens of Hamadryads stepped from the forest, each with a soft delicate song upon their lips that swam upon the breeze. Parker quickly pulled his lyre from his pack as a howl echoed from behind him. He looked around before striking the lyre and Zephyrus, the West Wind swam beside him spinning him in a circle.

"Oh, great...Zephyrus is here." Parker replied sarcastically being swirled off his feet.

Parker regained his composure, though remained sitting, and struck a beautiful sound upon his golden lyre to join with the Hamadryads song and hopefully put Zephyrus at bay. The sound of the lyre caressed the long blades of grass upon the valley floor, and they appeared to dance. Bill and Jenn stood in stunned silence as they watched their son create such profound beauty with such an ancient and simple instrument.

The professor, Myrtle and Battus along with a handful of Hamadryad stood before the group preparing to retell the recent adventure of Thrace and the Hundred-Handed. Battus would be playing the role of Thrace and the latter felt honored. The young Hamadryad whom Thrace had pierced with a pencil and later removed the mortal mist from Parker would be playing the role of Parker, who laughed as he watched her attempt a more clumsy walk than she was use too.

The crowd took a seat and embraced the performance. The parents of both Thrace and Parker continually gazed upon their children ever impressed by the events of their adventure. Their sons had shown maturity and strength even they did not realize. Sophos took a seat next to Thrace to watch the stage performance.

"Have you told your mother of the promise you made to Aphrodite?" He asked.

"Not yet," Thrace replied regrettably. "She's only been home a few days, and I don't want to worry her."

"Your mother is quite strong. I believe she can handle much more than you can imagine. She did give birth to the 'Seed of Destruction'." He reminded Thrace.

"Yeah, I haven't told her that either," Thrace commented quietly.

Thrace looked at his mentor and knew his words to be true though he did not wish to explain that either. He was not sure if he was the 'Seed of

Destruction' or if he could calm the wine dark sea. So much had happened in such a short time, and what he wanted more than anything else was some calm, some time. He wanted to be a high school kid again, but he wanted this calm with the immortals in his life as well, and he wondered if that was even possible.

Thrace watched as Halia of the Sea walked over and took a seat next to Sophos. Her look of affection toward Sophos was returned as their hands embraced. At the same time he saw Anthia approach with Deinus to take their seats next to him and his mother. First, he needed a word with his mother, Cybele of the Javelin.

"Mom, there's something I need to tell you."

THE END

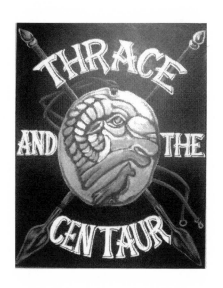

Glossary

1. **Achilles** (a-kil' –eez): Son of Peleus, mortal King and Thetis, Olympian Goddess. Fought at battle of Troy, defeated Hektor, prince of Troy and died at Troy when an arrow pierced his Achilles heel.

2. **Aeschylus** (ESS' –kuh-luhs): A Greek poet and writer who crafted such works as *The Persians, Seven against Thebes, Agamemnon* and *Prometheus Bound.*

3. **Agoge** (ag'-o-gay): The Spartan youth education and training regime where children attended for physical and stealth training, loyalty, song and dance and Spartan government.

4. **Alexander the Great** (al-ig-zan'-der):Son of King Philip of Macedon and student of Aristotle, and by the age of 30 controlled one of the largest empires in the ancient world with over 20 cities named after him.

5. **Aloeids** (al-oy-i-dz): Giant twin sons of Poseidon who declared war on the Olympian Gods. They first captured Ares and placed him in a bronze vase. Deceived by Artemis they fought one another and are now in Tartarus tied to pillars by living vipers.

6. **Amaltheia** (am-uh-thee'-uh): Foster-mother to Olympian Zeus and mother to the satyr Pan.

7. **Amenoi** (a-men-oy): The 4 winds; Boreas, Zephyrus, Notus, and Eures.

8. **Andromeda** (an-drom-i-duh): Princess and daughter to Cassiopeia, who was punished for her mother's arrogance and sacrificed to an ocean titan known presently as The Kraken, but was saved by Perseus with the help of the head of Medusa.

9. **Anaximenes** (an-ak-sim-uh-neez): Anaximes of Miletus, a pre-Socratic philosopher who practiced material monism, believing that all things in the world come from a single element, and believing that single element to be air.

10. **Aphrodite** (a-fro-deye'-tee): Goddess of Love and Beauty and one of the 12 Olympians.

11. **Apollo** (a-pol'-oh): God of Light, Prophecy and Music, son of Zeus and Hera and twin brother to Artemis.

12. **Ares** (ai'-reez): God of War and son of Olympian Zeus and Hera.

13. **Aristophanes**: A comic playwright of Athens whose works include; *The Clouds, The Wasps, The Archarnians, Lysistrata* and *Peace*.

14. **Aristotle** (ar-uh-stot-l): Student of Plato, teacher of Alexander the Great and started the Lyceum, where he taught a variety of subject to include physics, metaphysics, logic, politics, botany and zoology.

15. **Artemis** (ar'te-mis): Goddess of the Hunt and Virginity and twin to Apollo. One of the 12 Olympian Gods.

16. **Asclepius** (a-sklee'-pi-us): The father of medicine and son of Apollo and Coronis, he was raised in the healing arts by Chiron the Wise.

17. **Atalanta** (at-l-an-tuh): Boeotian princess and fierce warrior who fought alongside Meleager for the Calydonian Boar and joined Jason and his Argonauts for the quest of the Golden Fleece.

18. **Athena** (a-thee'-na): Goddess of Wisdom and Courage who was born from the head of Olympian Zeus and one of the 12 Olympian Gods.

19. **Atlas** (at'-las): Great Titan and brother to Prometheus, he holds the Heavens upon his shoulders.

20. **Atropos (**a-truh-pos): One of the Three Fates, she cut the thread of life.

21. **Bellerophon** (be-ler'-o-fon): Son of King Glaucus and one of the greatest Greek heroes. Captured the winged-horse Pegasus and slayed the Chimera, but later was killed by Olympian Zeus for his hubris in an attempt to reach the Olympic Gods.

22. **Boreas** (bor'e-as): One of the four Aminoi, the Great North Wind.

23. **Briareus** (bri-ar'-yoos): One of the three Hekatonkheires, or Hundred-Handed Titans.

24. **Cassiopeia** (kas-ee-uh-pee-uh): Queen and husband to Cepheus, known for her boasts and arrogance that led to her daughter, Andromeda, to be offered as a sacrifice to the Kraken to appease Poseidon.

25. **Castor** (kas'-tor): One of the Discouri, twin brother to Pollux. Participated in the Calydonian Boar hunt and rode with Jason as one of the Argonauts.

26. **Charon** (ka'-ron): The boatman of Hades who transports dead souls across the River Styx to the Tartarus.

27. **Chimera** (keye-mee'-ra)**:** Daughter to the Titans Typhon and Echidna, she had the body of a lion, tail of a snake and head of a goat and breathed fire. She was killed by Bellerophon.

28. **Cheiron** (keye'-ron): A centaur who was sired and educated by Cronus, he instructed heroes such as Ajax, Jason, Asclepius, Theseus, Herakles, and Achilles.

29. **Chrysaor**: (k-ri'-sor): Son of Medusa and Poseidon, born at her death, and brother to Pegasus, the winged-horse.

30. **Clotho** (Kloh-tho): One of the Three Fates, she spun the thread of life.

31. **Cresphontes** (kres-fon'-tes): Son of Ares and the Gorgon, Stheno, and brother to Deinus, the black-winged mare and step-brother to Thrace.

32. **Cronus** (kro'-nus): Youngest Titan and son of Ouranus and Gaia, married to Rhea and father of Zeus, Poseidon and Hades.

33. **Deimus** (Dey-mus): God of Panic and son of Ares and Aphrodite.

34. **Deinus** (dey-nus): Black-winged Syrian mare and Daughter of Ares and the Gorgon Steno and sister to Cresphtones, the Horned-One, and step-sister to Thrace.

35. **Delphi** (del-fi'): An ancient city of Greece and home of the Delphic Oracle offering foresight to those in need by the Phythia, a priestess of the sanctuary.

36. **Demeter** (dee-mee'-tur): Goddess of the Harvest and one of the 12 Olympians and sister to Olympian Zeus.

37. **Diomedes** (deye-o-mee'-deez): King of Argos and one of the Greek heroes of the Trojan War.

38. **Echo** (e-ko'): A mountain Oread with a beautiful voice who fell in love with a mortal, Narcissus, but when he dismissed her, she fell into dismay and now echoes the words to those who pass her way.

39. **Elysian Fields** (ee-li'-zhun): A place in Hades reserved for Immortals and Heroes, also known as the Isle of the Blessed.

40. **Eos** (EE-os): Goddess of the Dawn and Daughter of Hyperion and Theia. One of the ancient Titans.

41. **Eures** (yoo'-res): One of the 4 Amenoi, the East Wind.

42. **Euryale** (yoo-ray-l): One of the three Gorgon sisters, daughter to Phorcys and Ceto and Immortal.

43. **Fates**: The Moiria, or the three Fates relaying the destiny of mortals from the Gods; Atropos, Clotho and Lachesis.

44. **Gaia** (jee-us): Mother Gaia, the Great Mother Goddess who gave birth to all the Heavens and Titans.

45. **Gyes** (jeye-us): One of the Hekatonkheires, or Hundred-Handed Titans.

46. **Hades** (hay'-deez): God of the Underworld and son of Cronus and Rhea, brother to Zeus and Poseidon.

47. **Hamadryad** (ham-uh-drahy-uh-d): Immortal natural beings that support nature and the forests.

48. **Hekatonkheires** (heke-ton-ker-z) The three Hundred-Handed; Briareus, Gyes and Kottus, who fought for Zeus against the Titans and now guard the gates of Tartarus.

49. **Hektor** (hek'tor): Prince of Troy, son of Priam and Hekuba and killed by Achilles on the plains of Troy.

50. **Helios** (hee'li-os): God of the Sun and son of Hyperion and Theia. One of the ancient Titans.

51. **Hephaestus** (he-fees'-tus): God of Fire and the Smith, and son of Olympian Zeus and Hera. One of the 12 Olympian Gods.

52. **Hera** (heer'a): Goddess of Marriage, women and birth and daughter to Cronus and Rhea and married her brother Zeus.

53. **Herakles** (her'-a-kleez): Son of Olympian Zeus and mortal Aclmene, completed 12 labors for retribution after a fit of madness led him to kill his children by Megara. In his death, he was offered a place on Olympus by his father, Zues.

54. **Hesiod** (hes-i'-od): Ancient Greek oral poet credited with the works of *Theogony*, *Works and Days* and the *Shield of Herakles*.

55. **Hippon** (hi'-pon): A pre-Socratic philosopher who believed that water was the base of all things and that the soul arose from the mind and the water within.

56. **Homer** (hoh-mer): Ancient Greek epic poet and author of *The Iliad* and *The Odyssey*.

57. **Hyperion** (hi-pe-reye'-on): Lord of Light and son of Mother Gaia and one of the original 12 Titans.

58. **Kottus** (ko-tus): One of the Hekatonkheires, or Hundred-Handed Titans.

59. **Lachesis** (lach-us-sis): One of the Three Fates, the measurer of the thread of life.

60. **Leonidas** (lee-on-i'-dus): King of Sparta, who led 300 Spartans along with a few thousand Greeks against Xerxes and his Persian Army of over 200,000 at Thermopylae, or the Hot Gates.

61. **Lycurgus** (lahy-kur'-guhs): Leader of Sparta who originated the military lifestyle of Sparta in accordance to the Oracle of Delphi.

62. **Medusa** (muh-doo-suh): Daughter of Phorcys and Ceto who was cursed by Athena for being assaulted by Poseidon in her temple and turned into the hideous snake-haired creature who turned anyone who looked at her to stone. She was beheaded by Perseus.

63. **Meleager** (me-le-ay'-ger): Son of Ares and host of Calydonian Boar hunt, and though he won, awarded hide to Atalanta, who wounded the Boar and for his infatuation for her.

64. **Menelaus** (me-ne-lay'us): King of Sparta and husband of Helen of Troy and brother to King Agamemnon of Mycenae who lead the Greek army against the Trojans.

65. **Minotaur** (min-uh-taur): A creature with head of a bull and the body of a man that lived in the labyrinth in Crete under the rule of King Minos, and was killed by Theseus.

66. **Myrmidons** (mur'-mi-donz): Fiercest warriors in all of ancient Greece and commanded by Achilles at the battle of Troy.

67. **Narcissus** (nahr-sis-uhs): A beautiful young man who shunned all suitors, and gazing upon his own reflection in a pool of water, fell in love with himself and unable to leave, died. The God Nemesis transformed him into a flower.

68. **Naiads** (neye'-adz): Immortal natural being that support water, streams and rivers.

69. **Night**: Goddess of Night and born of the God Chaos.

70. **Odysseus** (o-dis'-yoos): Son of Laertes and Anticleia, fought at Troy, creator of Trojan horse, followed by a ten year journey home to Ithaca.

71. **Oread** (awr-ee-ad): Immortal natural being that support the hills and mountains.

72. **Ouranos** (oo-rey'-nuhs): Original God of the Sky and husband of Gaia and father to the Titans.

73. **Pan**: Saytr; half goat, half human and son of Amaltheia.

74. **Paris** (pa'-ris): Prince of Troy and brother to Prince Hektor. He led Helen from Sparta to Troy that brought about the Trojan War.

75. **Pegasus** (peg-us-suhs): Winged-horse and daughter of Medusa and Poseidon, and born at Medusa's death along with her brother Chrysaor.

76. **Pelops** (pel'-ops): King of the Magnets and husband to Hippodameia. Defeated Mytileus for the hand of Hippodemeia and is the founder of the cursed line of Atreus.

77. **Peirithous** (per-ith'-ohs): A centaur and lost son of Cheiron, husband of Theope and father of Sophos.

78. **Persephone** (pur-se'-fo-nee): Daughter of the Goddess Demeter and Olympian Zeus. Abducted by Hades and made his wife and Queen of Underworld. Spends winters with Hades and when she rises to join her mother, spring begins at her arrival.

79. **Pheathon** (fee-a-thon): Son of Helios and the Naiad Clymene. Rode the sun chariot too close to the Gaia, burning the surface and was killed by Zeus.

80. **Phidippides** (pahy-dip-i-deez): Ancient Greek Olympic runner who ran from Athens to Sparta (150 miles) in two days to request assistance at the arrival of the Persians, and later ran from Marathon to Athens to announce the Greek victory and died upon arrival.

81. **Phobus** (foh-buhs): God of Terror and son of Ares and Aphrodite.

82. **Plato** (pley-toh): Ancient Greek philosopher and student of Socrates. He opened the Academy, the first institute of higher learning in the western world and wrote such works as; *Apology, Phaedo, Symposium, Republic,* and *Sophists.*

83. **Pollux** (pol-uks): Or Polydeuces, one of the Discouri, twin brother to Castor. Participated in the Calydonian Boar hunt and rode with Jason as one of his Argonauts. Known for his excellent boxing skills as he defeated King Amycus.

84. **Poseidon** (po-seye'-don): God the Sea and son of Cronus and Rhea and brother to Zeus and Hades.

85. **Praxiteles** (prak-sit-l-eez): Ancient Greek master sculptor, best known for his work of Aphrodite and Hermes.

86. **Prometheus** (pruh-mee-thee-uhs): Ancient Titan and brother of Atlas and a champion of humankind. Stole fire from Zeus and was punished, though later released for Zeus' need for his insight and forethought.

87. **Proteus** (proh'-tyoos): The Old Man of the Sea and son of Poseidon.

88. **Pythagoras** (pi-tha'-gor-us): Ancient Greek philosopher and mathematician best known for the Pythagorean Theorem.

89. **Salamander** (sal-uh-man-der): River God who fought Achilles on the plains of Troy.

90. **Selene** (si-lee-nee): Goddess of the Moon, daughter of Theia and Hyperion.

91. **Stheno** (sthen'-o): One of the Three Gorgon sister, daughter of Phorcys and Ceto and Immortal.

92. **Styx** (stix): A water God or Naiad, living within the River that bears her name that runs to the center of the Underworld.

93. **Tartarus** (tar'-ta-rus): The abysmal plain in Hades' Underworld reserved for the worst of beings.

94. **Theia** (thee'-uh): One of the original 12 Titans, wife of Hyperion and mother of Helios, Selene and Eos.

95. **Theope** (Thee-o'-p): Centaur and wife of Peirithous and mother of Sophos.

96. **Thermopylae** (ther-mop-uh-lee): Or "Hot Gates", a narrow coastal throughway where Leonidas led Greek forces against Xerxes' Persian army.

97. **Theseus** (thees'-yoos): Son of Aegus and Poseidon, slayer of the Cretan Minotaur and founder of Athens.

98. **Zephyrus** (zef-er-uhs): One of the 4 Amenoi, the West wind.

99. **Zeus** (zyoos): God of the Sky, son of Cronus and Rhea, husband to Hera and Ruler of Olympus.

Made in the USA
Monee, IL
04 March 2020